LOSERS WEEPERS

Jessica Thomas

Bella
BOOKS
2008

Bella Books, Inc.
P.O. Box 10543
Tallahassee, FL 32302

Printed in the United States of America on acid-free paper
First Edition

Editor: Cindy Cresap
Cover designer: LA Callaghan

ISBN-10: 1-59493-127-5
ISBN-13: 978-1-59493-127-7

For The Woofer who has moved on to the Land of Filets and Fireplugs, after fifteen years of being my companion, my clown, my protector, my confessor.

And for Sweet Tater, my new canine adventure who is ever at my side because she thinks I saved her life . . . when it was really the other way around.

Other Books by Jessica Thomas

Caught in the Net: Golden Crown Literary Award Winner—Mystery/Action/Adventure/Thriller

Turning the Tables: Golden Crown Literary Award Finalist—Mystery/Action/Adventure/Thriller

The Weekend Visitor: Lambda Literary Foundation Award Finalist—Lesbian Mystery

Murder Came Second

Chapter 1

So Cindy had left us.

It had been less than an hour, and already the house seemed empty and rather chilly. Strange. Unless I had an early appointment, Cindy left us every morning about this time—Monday through Friday—and I simply poured another cup of coffee and mentally planned my day. Certainly, I did not usually feel bereft and at loose ends, as I did now.

The weather wasn't helping. Whoever wrote the Chamber of Commerce blurbs would probably have called the slow, endless light rain a romantic mist. I called it a miserable all-day drizzle.

I don't know what Wells called it. She had disappeared. Probably I would find all twelve pounds of her when I made the bed. If I made the bed. She was now a sleek and lovely black and white cat, but I smiled as I remembered the first time I saw her, as a scrawny, bedraggled, but feisty, little stray. She bopped Fargo on the nose when he asked her to play and then she leaped for the protection of Cindy's arms—leaving Fargo with wounded nose and pride.

I don't know what Fargo called the rain, either, but he sighed heavily and flopped into his bed, ninety pounds of dismal dog who knew he would not be going to the beach this day. Fargo was my partner, my pal, my clown, my confessor, my protector against all things bad . . . a black Labrador with a heart of gold, not steel, but we didn't worry much about that.

As a puppy, not much larger than Wells is now, he had quickly learned that when loud noises occurred or large cats hissed or strange people seemed to menace . . . the best place for him to protect me was cradled in my arms, and there he leapt, barking shrilly, and there he remained until the situation was resolved to his satisfaction. A fifteen-pound puppy I could handle. A ninety-pound dog usually put me flat on my back in a state of considerable embarrassment, not to mention at considerable disadvantage for any physical encounter.

But we didn't discuss it much. After all, he never mentioned the time I forgot to set the car brake, and it rolled slowly across old lady Fratos's flowerbed, onward across Commercial Street and onto the beach, with Fargo in the driver's seat looking keenly competent. He didn't rat on me the time I accidentally put laundry soap in the dishwasher, either. So we each had an unflattering secret or two . . . what love affair doesn't?

My lover Cindy was a different matter. This morning she came into the kitchen, did a little dance step and a brief chorus of "Singin' in the Rain," and then asked, "What's wrong with you two? A mere cloud and drop of rain got you down? Do something constructive. Organize your office, my love. See what all is buried under the cushion in your doggie bed, my other love. And smile."

I looked over at Fargo and said, "Kill." But he was too depressed to move. "What are you so happy about?" I asked.

"Have you figured out how to get around the security system in the bank?" Cindy was head of Fishermen's Bank's Personal Investments and Financial Planning Department. She loved her job, but usually not this much.

"In fact," I reminded her, "You should be teary-eyed. You are leaving us, aren't you?"

"Yes, but only till Tuesday, darling. Just think, you and Fargo can live on pizza and Chinese take-away. You don't have to make the bed, and if you get lonely, you can go cry on Joe's shoulder at the Wharf Rat Bar."

"Sounds ghastly," I muttered untruthfully. Actually, at that point, it didn't sound all that bad for a day or so.

"Seriously, Alex, I'll be at work till noon-ish today, then drive down to Providence and back to work Tuesday morning early. I'll be home after work Tuesday, darling, and I'll call you tonight."

Cindy's brother and his wife—mainly his wife, of course—had just had a new baby. Cindy was going down to take care of their two older children while Pete and Karol got used to their new daughter, named Hillary—either for her paternal grandmother or a U.S. Senator. It sounded like a trip to hell to me, but Cindy was all excited, so I tried to be, too.

"So you'll have three full days to admire Hillary—with any luck she'll look more like the senator than like Grandma—and play with Ken and Barbie, uh, I mean Butch and Abby. Have fun. My regards to your family." I carried Cindy's bag out to her car while she struggled into her raincoat and said fond farewells to her other darling and to Wells. She came out and we kissed good-bye. She got in the car, turned to me and caroled the ancient Al Jolson song about April showers bringing May flowers.

"It's September tenth."

"So it is." She put the car in gear and pulled away as she bellowed out that never-to-be-forgotten Broadway bit about the sun coming out tomorrow.

I loved her to pieces.

But not enough to turn my office into some pristine executive

3

suite. I knew where everything was—that was what counted. Actually, I was bone-tired. We'd had a bunch of actors living next door for most of the summer, and their antics, added to the murder of two of their number over Labor Day, had left me physically and emotionally a bit drained.

I was glad I had no cases active at the moment. I really wasn't sure I had the energy. Cases? Oh, I'm a private investigator. I handle mostly insurance fraud. While the majority of tourists spend money on vacation, there are some who try to make a tidy sum by claiming injuries that never really happened. At least not in the way they present it.

They think up clever accidents, cases of unlikely food poisoning, or get "clipped" by cars racing along Commercial Street at three miles an hour. I try to separate the barely possible from the purely frivolous. At other times, I investigate job applicants for local businesses—or current employees who seem to have invented tasty recipes for cooking the books. I look for runaways and occasionally for unfaithful spouses. Although I enjoy neither of the last two activities, they help when it's time to pay the bills. You get the picture.

Actually, it is pictures that I enjoy the most. My second career is that of nature photography, and I'm getting better at it. Fishermen's Bank now has several of my photos on display in their conference room. Four of the best galleries in the area now handle my prints—signed and numbered, I'll have you know. And Fargo and I have a great time on the beach and in the pine or beech woods taking them. Maybe someday I'll be good enough to switch which career comes first.

I lazily poured a second cup of coffee, tossed Fargo a biscuit and Wells a couple of crunchies. I let my thoughts wander to such deep matters as why the Red Sox can never seem to make it two years in a row. Could there really be a curse? And I wondered how unlikely people such as Andre Agassi manage to make such beautiful farewell speeches with just the right amount of tremor in their voices. Maybe having all that money helps.

At that moment, the doorbell rang, startling all of us. Fargo ran toward the front door with his muted announcement bark, and I followed quickly. Wells peeked around the dining room door. It was early for guests, and I anticipated no bill collectors. But I had the feeling that all three of us were so bored, we'd welcome almost anyone not stark naked and carrying a bloody axe.

As I looked through the glass-paneled door, I saw that the lady standing on our tiny front porch was fully clothed and carried no axe. She did not look in the least threatening. In fact, she looked rather sweet, and I placed my hand lightly on Fargo's shoulder to quiet him.

My visitor appeared to be around sixty, and was wearing a raincoat, hat and a tentative smile.

I returned the smile as I opened the door. "Good morning. What may I do for you?" She looked vaguely familiar to me, but I could not quite make the connection. Maybe a friend of Aunt Mae's.

"Good morning, Alex. You may not remember me, but I'm Marie Catlett, your . . ."

" . . . my fourth-grade teacher. Of course, Mrs. Catlett, please come in. Let me take your coat."

"Thank you. Alex. Do you have a few minutes to talk to me? I think I am in bad need of your help."

Nothing like a cheery reunion. "Certainly I have time. How about some coffee and something to nibble on?"

I settled us at our table-for-two in the corner of the dining room, overlooking my bed of rain-drooped asters, cosmos and chrysanthemums. With croissants and coffee served Cindy style—that's elegantly—I sat down. "Now, let's see if I can be of help."

It was not to be a short explanation, and several times I tried to push her along a bit. On the other hand, I figured whatever crisis there was, it was bound to be over by the time she got to explaining it.

"You remember my son, Reed?"

She looked over her rimless glasses at me, waiting for a reply, and for an instant, I felt I was nine years old again. I almost stood up to answer.

"Sure. He's now an architect here in town, quite successful, too, I believe." I knew. With all the new buildings and renovations up and down the Cape, the talented Reed Catlett had made a bundle and then some.

Mrs. Catlett sipped her coffee and continued. "He has three wonderful children. Starting with the oldest—Rob is nineteen and on his way to college. Zoe is just seventeen, extremely bright and a real beauty. Zoe is also a handful." She smiled. "Not a bad girl of course, just . . . adventurous. And then there is Marvin, age fourteen, our scholar with a military bent."

Where the hell were we going with this? It began to resemble a TV script. "It sounds like a lovely family," I cooed.

"It is. And naturally, you recall the tragic death of Reed's wife, Frances, some years back?"

"Uh, yes, surely." A plane crash. A bus, maybe a train. Something violent, but not criminal.

"Well." Mrs. Catlett rested in this saga long enough to take a bite of croissant, and I took the opportunity to top off my cup. "They were all just devastated, especially the children, as you would surmise. Reed had his work. His work has always been a passion for him. And at the time, in his grief, he simply threw himself into it. I was around whenever possible. And naturally, we leaned heavily on Mrs. Hengel, the housekeeper/nanny for the kids."

Naturally. I had a feeling that by the time this tale was told, I would be old enough to need a nanny.

" . . . evangelical pastor with a little church off Shank Painter Road. So good with runaways, you know."

I was totally lost. Where had I been? Where had she gone?

"You mean Larry Bartles?" I asked. Surely I wasn't going to have to tangle with him again.

6

"Yes. Well, it seems that an old school friend of Mrs. Bartles came to visit and somehow got introduced to Reed at some charity event. It must have been love at first sight, for the next thing you know, Reed and Merrilou were married . . . about six months ago, now."

"How wonderful for them." I gushed.

"Possibly. She's very attractive." Mrs. Catlett paused, seeming to expect an answer, so I gave her one.

"Ummm," I said with deep meaning.

"And very southern . . ." Another pause.

"Aha." I nodded as if that explained everything. Apparently my answers were correct, and she continued.

"But it seems the trouble with the children started with the new marriage. I suppose it's only natural the children felt some resentment against Merrilou. And I must admit, she doesn't seem a particularly maternal type who would know to accept that and slowly change it to affection, or at least tolerance."

"You mean there were quarrels, or unpleasantness?" I asked earnestly, as if I really cared.

"On the contrary. Everyone has been operatically correct." She mimed a bow and a curtsy from her chair.

"But shortly after the wedding, Rob decided that he is going all the way to the University of Tennessee for his forensic geological studies instead of the University of Massachusetts. It's so far away, he'll almost never get home," she added sadly. "It was then that Marvin shared his absolutely stunning plans to join the Marines at age eighteen and to attend some Marine-oriented boys' summer camp every year until then." She sighed and raised her hands as if in supplication.

"And it's when Zoe announced she is a lesbian."

Chapter 2

"I see." I pursed my mouth sagely. Now I knew why she was here rather than asking the advice of several ex-students I could think of who were married and had large, possibly even happy, families.

"Mrs. Catlett, did this announcement of Zoe's result in the end of the world for the Catlett family?"

"Oh, no. Perhaps it registered a weak three on the Richter scale. Reed reminded Zoe that being gay had some built-in problems, at least in some areas of the country, and with some people in any area, but if that was her decision, well, it was her life. Rob just said he thought it was 'cool' and laughed and said he wished he'd thought of it first. Now that caused Reed to raise his eyebrows, but Rob is always kidding around. Marvin came to attention, barked 'Semper Fi' in his squeaky voice and said if anybody gave her grief, just to let him know."

I reached for a cigarette. What the hell? I was well out of

fourth grade. And this was only the second of the five I allow myself each day. I chastise myself firmly for all the others.

"Mrs. Catlett—" I began.

"Please," she interrupted, "call me Marie. Mrs. Catlett makes me feel we should be back struggling with long division. And we did struggle, didn't we? And if I might ask one more favor, could I please have one of your cigarettes?"

"Certainly." I pushed the pack and lighter across the table, more firmly convinced than ever that the whole world had quit smoking cigarettes until they were within reach of mine.

"Marie, you've covered everyone but sweet Merrilou. Tell me, what was her reaction?"

"Oh, a really wonderful scene. Loud screams, followed by desperate calls upon God and Jesus, falling to her knees in front of Zoe, grasping her hands, begging her not to go to hell, demanding to know who had led her down this sinful path and a rather embarrassing emphasis on learning exactly how far they had gone physically. Oh, and she demanded that Reverend Bartles be summoned at once for prayer and counseling." Marie was fighting off a smile.

I had no desire to smile. "Is Larry Bartles now in the middle of this, telling Zoe he can 'cure' her of her sin and help her lead a 'normal' life?"

Marie looked surprised. "Not at all. When Merrilou called him, she sounded so hysterical and incoherent, he did come right over. He and his wife. And when he arrived and figured out what Merrilou was hiccupping about, he asked Zoe if she actually knew what she was getting into. Zoe said she did. He asked if she had been coerced in any way, or led on by some older person. Zoe said no, and Bartles just said this was a situation for the family to work through. If Zoe—or any of them—needed professional counseling, he could recommend several good people in the area. If any of the family wanted—and he accented wanted—to speak with him, he would try to be of service. He would pray for Jesus to help them through their troubles."

Marie puffed on her cigarette and tapped the ashes. "Then he took his wife Emily's arm and led her out, although I could tell she wanted to stay, probably in hopes of learning who the other young woman is."

I could hardly believe what I'd heard. A year ago, Bartles would have been calling for the whole town to hold a prayer meeting on Zoe's behalf. Maybe some of our heated conversations had led Larry to think a little deeper.

I sighed. "That's a relief."

"Perhaps," Marie admitted. "But we may yet need the offices of the good reverend. It pains me to say this, and I hope you will keep it in confidence, but Reed's is not a happy household. He doesn't seem to see it. But I think it's obvious to anyone else who spends time there."

"What do you mean?" If Zoe's announcement and a new wife weren't enough problems for the Catletts, what was?

And why ask me about it? I obviously had no children, had never been married to a man. My brother Sonny and I had lost our father when I was just twelve and Sonny fourteen . . . and in a horribly bizarre fashion. Provincetown was scheduled to be brushed by a Category 3 hurricane, and if we were truly only "brushed," I never want to be hit head-on by one. Our father stayed at work and did everything he could to board up and batten down the supermarket where he was manager, arriving home late and slightly drunk.

He was in a foul mood and had obviously stopped for a few belts somewhere along the way. By the time he got home, the power had failed, and the dark, chilly house and cold supper did nothing to improve his humor, and he retired to the living room with the battery radio and a bottle of Scotch. The other three of us huddled in the kitchen through a long, sleepless and terrifying night, wanting to hide from the rain beating against the house like machine gun bullets, shivering at drafts moaning through cracks we hadn't known the house even had, cringing from unidentifiable thuds and crashes outdoors and finally ready to scream back at a shrieking wind that never shut up.

The next morning Dad awoke cold, tired and hungover, with rain still coming down and the power still out. The sight of our neighbor's tree partially blocking our driveway was the final blow for him. Despite warning after warning on the radio to be careful of live wires, he grabbed the chainsaw from the utility room and flung himself out of the house to clear a path for his car, so he could go to work. Thirty seconds later, we were a family of three.

I think in one way none of us ever forgave him his stupidity. In another, I think we were all quietly relieved that he, his borderline alcoholism, his rotten moods and bitter sarcasm were gone. Mom had to go back to work. Career plans changed for Sonny and me. It was not easy. Only in the last eight or so years had our finances become really stable. But we were happier.

Anyway, I hardly felt this idyllic family history qualified me to help turn Marie Catlett's extended family into an ongoing *Leave It to Beaver* episode. I wondered what she expected of me.

"Reed loved his first wife and his children deeply, but he didn't show affection easily," Marie explained. "Frances, his wife then, was the nurturer. Occasionally she would book them all on an interesting, unusual vacation and simply tell Reed he was going, too. He would argue that he had important work to do, but usually he would finally agree, and everyone would more often than not have a great time. Then he'd go back into his shell. Frances was the one who comforted them all, from a skinned knee to a difficult client."

Another of my cigarettes snaked its casual way to Marie's fingers, and she went on. And on.

"When Frances died, Reed was absolutely lost. He simply disappeared into his office and was practically mute. I came up and stayed for a while, but obviously something permanent had to be done. Mrs. Hengel, a middle-aged widow, motherly and kind, had served as babysitter since Rob was born. I convinced her to rent out her house and move into Reed's third floor, to act as housekeeper and surrogate mother. Of course, she wasn't Frances, but she loved the kids and they were very fond of her. They seemed to be coming through their grief in fairly good shape."

She tapped her fingers on the table in obvious irritation.

"Then Merrilou arrived, announced that she could manage the house quite well with the day help and that the children didn't need a nanny, now that they were older and had a new Mother, that's with a capital M. So for the second time, the kids lost a caregiver."

I gave a short laugh. "I thought one mother was standard issue. You might be lucky enough to get a stepmother you learn to care for, but you don't get a new mother. I doubt anyone would ever replace mine."

"Quite right," Marie nodded sharply, as she used to do if I had answered a tricky geography question correctly. "Anyway, let me finally make my point here. Zoe wrote me a few weeks back, asking to come and live with Barbara and me. Barb is my dear friend, another retired teacher. We share a home down in Madison, Connecticut."

"I see." I wasn't sure if I did or not.

Marie grinned. "Some discoveries come a bit late in life."

Now I saw and returned her grin. "So is Zoe going home with you? Do you think that will work?"

"That was the plan." Now, strangely, I thought I saw tears in Marie's eyes. "We had discussed things that could and could not be done and agreed to give it a try until the end of the year. At that time, we'd reevaluate and see if all three of us wanted to continue the arrangement."

"Sounds sensible."

"It's immaterial." Marie dabbed at her eyes with a tissue. "At breakfast this morning, the maid came into the dining room with the news that Zoe's bed had not been slept in. She had gone out to meet some friends after dinner last night, and no one in the house has seen or spoken with her since."

"Did you call the police right away?"

"No, we did not." Suddenly Marie sounded very weary. "This has happened before—Zoe staying away overnight—not often, but two or three times. Reed thought she may have gone to a friend's house, lost track of the time, maybe had some alcohol, and decided it was better not to come home until today."

"Well, Marie, that's worrisome, but it happens all the time with kids. Have you called her friends?"

"No. Merrilou said it would be too humiliating, and frankly, we're not sure whom to call."

"Humiliating. Who cares?" I asked angrily. "The kid could be somewhere sick or hurt. She could have started home last night and, for some reason, never made it. Did you call the clinic? She could be in there with no ID."

"Yes, I insisted on calling them. She's not there. Nor had anyone of her description been in their outpatient care. Anyway, it doesn't matter. At about that point the phone rang. Merrilou answered it. She said later the voice sounded like a teenage male, and he said, 'We have your daughter, and it will cost you one million dollars to get her back.'"

"My God." I slammed my cup into the saucer and stood up to go to the kitchen phone. "I'm so sorry! No wonder you need someone to talk to, Marie. But we can't afford to waste time. The early moments are very important in a kidnapping. I'll call Sonny and see if they know anything more. Have they got a tap on the phone yet? Or do you know? Surely they've got the police there by now."

Sonny, by the way, is my older brother and a detective lieutenant in the Provincetown Police Department. He is very good at what he does.

Marie stood up as I did. "Alex, the police know nothing. As I told you, they have not been consulted."

"You mean you still haven't called them? What does it take to convince your family Zoe is in trouble? Do they think if they ignore this, the kidnappers will get bored and send Zoe home in

13

a cab eating an ice cream cone? She must really feel hopeless and abandoned. Kidnapped by a set of criminals and blessed with a family of lunatics. I'm calling my brother."

"Don't call the police!" Marie made a strong negative movement with her hands. "Reed and Merrilou definitely don't want them in it. Zoe and Reed have been arguing over some decisions about college, and Merrilou has convinced Reed it is a joke of some sort, or a trick on Zoe's part to get money out of Reed to spend on the college she wants, and perhaps run away with this so-called girlfriend. We don't even know who she is."

"Why would Merrilou think it's a joke or a hoax?"

"As I said, she thought the voice sounded young, maybe a teenage boy. Second, she thinks she heard a girl or woman, laughing in the background."

"That hardly constitutes a hoax. The laughter could have been on a TV in another room, or someone laughing nervously or drinking or on drugs. A dozen reasons. And the man who called could simply have had a young sounding voice or be a young man. So what? What did Merrilou say? Did she ask to speak to Zoe to see if someone really has her and she is all right?"

Marie grunted.

"No. Merrilou said, 'I'm looking all over my dining room and I don't see any million dollars lying around to give to the sorry likes of you. If you've got her, I guess you get to keep her.' And then she hung up."

Chapter 3

I stared at Marie Catlett for a full minute. I'm sure my mouth was open. I had never heard anything so stupid and so cold-blooded in my life. Playing finders-keepers with kidnappers could be a dangerous game.

"Let's get over there." I went for my jacket. "Maybe— hopefully—the kidnappers called again, and somebody went suddenly sane and talked to them and to Zoe, or maybe even called the cops."

Fargo wanted to go with me and I hated to leave him home alone for God knows how long, so I let him come along. If Marie found this strange, she kept her mouth shut about it.

In the car, she kept clearing her throat as if she wanted to say something. Finally, I asked her if the dog was bothering her.

He was sulking in the backseat with his head stuck between the two front seats, and she turned to pat his head. "Heavens, no. He's a lovely boy. No, I'm just trying to get up the courage to tell you that after my pleas, and those added by Rob and Marvin, Reed finally agreed we should do something about this situation, and that 'something' is to retain you to contact some of Zoe's friends and casually ask if any of them know her whereabouts. Perhaps I should have told you sooner. I didn't have the nerve."

I guess it was a good thing we were already turning into Reed's driveway at that moment. Otherwise, I would simply have circled the block and gone home and turned the TV on to cartoons or old western movies. Why not? I seemed to be in the middle of a combination of the two.

We parked under the carport and went in through the kitchen to avoid the rain, which had picked up some, making me wonder fleetingly if Zoe was in a warm, dry spot or someplace deliberately uncomfortable. I thought it sad that Zoe seemed to be not between a rock and a hard place, but a rock and the vacuum that should have been her family.

We entered the house and Fargo tracked daintily across the pristine white and gold kitchen tiles, leaving a rather artistic trail until we reached the dining room, where his paw prints didn't show on what was probably a very expensive oriental rug. In that room, we found the entire family gathered silently around the table with coffee cups and crumbled pastries spread carelessly here and there. A real breakfast sat untouched on the sideboard, looking cold and soggy with the warmer lights turned off under the servers.

"Anything new turn up?" Marie asked quickly.

I thought I could guess that answer from the universal gloomy expressions. Merrilou answered, and I had forgotten about the accent. "No. Not a single threatenin' cawl. But this mus' be yoah deah friend, Alex." She rose and offered her hand, cool and firm, as she continued her tungsten magnolia welcome, which I won't even try to duplicate. She introduced me to the family and then poured coffee for me and set a plate of pastries within easy reach. I introduced Fargo, and the two boys got up to pet him. Merrilou smiled at him, and Reed looked underwhelmed.

"If you'd like a hot breakfast. It would be no trouble at all . . ." She looked at me questioningly.

"No, thanks, this is fine." I sipped the first-rate coffee and wondered who was going to be the first to get the conversation going. It was, of course, Marie.

She announced, "Everyone, Alex thinks we're all wrong not to inform the police. Immediately. Time is of the essence." Marvin and Rob nodded. Reed and Merrilou shook their heads.

Merrilou answered gently. "Marie, Alex, I am convinced it really is some kind of misplaced joke, and bringing in the police would just make fools of them and of us and of Zoe. This has happened before. Without telling us, Zoe has spent the night with a girlfriend. Lordy, what a new meanin' that has taken on."

Reed finally was heard from. "Please, Merri, don't get into that again. We're all upset about it, but the immediate problem is Zoe's safety. Now, I'm inclined to agree it's some kind of prank. I think Zoe will come waltzing in here with all kinds of excuses and expect us all to laugh with her and compliment her cleverness, and she'll think I will be convinced to let her go to that damned acting school and—"

The strident buzz of the phone on the buffet froze us all. Merrilou was the first to jump up.

"NO!" I managed to shout. "Reed, you get it. Demand to speak with Zoe, talk as long as you can. We may hear identifiable background noise. Tell them you don't have a million, or even near it. Ask them for a couple of days to try to get some money pulled together. Tell them you're trying hard."

Reed was pushing Merrilou ungraciously aside, grabbing for the phone. I turned to Rob. "Tape recorder? Speaker phone?"

Marvin was already up and running into the living room. Rob motioned me back toward the kitchen, moving at a trot on the slippery tiles.

"Tape recorder's in the living room, speaker's in the kitchen."

He punched a couple of buttons and Reed's voice came

through, with that sort of echo effect speakers lend to any voice.

" . . . yes, I'm Reed Catlett. Who are you?"

"Right now, I'm Zoe's watchdog. Arf, arf." I heard a girlish titter in the background. "And if you want me to keep on being a friendly puppy, you'll keep that friggin' comedian who answered the first time, off the phone. And you'll tell me you've got that million all counted out, and I'll tell you how you are to get it to me. That is if you want Zoe back. Scarlett O'Hara didn't sound like she much cared one way or the other."

The voice did sound young, but not childish. The caller could be most any reasonably adult age. I peered back into the dining room. Reed was pale, and his hand that held the phone was shaking, but he hung tough.

"I don't do business with dogs or in vacuums. We won't even discuss money till I know my Zoe is okay. Put her on the line." His voice was flat and businesslike.

"My, my, aren't we the bossy one. That won't last long." The kidnapper turned away from the phone and said something I couldn't hear. There was what seemed a long silence.

Then a young girl's voice cried out, "Oh, Daddy! Daddy, come and take me home! They say they'll kill me if you don't pay them. Are you there? I feel awful about this. I'm so sorry things didn't work out."

Before Reed could say anything comforting to his daughter, there was some sort of scuffle as she was pulled away. The young man returned. "Satisfied, Daddy? Now here's what we do. You put a million dollars in fifty- and twenty-dollar bills in a couple of the smallest school backpacks you can fit them in. Unmarked bills, by the way. We're too smart for that trick. Then you bring—"

"Not so fast, sonny." Reed was getting mad, which was fine as long as he remembered who had Zoe.

"My first clue to your ignorance of what you're trying to do is that you are not of the business world. Bill Gates may have a million in cash in his house on a Friday morning, but I sincerely

18

doubt it. I tell you right now, I've got about three hundred in the house. And I have a little money in the local bank. If I get that and borrow what cash I can today from my friends around here, I'd probably have fifteen thousand. Or a little more. Will that do it for you?"

Our kidnapper sounded shaky. "Never you mind what world I'm in. And fifteen grand ain't even a down payment on one of Zoe's ears, which you'll get if you keep this shit up. I'll call you Monday at this time. Have the money . . . all the money!" The connection broke.

We found ourselves back in the dining room, all talking at once. "How did I do?" Reed asked me.

"You did just fine," I said sincerely. "One small thing, you let him know you picked up on his ignorance of the business world. That's a clue to who he is and it made him nervous, and you don't want him any more nervous than he is. Believe me, he's as scared as you are. You want him to think he's in complete control—right up to the last minute when the cops snap the cuffs on him. Don't give him any information. Just try to get what you can out of him. Like is Zoe warm, reasonably fed, healthy? Do they want new bills? The longer you can keep him talking, the more likely you are to learn something."

I wasn't giving Reed some information, myself. I'd heard something in Zoe's plea that I wanted to pursue. But not now. Not with this group.

"Yeah, sorry about that business world slip. It was just so obvious."

"No great harm. Just be aware when next you speak to him."

Merrilou's soft voice came from across the table. "Alex, honey, you did hear how young he sounded and how flip, didn't you? And that silly giggle. I still think it's a prank. If Reed had said fifty thousand instead of fifteen, I'll bet you anything that young man would have taken it." She leaned against Reed's back and put her head on his shoulder, her arms around his chest, hands rubbing gently. Reed looked embarrassed and moved away from her.

I answered before she could take him off to bed. "I doubt it. Our watchdog is still thinking of dining on filet mignon. By Monday, we'll try two hundred thousand, which will buy a lot of T-bones. Depending on how we phrase it, that may work." Merrilou's eyes widened, but she made no comment.

"Monday seems so far away," Marie was teary eyed again. "Poor Zoe sounds just terrified. My God, what do you suppose they've done to her?"

"Probably nothing serious. She's their asset, their only asset until they get the money. That'll be the time to walk very softly."

"What do you mean, 'nothing serious'"? Marvin asked. With his round face and unreliable voice, he seemed quite mild. Until you looked at his eyes. Maybe he really would be a Marine.

"Kidnappers like to humiliate their captives." I took out a cigarette, glad I had remembered to say captive instead of victim. "It makes it easier for the kidnappers to keep them under control if they're embarrassed and uncomfortable. So they probably took most of her clothes. They may make her eat food right from the can with her fingers. They probably have warned her not to speak unless they tell her to, or maybe won't let her use the bathroom alone . . ."

"And you call that 'nothing serious'? I call that enough to kill the bastards." Marvin looked ready to kill, and I thought Reed might burst into tears. Rob was bent over, petting Fargo, to cover his own emotion, I assumed. Poor Marie was sobbing outright. Even Merrilou looked distressed.

"Look," I explained, "it's just that if they belittle her, they feel bigger. It makes the captive feel powerless. It's not nice, but it isn't really harmful. She'll handle it." I took a sip of my now-cold coffee, tried not to wince and hoped to God I was right about a seventeen-year-old I had never met.

"Now, Reed, what's the real story on the money?"

"First, I was lying about the bank. Most of my easily convertible assets are at Fishermen's Bank. I just didn't think that punk needed to know that." I nodded in approval. And he went on.

"The problem will be getting it into cash over a weekend. In four or five days, I could have close to a million. I'm not sure to the exact thousand."

"Yeah." I thought it must be nice to have a million, even if it did vary a thousand here, a thousand there. "Anyway, Reed, naturally we would try very hard to settle for a lot less."

"Why? What difference does it make how much is in the knapsacks, when they'll only have them for a minute or two?"

"Uh, well, Reed, you've elected to go with one lonely private investigator instead an entire police force plus the FBI. There's only one of me and my only concern will be getting Zoe home in one piece. They may well get clean away with the money. I'll be in touch. C'mon, Fargo."

Chapter 4

Rob walked us to the car, so I had the opportunity to ask him about Zoe's friends. He seemed rather at a loss. "She has a million casual friends, but not many close ones. For all her fun-loving side, she is kind of a private person," he finally said. "But if it is just some scheme they've cooked up, I mean if she isn't really kidnapped, if anybody will know where she is, it'll be Dana Portman or Harry Maddock."

"And just who are they?" I opened the car door and Fargo jumped across into the passenger's seat, taking no chances of being put in the back. I sat in the driver's seat and pulled a notebook from the compartment. "Shoot."

He leaned against the open car door. "Dana is a great girl. Smart, nice and super rich. Her old man imports antiques of all kinds from all over the world. Sells 'em to dealers or museums and then has replicas made in a couple of factories he owns. Talk about a million. He probably keeps that in the cookie jar to tip the paper boy."

I looked up from my notes. "I'm surprised he's not in jail."

"No, no." Rob laughed. "He doesn't pass the copies off as the real thing. They're all clearly marked Portman Reproductions and the date, and the ones I've seen have a little booklet with the history of the original. Very classy stuff. They're very well done and cost a bundle even though they're reproductions."

"I see." I also felt a little foolish. "And Dana is the recipient of all this money?"

"Someday, I guess. She'll deserve it. Next year she's off to Yale to study art history, although she already knows as much as most dealers. She's wants to be a museum curator for a few years and then her dad wants her to go into the family business. She travels a lot with her dad, but I'm not sure she's all that sold on joining him in the business. I think she wants her independence."

"Where's her mom in all this?" I lit a cigarette, and Rob looked at me longingly until I passed him the pack and lighter.

"Living on Spain's sun coast with—according to Dana—a gorgeous guy about half her age. They may be married, not sure. Dana stays in touch with her, secretly, I think. I don't believe her old man knows about it."

"And is Dana Zoe's lover?"

Rob dropped the cigarette and tapped it into the gravel, as Merrilou walked out onto the large porch and began a careful survey of the potted plants.

"Sorry to waste it. It's easier than listening to her lecture on the subject later. Anyway, yes, I assume Dana is the girl. They're always together, make a great pair, actually. Dana is so well-grounded and Zoe is always so ready to sail away in a beautiful pea-green boat." I could hear the affection in his voice and was glad. At least Zoe had one white knight.

"Is Zoe interested in antiques, too?"

"Not professionally. She loves pretty things and is fairly knowledgeable as a layman, but she plans—oh, God, how she plans—to be an actress." He struck a pose and grinned.

"How exciting. And is an internationally famous producer going to spot her in the supermarket, strike his forehead with a salami and sign her for the leading lady in his next play?"

"Ah, there's the rub. Zoe wants to go to some acting school in New York next year. Dad thinks she's too young to be cut loose in a big city and says he wants her to live at home and go to the two-year college up the Cape or go to Boston College so she can be home weekends first. Then he'll send her to whatever acting school she wants."

"Sounds reasonable to me." I shrugged.

"But not to Zoe. She says by then she'll be too old for the good parts and have to settle for the maiden aunt-type roles."

"At twenty-one?"

Rob laughed. "Zoe does have her own schedule, and being a star by nineteen is on her calendar."

"Okay, I can see that. What about the Maddock boy? Wasn't he the kid who won all the state hockey prizes the last couple of years?"

I looked around at the porch. The flowerpots were all running over with water. Merrilou would have the plants floating shortly. Automatically, I lowered my voice. "If Dana and Zoe are gay, where does Harry fit in? Is he carrying a torch for one of them? Is he gay, too?"

"Neither, I'd say. I think Harry is hockey. It's his life. He's a good friend to both girls, but I don't think there's any romance— real or imagined. His problem is getting a sports scholarship, not a bedmate. And they aren't easy to get in hockey . . . scholarships. I mean . . . it's not as popular as football or basketball. I guess bedmates come pretty easily to any star athlete." He grinned and bent over, picked up the battered cigarette. Held out his hand for my lighter and relit it.

"The hell with it." He shrugged.

"Yeah, well with his reputation, you'd think any college with a hockey team would want him. I don't know about starting a harem. Where would I find him and Dana?" I asked. "I mean, not at home. I'd like to talk to them without parents for the moment. And do you have a photo of either or all of them?"

Rob thought for a moment. "My best guess on where to find them? Mickey's Pizza, anytime of the day or night. All the kids practically live there." Obviously, Rob did not consider himself any longer in that age group.

"Photos, I'll check later with Nana. Grandmothers always have those things don't they? Look, I'd better get going now or Merrilou will be pouring water into your gas tank."

Rob reached in and took my notebook and pen. "Here's my cell phone number. Call any time if I can help. And could I have your e-mail address so I can send you any photos I turn up?"

He wrote the address on a note page as I recited it, and raised his voice as he tore out the page and handed back my book. "Yes, he certainly is a fine dog. You'd never know he's really so vicious, especially around women." He winked and walked away, cigarette dangling crookedly from his mouth. I liked his style.

Backing carefully out of the narrow, old-fashioned driveway, I started slowly back into town. The rain had become a mist, but it still was not an outdoor day. A few minutes later, I pulled over to give Mickey's a closer look. Mickey's Pizza had a few small tables jammed inside the building and a more numerous collection outside on the widened sidewalk. Only one or two were in use by the brave. It was not a time for Mickey's.

Anyway, I wanted to get some information and possibilities straight in my head before I started interviewing potential suspects—if that wasn't too strong a word. Cohorts might be a better one. Shortly I'd find out if all three kids had disappeared and if any of their families had received calls from "kidnappers."

Just down the street from Mickey,'s I spotted a public phone that actually had a tattered directory dangling beside it, and parked nearby. I just wanted the addresses. I had no intention of phoning. It was too easy to lie or stall on a telephone. Face to face was a little harder. Both phones were listed, and because Daniel Portman's home was nearer, that's where I started.

25

I drove slowly through the open wrought iron gates, but stopped short of the house to speak with an older woman in a bright yellow raincoat who was snipping dew-covered roses and handing them to a sweatered maid who stuck them gingerly into a large vase.

I got out of the car as they stopped their activities to give me curious, but not unfriendly looks.

"Hello, I'm Alex Peres. I'm a private investigator," I announced, showing my license. "Nothing serious, as far as I know."

I had added the last words to assuage their obvious anxiety at my apparently alarming introduction. "Zoe Catlett didn't come home last night. Her family is assuming she spent the night with a friend, but they'd like to make sure she didn't fall ill or something. Knowing Dana is a friend of Zoe's, I just thought I'd check if she were here visiting Dana, or had been here last night."

"I'm Dana's grandmother, Mrs. Arlen. I was already in bed when I heard Dana's car pull around to the garage last night, and I know she came in. I heard her on the stairs. I think she was alone."

She turned to the maid. "Greta, what about breakfast?"

The maid answered, "Miss Dana called down for breakfast in her room this morning, said she didn't feel well. I took it up. No one else was with her, and she didn't say anything about serving a guest in another room. And nobody strange was in the dining room before you came down, ma'am."

Mrs. Arlen and I looked at each other and smiled at the maid's last sentence. Mrs. Arlen pretty well ended the interview, but nicely.

"Dana is apparently here, and I guess there are no strangers in the house. I do hope Zoe is all right, she's such a lively, fun-loving girl."

"I imagine it's just one of those parent/teenager mix-ups that happen sometimes," I said. She was so pleasant I felt I should reassure her. We murmured a few more cordial words and parted.

I would love to have talked with Dana, but felt the timing was bad. I was sure Grandma would have come along, and if I had asked to speak to Dana alone, all kinds of red flags would have flown.

I went down the hill, back toward town and up another small hill, stopping in front of a modest ranch house.

I rang the bell, but nobody answered. I walked around to the backyard with the thought someone might be doing yard work, but that small hope was dashed, so I retreated in good order, under the watchful eyes of a next-door neighbor.

"Hello," I called across the fence. "I was looking for Harry Maddock. Any idea where I might find him?"

"Why would you be looking for Harry?" Her expression grew even more distrustful.

"I'm a private investigator, and a friend of Harry's has gone missing, and—"

I was talking to her back. She vanished into her house with the slam of a door. Did she think I figured Harry for a kidnapper? Probably she just disliked PIs. I wondered what tale the first Maddock to return home would be treated to.

I waved merrily toward a window where the curtain was jiggling and pushed Fargo over into the passenger's seat. He looked at me with such sad, big brown eyes that I said, "Okay, we'll go to the beach." What the hell was a little mist?

The Provincetown beaches had all kinds of weather from time to time, and I loved most of it, from cloudless hot days with the ocean sighing softly onto the beach, to days of hammer-like surf and horizontal sleet that burned if it hit your skin. Today a fog bank hovered firmly over us with no signs of burning off, and the ocean moved slowly in on oily rollers. And our only companion was the reassuring deep-throated boom from the Truro lighthouse.

The last words Zoe had uttered before being pulled away

from the phone had made me curious. I thought about them as I watched Fargo tear down the beach in a sand-scattering run.

She had said that she felt awful about it. Very few kidnap victims apologize for being kidnapped . . . at least not until they've been happily and safely returned to their loved ones.

Then she started to say she was sorry about something that didn't work out. Again, an unusual remark. Most kidnappees understandably, simply feel extremely sorry for themselves and are more likely to scream, "Get me the hell out of here!" than to apologize for being there. Of course, some of them go through real agonies of guilt, but again, that is usually when they are safely home and trying to reconcile the sad fact that every cent of the family's assets went as ransom for their rescue, and has not been recovered.

"I'm so sorry it didn't work . . ." had been her last words before she had to relinquish the phone. Funny phrasing. Was she simply going to say she was sorry it had occurred and inconvenienced everyone? Not hardly. Sorry it happened on a weekend and Dad couldn't get the money? I doubted it. Sorry it all worked out wrong? Had Zoe in the beginning thought she had control over the plans, and now discovered she did not? A real possibility, especially if it had started as a more-or-less innocent prank, as Merrilou figured. Or knew? Now there was a thought.

I coasted into my driveway and cut the ignition before I really realized where I was. As I separated ignition key from the back door key and others, Fargo ran around the yard checking for invaders, leaving his spoor on various shrubs and rolling in the wet grass as a good excuse for a rubdown.

He got it, along with a biscuit, once we were inside. I checked the phone message machine in the little front entry hall we never used. One strident male, selling vinyl siding. One Cindy Hart, saying she was "outta here" and loved us and would call tonight. And couldn't we even wait till she left town to start carousing? I missed her already. Suddenly the house felt dank and chill and deserted and so did I.

A little cheer seemed in order. I went back into the kitchen and popped a beer, returned to the living room and lit the fire in the fireplace. Already life was better. I sat down on the couch, accompanied by the now dry Fargo, and stared at the fire. It's like the ocean to me. If it's there, I have to watch it.

I thought about the kidnapping. My flip notion that Merrilou had something to do with it—or at least some knowledge of it—became more and more a possibility in my mind. Maybe she had known what time the first phone call would come and had placed herself near the phone so she could logically be the one to answer it. And we had only her word for what had been said on the other end of the line. Keeping the police out of it seemed pretty much her idea, too. Reed may have been a success in business and able to hold his own when talking to the kidnappers, but he obviously didn't want a confrontation with his wife. I'll bet the family would have convinced him to involve the cops in a hurry if she hadn't been there, insisting that a call to the police would be embarrassing to Zoe's friends, would cause Reed publicity his business image didn't need and would humiliate the entire family, especially if it had anything to do with Zoe's lesbianism. Somehow, I had the idea that Reed Catlett was not the sturdiest tree in the forest when it came to emotional stability. If Merrilou used sex as a weapon, he had already lost that battle. I wondered how long it would take him to find comfort elsewhere.

Logically, I had no idea why Merrilou would want Zoe kidnapped. Surely, there must be simpler ways of getting her out of the house if Merrilou couldn't stand living with such a sinner. Hell, Zoe was considering living with her grandmother, anyway. Although Merrilou might not know that. And, obviously, there was that million dollars if it ever got that far. Merrilou and some number of other people could be richer. But, to me, that seemed a dangerous route. The kidnappers might well decide they had done all the work, taken all the risks—and deserved all the money. Merrilou could hardly sue them for breach of contract. On the other hand, if they were caught, certainly they wouldn't hesitate

29

a heartbeat to rat on her as their employer in hopes of a softer deal from the prosecutor.

My bottom line thought was that Merrilou was better off leaving things as they were and hoping Reed succumbed to an early death. Preferably natural.

Another question mark in my mental Merrilou file was her relationship with the Reverend Lawrence Bartles and his too-good-for-words wife, Emily. Bartles had a little storefront evangelical church over off Shank Painter Road. The property included the "church" plus the rambling house they lived in and a fair-sized barn. He and his wife specialized in helping runaway or homeless teenagers.

The girls stayed in the house with the Bartles. The boys lived dormitory style in the barn. The Bartles fed them and tried to reconcile the runaways with their families, tried to help the others get at least a high school education equivalent and a permanent job and to get—or keep—them off drugs and booze. I had initially had some serious doubts as to whether Larry and/or Emily had more than a religious interest in these kids, but apparently, all was on the up and up.

Larry was a little easier going than his wife. His theory was to take care of the kids' physical and emotional health first, that their souls would follow along later. Emily was rather more Middle Ages in approach. She would have demanded chastity, poverty and obedience before you got your first bowl of oatmeal.

Larry and I had been involved in a murder case last year. The beginning of our acquaintance had been stormy at best, and while we both still knew we were on opposite sides of many fences, we eventually realized we rather liked each other. I trusted him, to a degree. And he decided I did not have cloven hooves. I barely knew Emily and saw no reason to change that.

My mother, who contributed to their ever-needy larder, said Emily was "about what you would expect." My Aunt Mae said she was "sometimes difficult, but rather sweet, in her way." Of course, Aunt Mae would have considered Genghis Kahn rather sweet, in his way. I wondered idly if Emily's sweetness included starving young kidnapped gays into lifelong repentance. And I imagined even a small part of a million dollar ransom would look awfully big to Emily.

Thoughts of starving reminded me that it was nearly dinnertime, and I had had little breakfast and no lunch. The rain was with us again, and I decided to let the food come to me in my nice dry house. I called the Chinese restaurant and ordered too much of too many things as usual. No harm. There was always tomorrow's lunch.

Just as Fargo and I were polishing off an egg roll we didn't need, and Wells was playing mighty hunter with a shrimp, the phone rang. I said, "Hello," and a voice, obviously disguised came over the line.

"Hallo, is thees the Peres House of Ill Ree-pute for bee-oo-tiful womans?"

"Yes, it is." I was grinning now. "And I can tell just from your voice that we will hire you in an instant. Can you start work tonight? Of course, you realize that as the owner I have to check you out, as it were."

"Ah, no." I think I had her rattled now. "I cannot start until Tuesday, but, bebe, it vill be worth zee wait!" What the hell kind of accent was this supposed to be?

"Sorry, honey, if you can't get here tonight, I'll just have to hire this other gorgeous girl who's waiting outside."

"Well, if you've got the same weather we have, your other girl just drowned." Now the voice was wonderfully familiar.

"We do have a downpour working." I laughed. "But maybe drowning is better than having you stomp her to death with your stiletto heels. Hello, darling. I take it you arrived safely."

We settled down and chatted for half an hour, telling each other about our day's events.

Mine, I assure you, were more interesting.

31

Chapter 5

Saturdays seem to have a different feel to them, even though I don't work a standard Monday-to-Friday schedule. Fargo, Wells and I slept late, warm and cozy against the sudden autumn chill. I decided to have coffee before dressing and went for the heavier robe and slippers.

Fargo had just come in with the weather report: the grass was still wet up to his ankles, but the rain had stopped. I poured my first cup of special Blue Mountain coffee on that good news . . . and the phone rang.

It was Rob Catlett with photo information. I had to credit him. He got things done promptly. "Anything new going on?" I asked.

"Nope," he replied. "No phone calls, and the five of us hung around all evening. It was like we were all watching each other. Nana doesn't trust Merrilou. Merrilou doesn't trust her. Dad doesn't trust me or Marvin. I don't trust Merrilou or Dad. And

Marvin doesn't trust anybody. Aside from that, we are one close-knit family, warmly united by our troubles." He laughed, but he didn't mean it.

"Why don't you trust your father?" I sipped the coffee and lit the first of the five allowed cigarettes. Should I exceed that number, and I probably would, the way things are going, I'd give my wrist a good slap.

"I'm not sure. He seems to be . . . different than he used to be. He was always sort of remote, even before Mom died. But you had the feeling that in there somewhere, he loved you. After he married Merrilou, he still really didn't change, until this damn kidnap. For example, even before Zoe said she was a lesbian, Merrilou had been talking about this girls' school somewhere down south, run by the evangelicals. About how they teach premarital chastity, how you should always obey your parents and how later you're supposed to obey your husband that your parents picked, and have a lot of babies that you nurse. Sounds more like raising a cow than a girl. Anyway, Dad just laughed and said Zoe would have the girls into mutiny and the faculty into cardiac arrest within a week. Hold on a minute." I heard him say something in a low voice, and then the sound of a door closing.

"Just Marvin," Rob explained. "Anyway, Merrilou started in on this school again last night, and Dad said he'd think about it, maybe they'd go down and take a look at it. Nana said it would be a big mistake for Zoe. Dad snapped that it was his decision, and his alone. He never snaps at Nana. Marvin slammed out of the room—yelling shit! I was glaring at Dad, and Merrilou was licking cream off her whiskers. It's turning into the weekend from hell around here."

Suddenly he sounded very young. I tried to sound reassuring. "Rob, you have to remember, everybody is scared, and nobody has any control—or even real understanding—over what's happening. That never brings out the best in anyone. Try to stay cool and keep your brother cool, and look after your grandmother. She's a threat to Merrilou, and Merrilou knows it. The kidnappers aren't supposed to call again until Monday anyway, so at least we have today and Sunday. Now, the pictures you said you located, can you e-mail them to me?"

"Yes, there's a scanner in the library. Dad's at his office so I can use the scanner and get them to you right away. And thanks, I feel a little saner. You mean I don't have to strangle Merrilou and shoot Dad until Monday?" His laugh was shaky, but I figured it was a little more genuine.

"At the earliest." I smiled, as if he could see it, and said good-bye.

I took a drag on my cigarette and sent up a short puff of thanks that my name was not Catlett. The kitchen got suddenly brighter as the sun broke through outside. Maybe we'd have a nice warm day after all. I'd try Mickey's for lunch, and on the way I'd stop in the bank, which would be open till noon. With any luck, Choate Ellis, their high honcho, would be there, and I could talk to him about ransoms.

I exited the shower to hear the little bell that tinged when I had e-mail on the computer in my so-called office.

A few minutes later, I was gazing at two photos, somewhat blurry, but definitely clear enough to use for ID purposes.

One was of a grinning teenage girl with short, dark wavy hair, and a devil-may-care flash to her brown eyes—Zoe without a doubt. The boy with her in the picture was barely taller than she was, maybe five-nine, blond short hair and a nose that had been broken. He had a sweet smile as he looked down at a puppy he held. The other picture was more formally posed, a pretty young woman with reddish brown hair, carefully ragged in its cut, and warm, light hazel eyes. She wore a simple dress and leaned invitingly against a garden gate. In a few years, she would be beautiful. At thirty-five, she would be stunning. At seventy, she would not have faded. No wonder Zoe was in love with Dana.

These kids were going to need more help than I could provide.

They might have tried to pull an imprudent—and impudent—stunt and they might need to pay for it in some way, but they were by no means professional criminals. Certainly, they should not be placed in danger or serious discomfort. Nor should they serve as the means for Merrilou or anyone else to wreck a family—or families—just to ensure someone's financial future.

At some point very soon, I'd have to catch up with Sonny. Maybe some of the Catletts didn't want police help, but I did. And I didn't want to find myself guilty of not reporting a crime I was aware of. After the phone call I had heard, I could hardly claim to assume she was "voluntarily missing." Maybe her family—or some of it—could tell themselves it was a prank, but unless I wanted to lose my license, I had better be on the side of the angels.

And once in a great while, cops could be angels. Maybe it was easier in a small town, where things were a little more informal. I recalled a few years back when they handled a rather complex "kidnapping." A drunk and abusive husband beat up and threatened to kill his wife and baby, because, sick of his abuse and frightened for her child, she had sued for divorce. One night while he was passed out, she worked up her courage, took the kid and ran for her life. She made the mistake of calling her sister in Indiana to say she was coming to her, and let the conversation record on the answering machine. She took her own car, but stole some Michigan plates off a red Ford downtown as a clumsy attempt at disguise. Then she headed for Gary, Indiana, in her dark blue Honda.

Later, the husband woke up and wanted action before he left for Indiana to bring his son home "one way or another." He took the tape to headquarters just as an irate tourist from Michigan was there, complaining the license plates from his car had been hooked. It should have been cut and dried. Both husband and wife were suing for custody of the child, and neither should have taken him out of state. She should have been easily picked up and returned to Ptown with the child . . . if her husband didn't find and kill her first.

The cops got busy in a hurry and were unbelievably efficient. To satisfy the irate husband, Nacho got hold of the Michigan State Patrol and reported the missing plates . . . for a cream Dodge, with two wrong digits. Mitch tracked down the sister and told her to head off the mother and child to some different spot, preferably one the husband didn't know about, until things cooled down. Sonny interviewed the husband and was so snotty, the still half-loaded man finally took a punch at him, allowing Sonny to arrest him for assaulting an officer and putting him in a cell for two days until he could come up with the bail money. And the wife conveniently disappeared.

A few months later, the husband robbed a convenience store and pistol-whipped the clerk, thereby earning himself a twenty-five year prison term. Shortly after that, Nacho handled the sale of the trailer and household goods for the runaway mom and shipped her the money from the trailer plus a few small items she wanted, to an address in Marietta, Ohio. No one ever knew how Nacho had the information, or who actually signed the husband's name to the trailer's bill of sale. But then, nobody was around to complain, either.

I had a feeling that kind of expertise might well be needed in the Catlett caper.

Luck was with me. Choate Ellis was in his office and able to see me at Fishermen's Bank. I felt free to talk with him about the situation. I'd known him all my life. He was a good friend of my Aunt Mae and my mother. He'd like to have been more than a friend to my mother, I thought, but his rather prissy ways and short, pudgy height were against him. Anyway, Mom had managed to get herself romantically entangled with one of the actors who had been here last summer. She was currently in New York "visiting" him as the cast rehearsed the Broadway opening of the modernized, musical version of *Hamlet* that had resulted in two murders and a literal stampede in its single performance at our amphitheater over Labor Day. I really don't want to get into details. It's too bizarre.

"Hello, Choate. Thanks for fitting me into your schedule."

"A pleasure, my dear, always a pleasure. Sit down, sit down. May I offer you coffee?"

"Thank you, no. I don't want to take up your time, but as you may know, I'm working on Zoe Catlett's kidnapping. I just wanted to fill in a few blanks, if you'd be so kind."

"Kidnapping. Has that actually been established? We've been pulling a few things together, but I had the idea it was some sort of convoluted teenage scheme to hit Reed up for some money."

"I am not sure if it started that way. It's possible. But I don't think it's a joke, however poorly planned, at this point. I happened to be in their home when the kidnapper made his second call. Reed spoke briefly to Zoe, and there was no doubt in my mind she was scared to death and wanting her father to come and get her. I hope the parents have called the police by now. This stalling is getting dangerous. The kidnappers are asking for a million by Monday and getting a little nasty about it. Is that possible for you to achieve?"

"It would have been a lot easier if I'd known we really needed it," he said sourly. "I was laboring under the idea that we might—might—need one to two hundred thousand, which is no big problem. A million will have me scrambling to liquidate some of Reed's assets and get extra cash in here. No, Monday is a no. Tuesday soonest, and that's with luck. What the hell is Reed doing trying to handle this himself? Does he think he can bargain them down to a dollar ninety-eight?"

"I know I have no authority to say this, Choate, but my thought is you would do well to start scrambling, even though it's a weekend. And even though you may not need quite all of it."

He looked at me keenly. "You think it is real, that Zoe is in danger? That lovely young girl."

37

"Yes, I do. Enough that I plan to go against family wishes and report it to the police myself later today . . . if they haven't."

"Is it legal for you to do that? You can trump the family's wishes? I'm glad to hear it. Frankly, I'd feel better about it if the police were involved. A million is a lot of cash for me to get in here. And I've requested available marked bills from a small cache the . . . a certain agency keeps on hand. It won't be much, but it might help." He looked uneasy.

"I know marked bills are virtually impossible for most of us to spot. Would the kidnappers know how to do it?"

"Probably not. We've come a long way from putting an ink dot somewhere on the bill, you know. It takes special equipment to spot the mark. They might or might not have access to it or even know what it is. I wouldn't worry about that, especially if they're amateurs."

He cleared his throat and pulled out a slim cigar and an ashtray from his desk drawer. "I'll tell you frankly, Alex, I worry more that this is some sort of trick to pull off a bank robbery while I've got an extra million in tens and twenties sitting here, on a busy weekday with a dozen hostages lined up at the tellers' windows." He blew out a cloud of expensive, aromatic smoke.

I figured that was my passport to cigarette number—good grief—was it four already? "Frankly, I never thought of a bank robbery. It's hard to believe, Choate, that a fairly naïve young girl like Zoe and a couple of school pals would be involved with something like that. I can't imagine they would have even the vaguest idea of how to pull it off."

"I doubt that they would. There would have to be adults, probably even professionals involved. Zoe would be unwitting or unwilling bait. That's why I'm glad you're going to Sonny. No offense, my dear, but I think we need more than a charming young lady and an aging, worried banker to handle this."

One part of me wanted to pour his coffee over his head, but part of me knew he could be right. "Make me a bargain, Choate. I'll forgive you the sexist remark if you'll promise to get extra security and stay well into the background yourself. Don't get hurt in this, Choate. We need you around here."

He laughed and stood, extending his hand. "Very well, I will. And like it or not, you're a dear sweet girl."

I shook my head, patted his hand and gave him a dirty look.

Chapter 6

My mind was churning as I walked to the car. Opening the door, I tousled Fargo's head. "The plot thickens, Dr. Watson. How would you feel about pizza for lunch?" The increased tempo of his tail wag gave me my answer. I decided to leave the car in the bank lot, figuring Saturday was slow and no one would mind. I put Fargo on the lead and we walked the couple of blocks to Mickey's Pizza.

You could hear it and smell it before you saw it. Conversations were carried on at a mild shout to compete successfully with numerous iPods and cell phones ringing with tidbits of songs the owners thought reflected their personalities or looks in some way. Horns blew to summon friends out to the curb or to urge another car to move on. But the aroma—ah, now that made up for any minor faults I may have been finding with the ambiance.

The menu was beautifully simple on its blackboard behind the counter. Pizza by the pie or the slice, calzone, meatball or sausage grinder, small or large salad. Dessert was Italian ice or cannoli.

When my turn came at the counter, I ordered half a small pie with sausage and mushrooms, small salad and—remembering they sold no alcoholic drinks—a Diet Coke for me plus a cup of water for my friend tied to a table outside. Getting a firm grip on my tray of goodies, I eased my way through the crowd to the table Fargo had reserved for us and sat down beside him. I broke him off a crust of pizza—leaving a piece of sausage and picking off the mushrooms—and opened my Diet Coke for a sip.

I looked around, hoping to spot one or more of the kids. I really didn't expect to see Zoe, but who knew? I gazed until the scene began to blur and then stopped looking for a few minutes while I enjoyed some pizza and salad.

And then I saw him.

Harry was walking down the edge of the sidewalk, turning his head back and forth to check both cars and pedestrians. He, too, was looking for someone. When he reached my table, I called his name softly.

"Harry? Harry Maddock?"

He looked at me, his face a question mark.

"Yes. I'm Harry Maddock. Do I know you?" He was obviously on guard and untrusting of anyone who looked old enough to vote. Along with jeans and T-shirt, Harry also wore an unmistakable air of guilt.

"My name is Alex Peres. I'm a friend of Rob Catlett and also of Mrs. Marie Catlett. I'm a private investigator, and I am very quietly looking for Zoe. Marie and Rob fear she might be in some danger, and I'd like to be able to reassure them. Would you sit down and talk to me for a minute or two?"

He more or less collapsed into a chair, as if he had removed a suit of armor that was all that had held him erect. "Thank God somebody's doing something. I think I'm going nuts."

"Yes, I'm trying to do something, but I need all the help I can get. I noticed you were looking around as you walked. Were you expecting someone?"

"Dana. Dana Portman. She really got roughed up in the confusion last night. I hope she's okay. She's supposed to meet me here."

I wondered what he meant by roughed up. But I thought we'd better start at the beginning. "Harry, can you tell me from the get-go how this all came about? Is Zoe kidnapped or not?"

He looked at me for a long minute, then apparently decided he had to trust someone. He leaned over and stroked Fargo, probably to let his voice steady. "Okay, sure. Zoe and I will be seniors in high school when it opens next week. Dana is a year older and will be going to Yale in a couple of weeks. We didn't want the three of us to be separated for a year. We wanted to stay together like we are now. We tossed around various things we could do—like moving to New York, getting an apartment, Dana going to Columbia, Zoe and me finishing high school there. Then Zoe could either get a good role in a TV serial or on stage or go to acting school. I could either get on a pro hockey team—I'm pretty good—or get a hockey scholarship at a college in the New York area. With the money we could borrow from Reed Catlett, we could afford to do that until we started making money on our own. Then we would pay him back, of course. Excuse me a minute."

He stood and walked into the restaurant, leaving me to marvel at how teenagers could simplify the complex and complicate the simple. Harry returned with pizza and soda and resumed his "explanation."

"Dana thought we were being silly. She said we should leave things as they are. She'd be home from Yale plenty of weekends, or we could come down there to visit. I could try for scholarships or student loans either at Yale or at other colleges in Connecticut or Rhode Island for the next year, while Zoe made sure her grades were good enough to get into Yale next year as a drama major. But Zoe wanted us all to be together—in one town, if not one school. And she was afraid Reed would never come up with a cent for such an unusual—what he would call harebrained—scheme. Of course, Dana might not need any of it. She has her own money from her grandmother, but it's pretty well tied up till she's twenty-five. And, obviously, she's committed to Yale. I think she was kind of relieved that she is."

I took the last bite of pizza, splitting it with Fargo. "Dana seems to have some common sense. And Zoe might be going to Fairfield, Connecticut, to live with her grandmother. That's quite near New Haven. Did you know that?"

Harry nodded and swallowed. "Yes. But we weren't certain. And we needed to get things nailed down. Time was flying. And we still didn't know what I could do."

He took some soda and went on. "We all agreed that Reed or Mr. Portman wouldn't agree to any of this. We were about to give up when Zoe said, kind of dreamily, 'I have it. You can kidnap me. My father will pay the ransom, and away we go.' We all laughed, and started just some crazy talk about kidnapping her, my wearing a mask and carrying a hockey stick and demanding money, Dana blindfolding Reed and taking him somewhere to give us the money. You know, just nonsense."

I nodded and held the cup down so Fargo could drink part of his water. "I understand. But then it began to seem plausible, no longer just a joke. Where were you going to keep her?"

"We thought of Dana's house. It's real big with lots of unused rooms. But she says her grandmother—who lives there, too, since Dana's father travels so much—sometimes roams around the house, looking into the rooms, remembering years ago when she was a girl and they used them for weekend parties and dances and all."

He paused for a bite and a sip. "So we decided on the apartment over our garage. It's not rented for the winter."

I had to laugh. "Oh, God, Harry, your house or Dana's? I, or the police, would have found her in twenty minutes."

"Well, you won't find her in twenty minutes now." He looked frightened and angry. "We've looked all over town and can't

43

find a trace. She's just . . . gone." The tears rolled unbidden. He buried his face in his napkin, shoulders shaking.

Suddenly a hand appeared on his shoulder, and behind him stood what should have been a lovely girl. "Harry, what's wrong? Have they . . . found . . . something?" She looked up. "Who are you?"

"I'm Alex Peres, a private investigator. I'm looking for Zoe Catlett, and Harry's been giving me some background. And you're . . ."

She extended her hand. Her voice was perfectly modulated, her hair was professionally styled, her clothes informally fashionable. And she was a mess. Dark, dark glasses partially concealed a whopper of a black eye. She had a nasty scrape on one forearm and another on her right leg. Her left ankle was in a soft cast, and she carried the type of cane that hospitals give to you on loan from the emergency room. I had seen her picture just this morning. I preferred that version.

"I'm Dana Portman, and this is . . . ?" She stroked Fargo's willing head.

"He's my partner, Fargo, the brains of the outfit."

"They so often are, aren't they?" She smiled. Then sobered. "Have you any news of Zoe? Is she all right?"

"As of yesterday afternoon, her father spoke with her briefly. She was okay, just scared. As of this morning, no contact."

"This is turning into a nightmare." She took a wallet from her purse and pulled out a bill. "Harry, would you get me some coffee, please? My damn leg is killing me. And for you and Alex, too, of course."

"Thanks, black, please. Dana, what happened to you? You look as if you barely survived a train wreck."

"It all goes back to where this kidnapping stopped being funny." She pointed to a table near the sidewalk. "The three of us were sitting there, talking and laughing about how we could stage a kidnapping with enough realism to pry the money out of Reed. I never really took it seriously. And I didn't really believe

44

Harry and Zoe did, either. It was just childish play. Reed is so tight we all roared at the thought of his face when one of us told him the ransom was a million dollars. And Merrilou is so hungry for Reed's money and social status we just loved thinking of her not only watching him fork out a million, but doing it to save his lesbian daughter. She would be mortified beyond belief, and we loved the thought of it. No, we were not being nice, but I thought we were just playing. We talked of how it would make a great sitcom, and that's all it was to me."

Harry returned with the coffees in time to hear Dana's last remarks. "It was funny, but Zoe and I did need the money. You were all set financially, Dana, but I still thought you were going along with us."

She shrugged. "I was. I would love to have had Zoe stay with me, if that had worked. It would have been wonderful to be alone and play house together for at least a few days. Or I'd have taken food to her at your place, made phone calls, that sort of thing. But, to be honest, I thought Reed, or more likely Merrilou, would see through it fairly quickly. I thought Zoe would go home trying to make a joke of it or crying that she had been desperate for money to help Harry or some damn thing. She could always get around Reed. At least until she said she was gay. I doubt Merrilou has given him a minute's peace over that. Of all the scenarios I visualized, it never occurred to me she'd really be kidnapped."

I sipped my coffee and found it surprisingly welcome. The breeze coming off the water was turning chilly and the hot coffee felt good going down. "How in the world did you get from a sitcom to a real kidnapping? Who arranged it? Who are 'they'? Where did they take her? Did they do it to get the money for you? You hired them?"

They looked confused and guilty. Harry simply stared at his coffee. Dana sighed heavily and began to talk rather fast, as if she just wanted to get it over with.

"These two guys had the table next to us. I guess they had

45

been listening to us. God knows we hadn't been especially quiet about it. One of them leaned over and said, 'You kids are gonna fuck it up. The cops will find her in no time, and they'll know she was part of it, all tucked up comfy in her friend's apartment. Somebody will recognize your voice on the phone. And even if you get away with all that, you'll screw up the money exchange because you don't know what you're doing. You guys need help. You need it ba-ad.'"

I was more confused than ever. Kidnappers for hire in the middle of Ptown? Just volunteering like someone saying, "You say your yard needs mowing? I can do that for twenty bucks." And the three teenagers just went along with it? I'd had a Diet Coke and half a cup of coffee, but I had that three-martini feeling.

"Who were these men? Had you seen them before? What did they look like? Did you hire them to carry out this idiot plan? Were they serious?"

I probably would have asked another dozen questions, but Dana raised her hand like a traffic cop.

"Stop. I can't keep up with you. No, we'd never seen them before. They looked familiar, but I couldn't place them. I just assumed maybe I'd seen them around here. They were in their early-, maybe mid-twenties, just dressed like most people. Jeans, I think, T-shirts. One had on a Windbreaker. He had brown hair, average build, fairly good looking. The other one was shorter and skinny and had blondish hair." She paused and sipped her coffee.

Harry took up her tale. "At first I thought they were just older guys, having a little fun jazzing us. Then I thought they were hitting on the two girls. But they were telling us how they'd handle Reed and a lot of serious stuff. About then I realized something really funny . . . weird. The blonde never spoke. He smiled and laughed. He'd shake his head for 'no' or 'yes.' The other guy said it would take them three days to set it up, but the blonde shook his head and raised two fingers, so the other guy said, 'Okay, two days.' So we agreed to meet them, and they left.

I think we were all a little scared. It was becoming real now."

Dana shook her head. "I didn't believe them. I thought in two days, they'd just leave us sitting here. That we'd never see them again and they'd have a good laugh at the naïve kids." She laughed rather sadly. "Zoe was a nervous wreck. She believed every word of it. She even wondered what clothes to take. I reminded her you didn't pack a bag to be kidnapped. She said, well, at least she'd cram some clean undies and makeup in her handbag . . . and her diary. She might induce someone to write a play about it, in which she would star, of course. And she'd have to remember how to act, how she felt, et cetera. She thought the whole thing was a lark. I wonder how she feels tonight?" She dabbed her eyes with a tissue, and I patted her hand. Big help.

I turned to Harry. Maybe I could at least keep them crying only one at a time. "So you met them Thursday night?"

"Yes." He polished off his cannoli and wiped his mouth. "I could eat those things all day."

Even if bombs were falling around us, I silently completed for him. So could I. I asked, "They had a plan?"

"Oh, yeah. They knew a closed-down house with no immediate neighbors who might notice a little activity when the guys had to leave her and go to work. She'd have to make do with a sleeping bag, but the place was clean enough and the water was still on."

"What kind of work do they do?"

"Handyman stuff," he guessed. "They hadn't really said. But they assured her she'd only be there a night or two. They really knew how to pressure Reed, so he'd come across with the million in a hurry. And out of the million, they'd only keep five thousand apiece. And they laughed that they wouldn't even charge her room and board. They made it all sound so simple. They sounded like really nice guys who would enjoy a bit of adventure and a big chunk of money." He drained his coffee and looked wistfully at my cigarettes on the table.

I nodded for him to take one, continuing to prove my theory that while millions still smoked cigarettes, only I purchased them. These guys sounded too good to be true. If they were so "nice," why were they willing to put an entire family through a nightmare experience? Why were they willing to help steal a million dollars for someone else, and someone they didn't even know? Better yet, why were they willing to work so cheaply? Why was the blonde mute? Was he foreign, with a heavy accent? Obviously, he understood English. Did he lisp or stutter? Somehow I doubted it, and though I couldn't figure what it was, I'd bet it was something that made him easily identifiable. I didn't trust them an inch.

Dana echoed my thoughts. "I didn't trust them," she said. "I thought ten thousand was too cheap. They did the work, took the risks, and Zoe got all the money except a pittance. Something smelled about the whole thing. But Zoe was all for it, and so were you, Harry, so, I just tagged along. Stupid me. I should have stopped it somehow. And now everything, including me, is a mess." No tears this time, just good old-fashioned anger.

I finally got around to it. "Yeah, Dana, did you run into a sawmill?"

"You know it. We all met here Thursday night at nine. They said they had a van up the street, which they would get and drive slowly past Mickey's. They would stop for just an instant. The side door would be ajar. Zoe should open it enough to jump in and they would drive off, and in two days we would all be rich."

Dana shook her head as if she could not believe her own naiveté. "They reassured us that Zoe would be in a safe and reasonably livable place. Zoe was on a real high. I don't mean drugs, just excitement. I was excited, too, but I was also a bit scared. I wanted to know where this place was. The men had been a little vague, and I wanted to see that it was as livable as they claimed. So, I said I'd go with them, see Zoe settled in, and one of them could drive me back here to pick up my car. They agreed and left to get their van."

Harry was obviously on the masculine defensive. "Naturally, I felt I was the one who should go with Zoe and had said I would follow them in my car. They said a parade might cause attention on the back roads, so I agreed to stay and wait for Dana." He snickered bitterly. "It wasn't much of a wait."

The more they told me, the more my heart sank. "What happened?" I asked.

Dana answered. "This whitish van came creeping up the street, the blonde driving. Zoe and I stood on the curb. It stopped, the door slid open a bit, and Zoe hopped in. The van started to move away, fast. I jumped inside, off balance. Zoe grabbed for me, but someone pushed me back and I fell out. And here I am."

"I ran out and picked Dana up." Harry doused his cigarette in the remains of Fargo's water and got a dirty look from both of us. "I got her back to the table. A couple of people asked what happened, and I had sense enough to say she stepped off the curb wrong and sprained her ankle. Then I drove her to the clinic. We told them the same story. They patched her up and I drove her home, walked back and drove my car home."

He sighed. "And Zoe is just . . . gone."

Chapter 7

"We've driven all over the place with no results." Dana sighed. "I'm a pretty good artist. I could draw a sketch of you that would be recognizable. I drew a sketch of the two guys and asked around, but nobody bit. We don't know what else to do."

"Do you know anything about private investigators?" I asked.

"Just TV stuff," Harry answered for them.

Dana smiled. "Do you carry a piece and have all sorts of disguises and can wrestle a three-hundred-pound brute with one hand?"

"Occasionally, no and no. But I do have to follow a bunch of rules they never tell you about on TV. One of them is that I am technically an officer of the court. If I know of a crime, I am bound to report it." I lit a cigarette to Dana's moue of disapproval, and paused.

She looked politely bored, not really interested in Class

PI-101. Harry glanced up at me sharply.

"You mean you've been to the cops?" He managed to look both frightened and relieved.

"No. Nobody was a hundred percent sure there had been a crime . . . that Zoe was being held against her will. Merrilou is certain it's some kind of joke and has managed to convince Reed of it. We still can't prove kidnapping. She was not dragged kicking and screaming into the van. She's just not home and not happy about it. Perhaps illegal detention, or is she still acting? As part of your original plot?"

I took a drag on my cigarette. "But one look at you, Dana, proves assault, reckless endangerment and/or attempted murder. Depending on how bad a hangover the DA has when he hears about it. It gives the police plenty of reason to locate and arrest your two buddies. You could have been permanently injured or even killed if you had hit your head on the curb." I nodded toward the edge of the sidewalk. She paled at that. I don't think it had occurred to her. But her reaction fooled me.

"I won't prosecute or sue or whatever it is you do." Dana's voice grew hard. "I can't afford publicity around this mess. It could screw me up badly enough to be unacceptable for college. That kind of media hype wouldn't do Harry any good either. And it would be terrible for my father. We have to count on you to find her, Alex. Please do this for us. If money is a problem, I'll match whatever Reed is paying you."

She reached out and touched my hand. Her voice grew soft and appealing again. "Maybe the two guys are doing just what they said they would. And Zoe is going right along with them. I'll bet that's it. Never mind arresting the two guys. I'm not badly hurt. And I'm sure Zoe is fine. I've been worried sick. I love her dearly, but we have to be sensible about this. It'll all work out in a few days. When they call again, Reed can just tell them he now knows all about it, give them some small 'reward,' ask where Zoe is and go get her. No harm, no foul."

I couldn't believe what I was hearing. If there was one chance

51

in a million Cindy was kidnapped, I'd have the National Guard out looking for her and her captors under every bush east of the Continental Divide. And the phone call I had heard didn't sound particularly jovial, or ready to be written off as a blown gag for a "small reward."

"That's fine for you, Dana. In a week, you won't be limping or showing any scars. And, of course, it gets Harry off the hook, too. But are you that sure Zoe is okay? Aren't you being just a teeny weeny bit selfish, lover?" She had the good taste to lower her head. But I wasn't finished.

"Think about this: nobody now knows where these two men took her. You don't know where they came from. What if they get the money from Reed, kill Zoe and disappear? You have no idea where they might go. Then how would you feel? What kind of publicity do you think that would get, once I tell what I know? Would you still be saying, 'No harm, no foul?'"

"She's right," Harry said slowly. "The police have to know. Maybe they'll keep it quiet until she's found, at least. They sometimes think that's better for some reason. And maybe once we're all sure she's safe, Reed will drop any charges." He looked at me hopefully.

I wasn't ready to let them off the hook yet. They had pulled a stupid, childish trick, and quite possibly, it had backfired disastrously. At best, they had caused a lot of worry and trouble.

So I answered, "Sure, he might, unless he wants to pursue a little matter of conspiracy to extort. And I forgot to mention attempting to bribe me. I'm leaving now. Do either of you need a ride? No? Well, I'm sure we'll talk again soon. Thank you for the coffee."

I picked up Fargo's lead and we left. I felt a great desire for some quiet time. Maybe it was warm enough to sit in my backyard with a cold Bud and someone with the good sense not to babble . . . like Fargo or Wells.

The ride home was slow. There were still plenty of tourists on our narrow streets. My mind, however, was not in an unhurried mode. By the time I reached the house I had worked myself into an uneasy feeling of pity mixed with anger and seasoned with despair for most of the principals in the case.

Reed was simply being pulled apart: his sexy new wife on one side, his sensible family on the other. He was trying to placate everyone, including the kidnappers, and that never worked.

Even Merrilou had a point. From all I had heard, Zoe was quite capable of making Merrilou's little "mother" act look as silly and feigned as it was—and would prefer to do so as publicly as possible. And Zoe did have a history of staying out long past any reasonable curfew. Where and with whom?

Certainly I knew that many teenagers made those "nothing will ever separate us" pacts of friendship or love. My last year in high school I had been through it. My girlfriend, Polly, got a summer job at a resort in Maine. We agonized over the impending separation. We wrote pages of letters about everything from the cat's new kittens to turgid declarations of our undying love and faithfulness. They worked about as well as most declarations of that sort. By August, I had met and fallen for a different girl. Polly, to my total surprise, had gotten pregnant by a wealthy older guy, married him and now lives on a giant ranch in Arizona, along with several kids. Happy? I hope so. At least I'm sure her allergies are.

The Dana/Zoe/Harry triumvirate would likely work out about the same way, assuming no tragedies occurred and none of them actually went to jail, which I really did doubt.

Tweedledee and Tweedledum were the only ones for which I could feel no sympathy. For one thing, they weren't kids, and if they were straight, I doubted Zoe stood a chance of not being raped. And more than once. For another, they weren't in this plot with a one-for-all-and-all-for-one attitude. They were simply after a fee, if indeed, they planned to turn the other nine hundred and ninety thousand over to a cute teenage girl who had simply sat in an empty house for two or three days to earn it. There was something frightening here, something in this silly plan held a whiff of evil. But I couldn't trace the odor to its putrid source.

Yet.

Finally, I was home, greeted with indignant meows from Wells. She and Fargo sniffed and circled as if they had never met, and then in some canine/feline agreement, walked to the back door and virtually said, "Treat." I let us all in, took care of treats and water bowls and popped a cold beer. Treats all around and well deserved.

We all trailed back out and found places in the sun. I sipped the beer and lit a cigarette, and tried to remember how many it was. Maybe three. Maybe six. It was hopeless to try to count when I tossed them around to others like Mardi Gras doubloons from a float. I was tired, but it was no day to take an afternoon nap. I needed help rather quickly, and so, I feared, did Zoe.

I reached in my pocket and, miraculously, my fingers closed on my cell phone. Usually I left it in the car, or the bedroom, or the kitchen, or the clothes hamper or just about any place I was not—including, once, the washer. It was time to talk to my brother, but first, I'd check with the Catletts.

I looked in my pocket notebook for their number and dialed. Reed picked up on the first ring. "Hello, Reed, it's Alex Peres. Sorry to startle you, I just wondered if we had anything new."

"Not much. Overnight I got a cell phone in my mailbox with a note that said all future calls would come in on it, for some reason. But it hasn't rung yet, and I wish to God it would. I want this wrapped up."

"It's surely one of those prepaid phones, so we can't trace the call. They're getting cagey."

"Yes, this is going on too long, Alex." He sounded worried, but stronger. Maybe he was getting his act together. "I think you are right. I'm going to call the police and the hell with whether it's a joke or not. The worst it can do is make a bunch of us look like fools, and that's not fatal."

"You're making me very happy, Reed, but first let me tell you what I've picked up." I told him most of my afternoon, leaving out the kids' names and the part about Dana getting shoved out of the van. I didn't think he needed to know the two men had made very sure only they knew where Zoe was, and had used considerable violence to make it so.

"And so, Reed, just one other small thing. It is possible the kidnappers are watching you, and it will be obvious if you go to the police or if they come to your home. At this point, they might as well think they are dealing only with you. We'll get the phone company to put a tracer on your landline just in case. For other matters, I'll be around. Doubtless the 'nappers already know I'm involved. Okay?"

"Yeah," he said reluctantly. "I guess that makes sense."

"Everybody knows Sonny is my brother. If he and I are seen together it probably won't ring any bells. So I'll bring him up to date and let him decide who sees whom and how."

I took the last sip of the now-tepid beer, made a face and continued. "I'll talk to Sonny, and he or I will get back to you tonight. If you hear from Zoe or the Tweedles, let me know. Here's my cell number."

After we hung up, I carefully put the little phone back in my pocket and went inside to call Sonny. First, I would try my mother's house, where he technically lived. It was about all he could afford with an ex-wife and two kids draining off a good portion of his salary. Fortunately his other ex-wife had remarried, which helped. Now if we could just find a suitable husband for the first one.

If Sonny wasn't at Mom's, I'd try Trish's apartment. She was Sonny's current affair, a nice young woman, bright, as independent as Sonny and apparently blessedly uninterested in marriage. She was a lawyer, assistant to John Frost, and seemingly headed for a successful career in criminal law. If Sonny wasn't there, I'd call the station and let them chase him down. They'd know where he was.

He was at Mom's, surprisingly, until he told me why. "Got a card from Mom in New York. The opening of the show is tonight, and she'll be home Monday. I'm just, uh, doing a little housecleaning. Not that it really needs much. Just a little vacuuming and dusting, you know." His voice got oily like it always did when he was lying or wanted something.

"Yeah, I'm sure. I have something that may take you away from your domestic chores. You'd better get ready to shell out some bucks to The Super Scrubbers, or just borrow a fire hose and a backhoe from the town. Can you come over soon? Park in Carla's driveway and wear dark glasses or something so you don't look like you. Come over the back wall."

"Are you serious?"

"Never more so."

"Give me twenty minutes to grab a shower. I'll be there." I could feel his entire demeanor change from naughty little boy to competent young professional. I'd have been willing to wager he stood straighter and his shoulders were squared. No good-bye, I just heard the dial tone.

It required a double take for me to recognize him. He came sauntering across my backyard with a slightly effeminate sway, and sporting black sunglasses. He was wearing sandals, white duck calf-length trousers and a wide-stripe Cote d'Azur black and green polo shirt topped by a white Greek fisherman's cap. I wondered if he and Trish were planning a European trip.

We went inside, and he removed the cap and glasses. I asked him about the clothes and he laughed. "No trip this year. But Trish and I met a couple down at Brewster that we enjoy. They are a little more formal down there. I don't think I'd wear these clothes in Provincetown unless I felt like defending my virtue. Now what's the deep secrecy all about?"

I'd made a pot of coffee and poured us both a mug. Then

I sat and told him. When I finished, he sighed. "I wish Reed had called me right away. Now that they're on the prepaid cells, it pretty well eliminates any trace. Dammit. Parents just will try it alone. Usually the cops can save the kid, even if they lose the money. And even then, we often recover a sizeable amount and catch the doers. It's so strange. The parents wouldn't set a broken leg, or try to fix the microwave or the furnace. They'd call a pro. But when it's their kid—surely more important than the microwave—they get all secretive and think they can handle it better themselves."

"It is not sensible or smart, Sonny, but when it comes to kids, most people panic easily. Some tough guy on a phone says he'll kill your kid if you call the cops. What do you do?"

I lit a cigarette and pushed them and the lighter across the table. I figured I might as well save his asking. "You think of the rather dull-looking cop with a wilted shirt collar who gave you a parking ticket last week, and you don't rate him very high against a bunch of professional criminals threatening your child. You think if you come up with the money, it's a simple cash transaction."

"I guess." Sonny sighed, then straightened. "Okay, we'll tap their house phone just in case. We'll set up a tape for incoming cell calls. Mitch or I will see if there's anything they forgot to tell you."

I laughed. "You'd better talk to Miss Scarlett. She'll chew up Mitch and spit out the seeds."

"He's getting better. And tougher. We'll see." He sipped his coffee, smiled approval and reasoned, "I can understand Harry Maddock getting himself involved in this Grade C drama. Kid's kind of shy, except with a hockey stick. And his family is anything but rich, but what the hell is with the Portman girl? Dan Portman's got more money than God."

I shifted in my chair. It was turning into a long day. "She wasn't going to use any of the ransom money. It appears that she's loaded in her own right. Although there are evidently some restrictions

57

on how much she can tap at a time. She was just being supportive. According to her."

"What's her family setup?"

"There is none that I could see. Daddy Dan travels a great deal. Mums is off on the Costa del Sol with a very handsome, very young man. I don't know why they split up and thought I better not ask. Dana rattles around in that big house with her grandmother and the servants most of the time. Occasionally Dan takes her with him on a European buying trip."

Sonny shrugged. "Aw, poor baby. Nothing to do but sit around and count the bearer bonds. We've got plenty of local kids in worse situations. But how about Zoe, is she nuts?"

"I have no idea. To my knowledge, I have never seen her. But if I had her stepmother, I might advertise for kidnappers to come and get me, too." He was beginning to irritate me.

"Kids today, they don't know how lucky they are." He leaned back, the chair resting on the back legs, which always aggravated me. "We didn't do things like that growing up."

"Put the damn chair down. And since I am approximately only fifteen years older than they are, I don't consider myself from another planet. Neither should you. Who was it at age sixteen who had the bright idea of building a rocket ship and blew the roof off our garage?"

He crossed his arms and stuck out his chin. "No comparison. That was a scientific experiment that needed more research, not some idiotic, childish, criminal plot." He smiled smugly.

"And, Mr. Einstein, just where did you get the gunpowder for the rocket?"

The phone rang, sparing him from admitting he had stolen it from our neighbor who liked to make his own bullets for his antique rifles.

I picked up the phone and found I was speaking to Rob Catlett. "Rob, my brother, Lieutenant Peres, is here. Do you mind if I put the phone on speaker?"

"Not at all. I just wanted to update you. I've got a feeling Dad is trying to handle this himself. I think he's out now, meeting the kidnappers, and I'm pretty sure he's got two hundred thousand with him. Or nearly, anyway."

"Where did he get the money?"

"Right after lunch, Mr. Ellis from the bank came over with two big guys carrying two big briefcases and another carrying a shotgun. They went into Dad's office and locked the door. You can't hear much from there, but I could tell Mr. Ellis was arguing about something. Then he came out, saying he'd have the rest in a day or so, and that this hundred and eighty grand wasn't lunch money, so Dad should call the cops. He said he was worried about Zoe. Dad said Zoe was his daughter and he'd take care of her. So Ellis and the gorillas left looking grim."

He took a deep, shuddering breath and picked up his tale again. "Then Dad and Merrilou got into it. She kept wanting him to call Mister—I mean Reverend Bartles and his wife, so that they could all pray for wisdom. Then Nana said we didn't need prayer, we needed somebody to knock some sense into Dad and to shut Merrilou's mouth. Merrilou kind of lightly smacked Nana. I grabbed Marvin before he could clock Merrilou. Dad banged the silver coffeepot down on the table so hard he broke off the handle and made a gouge in the table. He screamed we should all go to our rooms and if he heard a word out of anybody, he'd lock in whoever said it. Alex, can somebody help us? There's going to be a murder over here."

I looked at Sonny and he spoke up, calm and reassuring. "This is Lieutenant Peres, Rob. Sounds like everybody is very much on edge at your place. You can't really blame them. It's a nerve-wracking spot to be in. I'll be over in a few minutes, and we'll see what we can do to get some positive action going. Right now, just stay quiet and try to keep your brother and grandmother quiet. Maybe I can get your dad to accept some assistance."

"Not now, you can't." Rob giggled nervously.

"Why not?" I asked.

"A minute or so after the blow up, the cell phone rang. Dad

59

grabbed it and ran into his office and slammed the door and locked it. And, by the way, he yanked the recording tape off of it."

Sonny muttered, "Shit," but Rob just continued his report.

"I went out and tried to listen under the window, but it was closed. However, a few minutes later he went out to his car, carrying the briefcases like they were heavy."

"What kind of car?"

"Lincoln Town Car," Rob said. "Maroon, oh-seven model. Oh, I meant to tell you, the handle of his gun was sticking out of his jacket."

"He's got a gun?" Sonny rolled his eyes at me and made that twirling motion to his temple with his forefinger. I agreed. The man had flipped. "What kind of gun does he have?"

"I—I really don't know. It's a big old pistol his father had during World War Two. But I think maybe it's German. Granddad captured it or something."

"Oh, God, probably a Luger that would take out a tank. Where is he now?"

"I don't know. He just drove away."

Sonny slumped and closed his eyes for a moment. Then he straightened and spoke, sounding composed and in control. "Okay, Rob, you've done a good job getting all this data together. I'll be along in a little while, after I've made a phone call. Keep cool. Everything's going to be okay. 'Bye."

"Dear God," I said.

"Apparently is not in His Heaven, and very little is right with the world. Is there more coffee?"

Chapter 8

Whenever a mechanic, a doctor or a cop tells me everything is going to be just fine, I begin to sweat. There were a dozen scenarios that could be playing out right now, and only one of them was good. Of course, with the tape disconnected, we now had no way of knowing where or when Reed was to meet the Tweedles, although, given his speedy departure, one would imagine it was eminent. Was Zoe with them? Would they accept the lesser ransom and free the girl? If not, would Reed try to shoot the Tweedles and rescue Zoe? If Zoe was not with them, would Reed try to force them to tell him her whereabouts with his trusty pistol? Did the Tweedles have guns and would everyone shoot everyone else?

I finally realized Sonny was gesturing for the phone and handed it to him. He punched my speed dial for the police station. "Nacho, it's Sonny. Patch me through to Mitch wherever he is." Mitch was Sonny's right-hand man, a young detective sergeant with a natural instinct for the job. There was a considerable pause, and Sonny's mouth grew tighter by the second.

Finally he spoke. "Mitch, we've got a freaking mess with a two-day-old unreported kidnapping here. Now listen." He gave a surprisingly brief but cogent report, ending with the news of Reed's disappearance. "So we have no idea where he is. I'd say he left the house close to thirty minutes ago now. I hope he is still in town and meeting a white or light tan van, but he could be meeting a boat, or he could be headed for Boston. But concentrate on Provincetown. Tell Nacho to get his plate number, I forgot to ask the kid. Have her alert the state police and the locals down as far as the canal bridges. Tell everyone to exercise caution, Catlett is armed. I don't know about the other two. Stay in touch."

He stood and drained his coffee cup. "Want to come?"

"No. I want to eat my dinner and watch something silly on TV. Also if Harry or Dana should hear anything, they might try to reach me here. They don't have my cell number."

"Good idea. Okay. Talk to you later."

Although it was early for dinner, I was hungry and tired and had just lined up the ingredients for one of my famous grilled cheese and tomato sandwiches, when the phone rang. "Is Sonny there?" It was Mitch.

"No, he left about five minutes ago."

"Damn."

"Anything I can do?"

"No. Thanks. Oh, God, Alex, if only we had known about this an hour earlier, we had four cars just inadvertently in position to bring them all in, neat as a pin. Maybe not the girl, but everybody else. Now we're going to look like idiots. Why didn't somebody clue us in?" He sounded petulant.

"Because nobody knew. What happened?" I put the phone on my shoulder and started constructing my sandwich.

"Well, uh, you know how sometimes two or three of our cars

take a break around four up by the amphitheater, if things are quiet. Just coffee or a Coke, maybe a snack, you know."

"No I don't know, Mitch. Why don't you tell me?"

"It's a time-honored custom," he said magisterially, "has been for years. We just catch up with what's been going on, you know. And we are entitled to a short break. Well, we are. And we only take ten minutes or so, just a brief period to loosen up, and a little caffeine intake to keep us alert. We don't really waste any time, you know?" He was having a hard time selling himself on whatever he was talking about.

"This time-honored custom seems to have upset you, Mitch. But it is not me you have to explain it to."

"I'm not explaining it to anybody. I'm just telling you it may look a little strange on the surface. Four cars just happened to be there at once."

"And the bank was robbed at the other end of town?" I had the sandwich put together and got out the skillet.

"Worse. In one car, Nichols was just leaving to go back into town, even though everything on the radio was routine. As he pulled out of the parking lot, an off-white van pulled up with two young men in it. They looked a little startled to see all the cop cars, I guess, but they parked anyway. One guy got out and stretched, looked at the scenery for a minute. They swapped drivers, got back in and left."

"And nobody stopped them? Well, no, why would they?"

"Right. They did nothing wrong. They didn't run or try to hide or anything suspicious. Maybe looking for a spot to have a little sex, and this sure wasn't it, so they moved on."

I was using both hands to butter the skillet and almost lost the phone, as he continued. "Nichols and Brandeis left. Pino was still there, and Mendes was there in an unmarked. A couple of minutes later a maroon Lincoln pulls up with a man in it."

"Ummm." I was licking some tomato juice off my finger.

"He jumps out of the car and shakes his fist at them and yells, 'You lousy cops. You tell that Peres creep if he's gotten my daughter killed, I'll kill him.' He jumps back in and takes off."

"Didn't it occur to Pino or Mendes to go after him or to call dispatch and have them warn Sonny?"

"Frankly, I couldn't blame them in a way, Alex. For one thing, they were startled themselves. And then, this guy was raving about his daughter. They thought maybe Sonny and she . . . well, I'm not sure what they thought. But they wanted to tell him in private. You know half the retirees in town listen to the police scanner instead of TV for their entertainment."

"Yes. I can understand. I really can. But, God, what a mess."

"I'm almost to the Catletts's now. I gotta talk to Sonny."

I hoped Sonny was alive to hear it. I turned the heat down under my sandwich, flipped it . . . perfection. And poured myself another mug of hot coffee.

The back door flew open with a crash that announced the arrival of Reed Catlett, pointing a pistol with a barrel the size of the Lincoln Tunnel. I don't know why I did it. Maybe I was just tired and had had enough of the Catletts that day, or maybe I was just pissed to smell my beautiful sandwich burning. Anyway, I did it.

I threw my coffee, still surrounded by the mug, into Reed's face and then hit him on the head with the hot skillet. He went down without a murmur.

The door crashed again to admit Officer Mendes, Ptown's baby-faced rookie on the force, and perhaps the only person associated with the police to do anything well that night. He had cruised my house as a precaution, noticed the Lincoln parked up the street and come a-running.

He cuffed Reed as he lay on my kitchen floor, now conscious, sort of, while Wells and Fargo took tentative bites of the still-hot sandwich from his hair, carefully spitting out the tomato.

Just to be on the safe side, we called the EMTs, but Reed was fully awake and talking by the time they got there.

64

Yes, he had been supposed to meet the kidnappers in the parking lot. Yes, he'd had the money with him. It was now in the trunk of his car. He hadn't really meant to shoot me. He just hoped I'd discovered where Zoe was. He thought his nose was broken. By the amount of blood leaking onto his shirt and then spattering onto my kitchen floor, I agreed with him.

The EMTs got the blood slowed down. They put some kind of goop on the top of his head, where there was a sizeable lump and probably a mild burn. Mendes pronounced him under arrest for carrying an unlicensed firearm and for trespassing and aggravated assault. And they all left.

Fargo figured it was now safe to bark and began to do so, sounding like a killer dog if I ever heard one.

"Fargo, shut up. The cameras are not rolling."

I looked around at the kitchen at the shattered mug and spilled coffee. The rather sickening remains of my sandwich was now tracked all over the floor, with both animals licking at it here and there. There was a small puddle of blood with a white towel casually tossed over it, and grease and tomatoes all around.

A drink. I wanted a strong drink, and I wanted food I hadn't scraped off of tile. I did not want to mop a floor and sweep up shards of a mug and scrub a charred skillet. I walked out, leaving the two animals stunned. I didn't care.

The Wharf Rat Bar had never looked cozier. Some of our tourists had departed vacationland, and mostly locals lined the bar and occupied a few of the tables. The Rat's determined sea-going look of anchors and shells and oars and lobster pots that so pleased our visitors was back to its old tatty, dusty self for the natives . . . complete with a ship's telegraph, frozen in time at Dead slow astern. If the Wharf Rat had an heraldic shield, that would be on it.

I selected a table in the emptiest corner and ordered a drink I usually have sense enough to avoid—a very dry gin martini, straight up, with two olives.

When Joe, the bartender, got the order, he grinned and called over, "Having a fun day, Alex?"

"Shut up, Joe, or make it a double."

"Oooh, well pahdonn moi."

Someone slid into the chair opposite me, and I turned back, loaded for bear. Seeing who it was, I adjusted my attitude and managed a smile. "Marcia. How nice. It's been a while. How are you?"

"I am fine, my dear Alex, and will not keep you from your recovery." She smiled, and I felt better already.

Marcia Robbie was somewhere in her forties, probably closer to getting out than coming in. Her curly black hair had two dramatic white wings that somehow made her look younger, and very dramatic. She spoke perfect English with just enough of a different cadence to tell you it was not her first language. She was originally from Canada and owned a top-of-the-line antique shop not far from me. She had a sort of vague reputation for having a number of male lovers, but nobody could prove it, and I personally rewrote the script to read: there were a lot of men who would like to be her lover and therefore, in the way of men since condos were caves, insinuated that they really were.

"Is it true that Zoe Catlett either ran away from home or is kidnapped?" she asked.

"Now where would you get that idea?" My martini arrived. I sipped it. Joe had done me proud.

"Ah, Alex, you know I am the original operator of the jungle drum network. Is it true?"

"Please don't spread this around, Marcia, no matter what you may have heard. Unfortunately, it could be true."

"I thought she looked . . . strange." Marcia actually offered me a cigarette!

I took it, my faith in humanity restored, and asked, "What do you mean? Have you seen her?"

She sipped the drink she had brought to my table. "Thursday

night, something after nine, I was walking Napoleon." Napoleon was her marvelous French bull terrier, who looked frighteningly ferocious and couldn't even spell bite. "As we walked, a light-colored van went by, a rather noisy machine. I thought it was Zoe in the back, looking out nervously. I believe she ducked as they passed us by. If it were she, she did not want me to see her."

"I don't suppose you noted the plates?" I had little hope.

"Damn. How silly of me. I shall keep my day job. I will never be a detective. No, I never even thought of it. I am so sorry, and they were right in front of me."

"Don't feel bad. Most people don't get the numbers. They're too busy watching whatever is happening." I waved at Joe and made a circling motion with my hand. He nodded, and shortly our refills arrived.

Marcia looked thoughtful. "She certainly was not gagged. I would have seen it. I'm sure she did not yell, or I would have heard her. No, I am almost positive she ducked down on the seat."

"That would have made sense at that point," I said. "That early in the game it was all still some silly idea of hitting Reed up for a big handout to allow Zoe to go to New York and enroll in drama school. Do you know Reed and his new wife?"

Marcia sipped her drink and smiled. "I've known Reed for years. Perhaps a little protective of his wallet, but I understand he can be generous when the occasion calls. He asked me out a couple of times, but I declined. He was very polite, but somehow, I was a little afraid of him. He brought the new wife by the shop not long ago. She has no finesse, no class, no hope."

I roared. "Maybe we could tattoo that on her forehead. It certainly fits."

Marcia smiled, but her eyes were serious. "Watch her, Alex. She is out of her depth with Reed and his friends. She knows it. That makes her dangerous."

"She certainly has been obstructive around Zoe's little caper, which I'm afraid has now turned into the full monty . . . probably no longer a joke with her, either. Incidentally, have you noticed any empty houses or shops out your way?"

She thought for a moment, then shook her head. "No, the houses all have locals in them, or are B and Bs still open. I think all the shops are open, too. I'll have a look around."

"Don't try to get in it, if you find one closed. Don't even pay attention to it. You could find yourself in there with Zoe. Just call Sonny pronto."

"Napoleon would protect me." She stood up. "Like Fargo looks after you. Oh, Alex, one thing I did notice. The van had a little dent and a small smear of blue paint on the side door—on the passenger's side. Does that help?"

"Very much. There are dozens of vans around, but I doubt many of them are marked with blue paint. Oh, Marcia, you may be our lifesaver—literally." I was already reaching for my cell phone, and when I hung up, Marcia was gone.

I had another drink while I waited for my steak, with duchess potatoes and a plain lettuce salad. No tomatoes if you please. There were enough of them waiting for me at home.

Dinner was delicious. Joe's wife Billie Jo was a super cook. And in my indulgent mood, I ordered a glass of claret to go with it . . . a sturdy little wine, able to stand up to the beef yet not eclipse its . . . oh, well, you know.

My after dinner coffee was accompanied by a brandy, sent along by Peter and the Wolf, who were at the bar, They owned a B&B that catered—in most any way you could imagine—to older gay men. They were also good friends, and ordinarily I would have waved them over. But I was willing to bet they had heard something or other about Zoe, and I was in no mood to play Inquisition. I just blew a thank-you kiss.

As I walked home, I realized I was slightly drunk. Maybe a little more than slightly. At any rate, I was glad I didn't have the car. I sang patches from "Singin' in the Rain," although a light fog was all I could muster, and that may have been in my head. I let the two irate pets out, checked their water, provided goodies and let them in. Looking around the wrecked kitchen, I gave a fast chorus of "Mañana," retired to my boudoir and got rid of most of my clothes before I fell into bed.

Chapter 9

From far away, I heard my name. "Alex. Alex. Are you all right?" Someone shook my shoulder and my head fell off. I groaned. The voice moved closer. "You smell like a bottle of gin. And what the hell happened to the kitchen? Did we have an earthquake here?"

"Yes, that's it." An earthquake was all I could think of to make me feel this way. "Is it Tuesday already? Have I been unconscious under the rubble? I think I may be badly injured."

Cindy plopped down on the side of the bed, and my stomach gave a gravity-defying lurch. "Oh, God! I'm dying."

"Before you go, tell me what happened."

"Tell me why you're home three days early," I said cleverly. Maybe by the time she did that, I could remember what happened to the kitchen. "Is everything okay in . . . wherever?"

"Oh, yes. Just fine." She reached across me and took a cigarette from the table. She does this about once a month, and it consistently amazes and, frankly, pisses me off. How do you smoke one cigarette a month?

"So, what happened?" I thought of a cigarette, but graciously declined, although none had been offered.

"So, I wasn't needed on the voyage. Ergo, I came home."

"What the hell are you trying to say? And stop calling me Ergo."

"There was a cast of thousands. First, you have the core family. My brother Pete, wife Karol, two older kids and now kid number three, Hillary, who's adorable, by the way. Then there was me, in the guest room, all ready to look after Butch and Abby, so the new parents could look after Hillary and still get some kind of rest."

"A solid plan." I was beginning to regain consciousness. I wondered if there was coffee.

"Quite solid." Cindy rolled her eyes dramatically. "Until . . . until, first, my mother arrived. She knew my brother needed to get back to work, so she came along to help with Hillary, and there went the other bed in the guest room. No more private, quiet moments. And here came a lot of advice on how to raise children."

"Daunting."

"Oh, I didn't give up. I am sturdy. I know my duty. I smiled, and Karol smiled and Pete smiled. And Pete and I drank rather a lot that night. Then Karol's mother decided she'd better add her assistance now instead of next week as scheduled, and flew in unannounced from Ohio."

"On the wings of a pure white dove, no doubt." I'd have been out of there in a nanosecond.

"Something like that, yes. And there went my bed in the guest room. I was now on the foldout couch in the living room, more aptly named Grand Central Station. I was bloody but unbowed. But when Karol's sister arrived from Pennsylvania—or was it Transylvania?—I knew we would be sharing that miserable couch. I do not share miserable couches in living rooms with vampire bats. I 'slept' in an easy chair for a few hours, quietly left at dawn and made good time. However, I am tired. And not prepared for this." She swept her arm around broadly, narrowly missing my nose.

"Did you also by any chance make coffee?"

"No. That mess in the kitchen—a chair turned over, God knows what all over the floor, Wells and Fargo actually huddled together in his bed. Your stuff tossed all over the bedroom. I was afraid you really might be dead. It must have been one helluva party." She apparently couldn't decide whether to look hurt or angry.

I reached for her hand. "It was. But not the kind you're thinking of. If you will make a pot of coffee—I believe the coffeemaker survived—I will shower and meet you in the dining room. I promise to tell all."

She looked unconvinced. "I suppose Cassie figures prominently in this and will swear to everything you say."

Cassie is my best pal and runs a chartered aircraft business. Right now I wished she and I were far up in the blue, headed most anywhere. On oxygen.

"No, my love, Cassie plays no role in this. My witnesses include such paragons of virtue as my fourth-grade teacher, an architect, his evangelical wife and the entire Provincetown police force. Now go, before I put me out of my misery."

Coffee helped. So did toast. Fargo and even Wells forgave me. I told Cindy about the whole convoluted mess, including that in the kitchen. Her entire attitude changed when I told her of Reed and his jumbo pistol.

"My God, he could have killed you."

"I think the safety was on. Anyway, I don't think actual murder was on his mind. I think he is just totally distraught and frustrated that everything went wrong. Imagine thinking you're going to meet some people to whom you will give money in exchange for the safe return of your beloved daughter, and all you see is two-thirds of the Ptown police force laughing it up over coffee and doughnuts. It's not a smile maker."

"Well," she said indignantly, "He didn't have to take it out on you."

I laughed. "My headache is better. His will be with him awhile. And his nose has definitely lost its virginity. I traded fatigue, stress and hunger for a whopping hangover. I'm still ahead of poor Reed."

"Yes," she poured us more coffee. "That's a terrible thing . . . a kidnapping. I can't even imagine the fear and anger they must feel."

"It must be ghastly," I agreed, "and add to that a bunch of very different people trying to deal with it. A man who's never been a hands-on father. A new stepmother of dubious character. A grandmother who blatantly much preferred her first daughter-in-law to this one. Two teenage boys trying to be adult, but frightened, motherless and antagonistic toward the new wife. It must be a barrel of fun around there even when nothing serious is wrong."

"God. Who did it?"

"I don't know." I poured another cup of coffee. I was slowly returning to life. "The two young men actually did it, of course, and that could be all there is to it. But I cannot imagine myself overhearing some kids fantasizing about how to get some money, and publicly offering my services to commit a capital crime for a mere five thousand dollars."

"You mean someone else may have hired them first . . . to kidnap Zoe for a lion's share of the money or for a reason we don't know."

"Right."

"There's Reed," Cindy said thoughtfully.

"Why Reed?" I was surprised at her choice. "How would he profit? Other than possibly getting rid of a sometimes troublesome daughter? And placating his wife."

"Oh, one very good way. Suppose he's been over billing

clients, saying he's built their structures to certain top-notch specifications, when actually he's been using very inferior materials and shoddy workmen. Maybe everything is literally about to fall in on him. This is a fine way to liquidate all his assets in a hurry and even get some hefty loans without rousing suspicion. Everyone is busy raising money for the poor panic-stricken father."

She gave a wicked grin. "Reed's next communication might have been a postcard from Brazil if the cops had picked another place for their picnic last night." Suddenly she sobered. "My God, Choate may have the bank in this up to his neck without even knowing it."

"It's difficult to believe," I said. "Reed's had a good reputation for years around here."

"He's got a new wife who sounds high maintenance. And he's facing college with three kids."

"Yeah. There's that. I guess you'll want to call Choate and give him a heads-up. And call Sonny. He may not have thought of this. I need to talk to him, too, when you finish. Please," I added.

Cindy moved immediately for the kitchen phone, and I could hear her voice, fast and urgent, as she spoke with her boss.

I lit the first cigarette of the day and let my thoughts move on to my favorite villain. The attractive, sexy, bitchy, rapacious, social climbing Merrilou. Gee, was there something I disliked about her? Well, yes. Upset or not, you don't go around slapping old ladies. And you don't threaten young girls with going to hell because they're gay.

The way Merrilou handled the first call was suspicious. But her reluctance to involve the police was not unusual with the families of kidnap victims. However, I didn't think Merrilou's disinclination stemmed from fear for Zoe's safety. If it were not indicative of her involvement with the plot itself, it was simply that she wanted no scandal to make her entry into Cape Cod society more difficult than it already was. If they had called the police and the "kidnapping" had proved to be just another way to say, "Hey, Dad, all I needed was a loan," the media would have had a field day.

Actually, I had to admit, nothing Merrilou had done was particularly dubious. Cold, self-serving, unforgivable if anything happened to Zoe, but not criminal. I was probably letting my dislike run away with me.

On the other hand, what about her friend Emily? Emily Bartles came into daily contact with unemployed, broke young men whose morals might be of dubious strength. Five thousand dollars would look like a fortune to most of them. The Bartles drove a beat-up, noisy, off-white van with numerous dents and scratches, as well as remnants of past colors, which might prove interesting. Obviously, Emily had access to it.

If you figured that Reed had somehow added twenty thousand to the hundred and eighty thousand Choate Ellis had brought, that made two hundred thousand. Ten to the two young perps left one ninety. If Merrilou gave Emily, say, fifty thousand, that left a hundred and forty for her. And everybody had a loverly nest egg.

In some of my contacts with Larry Bartles in the past, he had let slip that his marriage was not the happiest. Maybe Emily was building up some getaway funds.

Why did Merrilou feel she needed money? She had a wealthy, obviously doting husband. Or was he as dumb as he seemed? I wondered if there had been a prenuptial agreement Merrilou disliked. I wondered how Reed's will read. I wondered how much Rob knew. I would find out.

Of the family, I figured Rob and Martin were non-starters for being the kidnappers. So that left Grandma, and somehow I couldn't see her having anything to do with Tweedledee and Tweedledum. She'd be more likely to brush up their manners and their long division than to stage a kidnapping, even if she could use the money. And I imagined she was not buying day-old bread. So that took care of my current cast of characters.

Cindy came in with the walk-around phone. "Here's Sonny." She went back in the kitchen and I heard sounds of a beginning clean-up operation. Bless her neat little heart.

"Hi, Sonny."

"Hi. I hear you had quite an encounter with Reed last night. Are you okay?"

"The kitchen and Reed are the casualties. I'm fine. How's Reed?"

"Tape on his nose, bear grease on the balding spot/cum lump on his head. Very subdued and apologetic. If you can believe him, and I'm not at all sure I do. But seriously, Alex, the prosecutor wants to know what you plan to do about this."

"Nothing. I realize the gun might have somehow gone off, but he wasn't here to hurt me. He's a little crazed, I guess, but I think he needs tranquilizers more than jail time. Get him for the unregistered pistol and forget the rest. Doesn't he have any men friends to help him through this?"

"Choate, John Frost. That's about it."

John Frost was a lawyer here in town—bright, sardonic and certainly a loyal friend. "Are they spending time with him?"

Sonny cleared his throat. "Merrilou doesn't like them."

"Screw Merrilou."

"No, thanks. Fortunately, she does not like me, either. But me, she can't throw out. Look, we've got all the tapes set up again, but have had no calls. We're watching for the van with the blue paint. I got your message from Marcia last night. At least that narrows it down. We're already checking empty buildings all over town. Any other ideas?"

"Not really." But I couldn't resist. I told him my thoughts about Merrilou and Emily.

He said, "Hmm," which meant he didn't think I was nuts, but he wasn't excited, either. "Those are possibilities. We'll nose around, check the colors on that derelict van."

"Look, Sonny, I gotta go help Cindy rebuild the kitchen. Keep in touch, okay?"

76

"You got it."

Actually, Cindy had the kitchen about done, to my great relief. It was too late to take the dog to the beach . . . too many people still around. So I put on his lead and took him with me to get the Sunday papers. It was a legitimate excuse for an exit. If you didn't get there fairly early, they ran out of the *New York Times*.

Chapter 10

I figured that jeans and an old sweatshirt really wouldn't do, so I changed into light wool tan slacks, a pale green blouse and dark green blazer. Cindy wasn't thrilled that I'd accepted Dana's last-minute invitation to lunch, but it really was business—I assumed—and could be important. Surely, Cindy didn't think I was interested in the girl. In thirty years, I might be chasing eighteen-year-olds, but not yet.

Dana met me at the door, and I was glad I had changed clothes. She was in a blue dress that complemented her coloring, and I thought had been chosen to make her look older. From the beginning, she was the gracious hostess. From the beginning, I was amused.

We went immediately to the large dining room, where places were set at the head of the table and the first seat on the right. Cozy. But it also meant we wouldn't have to speak loudly down the table length. At the tinkle of a bell, the maid served a luscious fruit cup of mango, pineapple and avocado with sesame seed dressing. It was followed by a thick slice of cold roast beef with Stilton cheese, beet salad with all the trimmings plus warm French bread. In her most adult voice Dana said, "We have most anything you want to drink, but I find a good dry beer goes best. At least that's what I'm having." She glanced at me quickly, judging whether I would make some reference to her age. I didn't give her the satisfaction of making what I am sure would have been a clever retort.

"Beer suits me fine," I agreed. Dana nodded to the maid who disappeared quickly and returned shortly with chilled glasses and two bottles of Lee's Manchester Beer, which I'd never heard of. I assumed it was English. The maid poured my glass and got it just right with a head that would have measured exactly a half-inch with a ruler.

After she poured Dana's, I lifted mine and said, "To Zoe."

"To Zoe," she replied, and I noticed her hand shook a little.

If I ever get rich, Manchester Beer will be in my larder. Somehow the beer, the beef, the beets with enormous black olives, capers and celery on Boston lettuce, and the warm crusty bread came together perfectly.

I complimented Dana on her menu and she demurred sweetly. "It was mostly the cook's idea—except for the beer. And Dad swears she and Nana drink a lot of that." She laughed. "By the way, Nana sends her regrets that she isn't here to join us. She's in Boston for the day."

I just smiled. It sounded pretty handy to me. I wondered if Grandma even knew I was here or remembered who I was in the first place.

Dana looked a lot better than she had a couple of nights ago. The dress sleeves concealed the scrapes, an Ace bandage had replaced the soft cast on her ankle, and lightly tinted glasses pretty well covered the black eye.

"I invited you to luncheon mainly to apologize for my behavior Friday. I was taking pain pills, and I think they must have made me a little crazy. Not that it's any excuse. I really behaved badly, and I really do love Zoe dearly, although it certainly didn't sound it."

She looked at me closely. "Do you think we are too young to really be in love? I adore being with her. We talk seriously about all kinds of things, and we also laugh a lot and, of course, other things." She blushed slightly, the first genuine gesture I had noticed, and it was inadvertent.

"I think you are just the right age to be deeply in lust. That always comes first, you know. If you are lucky, love arrives a little later. Even if it doesn't, you've had a helluva good ride. Some people fall in love at sixteen, and it's life-long. Others are thirty. I know one lady who fell really in love for the first time in her fifties. Who knows?"

"Oh, dear, I hope I don't have to wait that long."

"I think that's probably a bit unusual. I wouldn't worry about it."

She turned serious again. "What I worry about is Zoe. I mean, as well as this kidnapping thing going wrong. I think she is maybe too intense. About us. Insisting I should rearrange my life and cause an uproar with my dad over changing schools, just so I can be in New York all the time with her. Anyway, she will probably be living in Fairfield in Connecticut—a half hour from Yale. And this whole kidnapping thing, I know, I went along with it, but it need never have happened. It's not even halfway sensible, even if nothing terrible happens. But anytime I brought up objections to anything she wanted, like what made her think she could just walk onto a stage and be an instant star, she'd cry and say I didn't love her."

I finished my beer, and a new one miraculously appeared and was poured into a fresh glass. "Slow down, Dana. You're beginning to babble. I have the picture. I've thought from the beginning Zoe sounded pretty spoiled. But so are you—in a different way. Face it, kids with your kind of money and Zoe's are used to getting most of what they want. Now the two of you want some important different things, so it's causing problems." I paused for a moment to sip this beer of the gods.

I wiped my lips and continued. "I met some quite successful actors last summer, and I can tell you, Zoe has a long, tough way to go before she even gets a role with twelve lines. And you can add in the fact that Zoe seems a bit immature to boot. The time to have thought up the kidnap plot—as it originally stood—was when she was thirteen, not seventeen."

"I never thought of that. You're right. And Harry fits right in. He thinks all the world spins around a hockey puck. His grades are iffy. Unless he gets into a school with big-time sports, he'll never get a scholarship. He'll be lucky to pay his way into some college. But with Zoe picking up the tab, he could live in New York and maybe get on some second-rate hockey team. He is good at that. But that worries me, too."

Dessert arrived: Italian ice, some marvelously delicate cookies that melted on your tongue and good strong coffee.

Dana clarified her last statement. "Zoe sort of looks upon Harry as her mission in life. I think they both know if he doesn't play hockey, he'll pump gas. A large part of this is for him. God, I hope he's not the one who got us all involved with those two creeps."

Startled, I almost spilled my coffee. "Why the hell would you say that?"

"A lot of not-so-nice people hang around athletes. Harry has been approached to throw games, although he says he never has. And I believe him. But he would know where to find the type of people who would know how to set up this kidnap thing. You know, make it for real, take Zoe God knows where, toss me casually out of a car, hold out for a bigger cut . . . or just disappear with all of it. Minus a nice amount for Harry, maybe."

"He seemed genuinely upset the other day," I answered rather weakly.

"Yes. He would be. It's out of his hands now and he's afraid of what he's gone and done." She dabbed her eyes with her napkin.

"Or maybe I'm just being bitchy again." She tried to smile. "What can I blame it on this time? The beer?"

"Maybe we'd better just take a closer look at Harry. This beer is too good to blame anything on, except maybe greed."

We chatted about beers in general for a few minutes, graduated briefly to the weather and the tourist exodus. Then I thanked her for lunch, she thanked me for listening, and we parted with a cool, brief hug.

As I got to the end of the driveway from Dana's castle, I pulled over and took my cell phone from the glove compartment. Okay, it wasn't on my person, but at least it was with me, not home in last night's dirty shirt. Fortunately, Rob picked up and agreed to meet me at Mickey's in a few minutes.

I got there first and managed to secure one of the few indoor tables. It was clouding over and the breeze felt like rain was due any minute. When Rob came in a few minutes after I did, I noticed a few scattered raindrops on his jacket. I was pretty good at predicting weather. Why couldn't I apply that to kidnappings? The only thing I seemed to do was add suspects, when the whole idea of an investigation was to eliminate all but the one who was guilty.

We ordered coffee—a little rough and ready after the smooth cup I had just consumed. I casually mentioned the idea of Harry Maddock's being involved criminally in Zoe's kidnapping, and was answered by a deep, genuine laugh.

"Harry? Involved in this kidnapping as some sort of mastermind? Alex, you may have noticed the Catlett family does not own a dog. Harry is Zoe's. He adores her and is content with the occasional pat on the head. She takes care of him. You might call him her mission. Trying to get him onto some hockey club is just one part of it. If he doesn't go through life carrying a hockey stick, believe me, he'll be carrying a waiter's tray. Harry is not the brightest light on the tree."

The vote was beginning to seem unanimous.

"Okay," I shrugged. "Moving right along. Rob, do you, by

any chance, know anything about a prenuptial agreement or your father's will? Anything that you'd be willing to share?"

He thought a moment. "As long as you leave Grandma out of this, yes."

"Unless she's criminally involved somehow in the kidnapping, I can't imagine why she would be of any interest. That said, anything about her stays private, I promise you."

"Okay. Her first. There's a trust fund in case she ever needs it. She can draw on it with the approval of the executor, John Frost. Whatever she doesn't use reverts equally to me, Zoe and Marvin on her death."

"Nothing unusual there. What about Merrilou?"

His mouth tightened. "All the whipped cream. She gets the house here in Ptown, which she'll have us evicted from in an hour. All the furnishings except a few specified things Mom wanted us kids to have. Insurance policies, stocks, bonds go to sweet M. We get money for education, including post grad if our grades are good. We get the little house of Mom's down in the Poconos—though I wonder how we're supposed to pay for its upkeep. And we each get a trust fund we can't touch till each of us reaches thirty—and it ain't no giant, anyway."

"Oh," he added, "there are some bequests to people who have worked for Dad, and quite a bit to charity."

"So Merrilou makes out quite well." I badly wanted a cigarette. The rain was still just a sprinkle, so I suggested we move out under the awning. We took another cup of coffee along and I began to get that over-caffeinated feeling. I zipped up my jacket. It was definitely fall.

Rob gave a grimace. "She makes out too damn well. But she better stay married to Dad. The prenuptial ain't so hot. John Frost must have been on the ball that day."

"Oh? She comes up short?" I could understand his father possibly informing him about the will. Or maybe telling Grandma, who decided to share the information with Rob. But the pre nup? Did Rob really have the details of that, too? And if so, how did he get them?

"She comes up financially amputated. Under certain circumstances. If she gets the divorce because of his proven infidelity and/or physical abuse, she gets a hundred thousand a year, plus a one-time payment of two hundred thousand. If either of them gets a divorce on general incompatibility, she gets seventy-five thou a year. And—I love this one—if he divorces her for infidelity, she gets ten thousand dollars for moving expenses. Period. Not even attorney's fees. Moving expenses. I'm sure you know which one we're cheering for."

"I believe I can figure that one out. But tell me, Sherlock, how come you know all these details? I can't see Reed sharing this with the family at-large over Sunday breakfast."

"Oh, no." He stared distastefully at the bottom of his coffee cup and set it down. "No, Marvin and I check his papers now and then—like when he married this money-grabber. We wanted to make sure at least Grandma was still okay. She's the one we have to take care of."

"And how did you do that?" I doubted they were tacked to the refrigerator door with a Disneyland magnet.

"Oh, Marvin and I figured out the safe combination years ago. We fiddled with birthdays and holidays and anniversaries, et cetera. It's Mom's birthday, backward. And his computer password is the three kids' birthdays by month. Two figures per kid. Oh!" He looked embarrassed. "I guess you know them, too, now, if you just look up the dates."

"I've already forgotten everything you said. But, Rob, that final clause in the prenuptial agreement sounds awfully tough, and it's a little unusual to have that sort of clause at all, at least not worded so blatantly. Usually it just says something like if he divorces her with cause, or something along those lines. Is there some reason to think that might occur?"

"I don't know. All I know is she was married before, to some Episcopalian minister down south in some rich parish. I have no idea what happened to him. Marvin heard her talking to Emily

Bartles about it. She also said that the women in the parish had been out to get her. That's all I know. I have to run, Alex. It's my turn to be home in case the phone rings."

"Oh, don't let me make you late for that." I stood. "But don't be surprised if the Tweedles go silent a few days. They are probably confused, mad, a little scared . . . and they're going to let you suffer, too. Silence is hard to bear, but hopefully they'll call tomorrow as they said. Thanks for all your help. Hang in, we'll get 'em yet."

He took my hand for a moment. "I'm glad you're around, Alex." And then he sprinted to his car.

The house was spotless. So was Cindy, curled up in front of the TV watching the Ravens flying all over the Bengals.

"Go, Baltimore," I cheered as I kissed the top of her head hello.

"How was your lunch?"

"Delicious roast beef and other goodies. And Dana will make someone a gracious hostess someday. For dessert, I had coffee at Mickey's with Rob Catlett, gentleman to the core. Maybe there is something to this kid stuff."

"Gee, that's too bad," she sighed. "I had thought we might enjoy some old-time stuff on a rainy afternoon."

"Old-time can be good, too."

And it was.

Chapter 11

Early Monday morning was devoted to a run for Fargo on the beach, which improved his attitude—and mine—no end, although several seagulls were slightly put out of humor. That interlude was followed by a swift cup of coffee with Cindy before she went to work. After she left, I noticed that tucked under her saucer lay a list of errands I was to perform. Normalcy for a weekday and a very welcome change from the recent past.

There was still no change in the Zoe situation. Sonny said that a lull this long was normal after a mix-up. They left you to wonder if they had just killed the victim and said the hell with it and gone home to plot something new. He said it was to soften you up, and I could well imagine that it would. The police, of course, were still active. The rest of us were almost taking it for granted. Zoe Catlett was missing. Old man Alton was sick again with bronchitis. Oh, yeah.

I had stopped by the police station and told Sonny what I had learned yesterday from Rob about Merrilou as Reed's heir. His eyebrows went up, and he looked thoughtful. I knew what he was thinking. Trish was John Frost's junior associate. Trish was Sonny's girlfriend. What could, or would, Trish find out about Merrilou's first marriage? And would she share it with Sonny? Who would probably share it with me. We would soon know.

I sat in the car a few minutes, checking my errand list: all done, in something like record time. I had felt a mild undercurrent of excitement throughout the day, which had probably inspired me to move faster. Cassie was meeting Mom's commercial flight at Logan airport in Boston and would fly her the last leg homeward bound. I would pick her up at Provincetown airport around three.

My watch said twelve. I had been neglecting what some people called "my other office" of late, so I headed toward the elegant Wharf Rat Bar for my lunch. A cloudy, chilly September Monday noontime found few tourists as patrons. Weekends would still be crowded, but weekdays had pretty well reverted to the usual local clientele. Even Joe was taking a day off, the bar delegated to his wife, Billie Jo.

She was a capable bartender and a better cook. The thing you had to watch about Billie was her syntax, which had her own unique formula. "Hello, Alex. I hear your mama's comin' home today. Had enough of that actor guy and the big city? Like he was always polite and friendly, however."

"Yep. Cassie's bringing her in around three. What's to eat?"

"The usual, and only one special today. You tell her hello for me. I been busy enough making stuffed clams without Joe." It sounded as if parts of Joe were usually included in the dish. I immediately changed thoughts before I lost my appetite for stuffed clams.

"Ah, I'll have a couple with a few fries and some coleslaw, please." Billie's stuffed clams were lots of clam, little stuffing, and delicious. I thought of the perfect drink to accompany them. "Say, Billie, you don't happen to have any Lee's Manchester Beer, do you?"

She laughed scornfully. "You crazy, Alex? Even if we had it in stock, have you ever seen anybody in here ready to pay twelve dollars one bottle for beer, which we don't."

"Just asking. Twelve dollars? Wow."

"Yeah. Ain't no beer going to bring that price around here. The minute my back is turned, call me if anybody comes in." She went toward the kitchen.

I sipped my Bud and contemplated one of life's little mysteries. Just how good could a beer be, to be worth twelve dollars a bottle? I remembered once being in a restaurant in Boston where filet mignon was fifty-five dollars a la carte. How much better could it be than one for twenty-five dollars? Didn't taste and price have to level off at some point? Or was there a steak out there somewhere for a hundred dollars? Probably in Tokyo.

A warm breath about equal parts onion and beer told me that Harmon had joined me at the bar. Harmon Killingsly held the uncontested title of Provincetown's Character-in-Chief.

He made some kind of living by beachcombing, helping out on the occasional fishing boat and doing various handyman jobs around town. He was a friend to most of mankind and all animals, but he hated drug dealers. It was his bounden duty in life to put a stop to their evil activities. And he was certain that Provincetown was rife with them.

According to Harmon, they came by boat from elusive mother ships at sea. They came by private plane if he did not personally know the pilot. They came disguised as housewives from Ohio on tour buses. They came in any car that was not registered in Provincetown—and a few that were.

He drove my brother to distraction with his "reports" of drug exchanges he had witnessed—one of which had actually included a live alligator and a naked lady. As Sonny said, Harmon had reported twenty of Ptown's last three drug sales. And if he couldn't find Sonny to tell about them, I would do.

"Hiya, Harmon. How about a beer? As soon as Billie gets back. She's just getting me some lunch." And I was beginning to sound like her.

"Thanks, I'd appreciate that. Say, Alex, I know you're working with Sonny on that Catlett case. I got some information that might help. You know I try to stay on the alert. I ain't no stranger to certain activities in this town." Billie returned with my platter, and I ordered two more beers.

Harmon lowered his voice to impart the important information, and I attacked the clams. Harmon's scorecard didn't warrant letting my lunch get cold. Of course, one day he would be right, and none of us would be paying the slightest attention.

"You see, Alex, a couple of weeks ago, there was this drug payoff out on Macmillan Wharf. There was this man in a car with out-of-state plates and two women drivin' a van. I figure they was using the women as a moose, because there ain't many women dealers."

"A moose? The women were disguised as moose?" That certainly would avoid any undue attention.

"Yeah, you know a scam, a trick, something that looks like what it ain't."

Now I knew—a ruse. I rapidly readdressed my clams. "Gotcha, go on, Harmon."

He sipped his beer. "They pretended they had had this little fender bender, and the guy, he was handing them some money, like you do if you don't want the cops and the insurance folks involved. Naturally, he was paying them for drugs they had give him earlier. And probably for that girl Zoe they had sold him," he whispered, "to put into white slavery."

"I see." I lied. I didn't see drugs, nor did I see Zoe's kidnappers sailing off to auction her in a Moroccan bazaar. Harmon had never been right yet, and he didn't look like he was starting today.

Then he added a comment that straightened me up. "You see,

the van was kinda white, and the car was blue, so I thought maybe there'd be some blue on the van's passenger side, just to look like they really did collide, although I didn't get around to look."

"Terrific, Harmon. Did you happen to get the plate numbers? Do you remember the day?"

"No plate numbers." He shook his head. "Some folks behind me was blowing their horn to bits, and by the time I could pull off and walk back, they was gone. I think the man was Hispaniel, and the ladies was just about the same color as the van. The ladies was taller than him. But I remember the day—last Thursday."

The day—or night—Zoe disappeared. "That's great, Harmon. I'll get this to Sonny as soon as I can. It's a real big help. You keep this up, you're going to make police chief yet."

He laughed, but squared his shoulders and swaggered a bit as he returned to his friends at the large front table.

I reached for my cell phone, but I guess it was in the car.

It wasn't, and I remembered now. It was on the kitchen table. No harm, I had to go by the house anyway to freshen up. I didn't want to meet Mom reeking of clams and beer and tastefully attired in a sweatshirt with a small smear of ketchup.

I called Nacho and gave her Harmon's latest observation. She said she'd check around for any reported accidents that day. Particularly involving a van and a blue vehicle.

I was early getting to the airport, and just as well. I had just gotten out of the car when I saw the sleek little twin-engine Beechcraft enter the traffic pattern and begin its approach. The wind was northwest that day, not too usual and a definite crosswind. But Super Pilot had the plane in a slight slip, gunned it just a tad as she straightened it out over the end of the runway. And greased it in with last-minute flaps. Oh, Santa, I have been so good. Can't I have one of those for Christmas? Please! Please! Please!

I walked out on the tarmac as Mom came down the few steps

of the plane, and we had a big, tight hug that felt just great.

Cassie was right behind her with a wide grin. "I do believe you two must have met before."

"Thank you, Cassie, for a lovely flight."

"My pleasure, Jeanne. If all my passengers were as nice as you, I'd have fewer wrinkles."

"If I may interrupt this love song," I said. "Would you like a ride home, Buck Rogers?"

"Thanks." Cassie shook her head. "I've got a four o'clock to Bridgeport, might as well stay here. See you tomorrow maybe. Let me help you with the luggage."

It was a good suggestion. Together we wrestled it to the car, while Mom and Fargo enjoyed a noisy reunion, which somehow ended with Mom in the backseat with Fargo and me alone in the front, lacking only my chauffeur's cap. Fargo sat at attention beside Mom. All we needed was for Her Majesty Mom to wave her white-gloved hand tick-tock at people along the way.

We got to her house and she changed into jeans and a sweater and loafers, which made her look more like Mom than the silky maroon and yellow dress and maroon T-strap heels she'd been wearing. The new hairdo, however, was still there, carefully casual and I swear boasting a few new auburn hairs.

We dragged some chairs from the backyard over to a warm and sunny sheltered nook, where the house made a small ell. I moved a little round table between us, and Mom set our iced tea glasses on it. We just held hands and looked at each other for a moment.

"Everything went fine," I said. "I can tell just by looking at you."

"Yes, it did, darling. It was a wonderful time. New York is a different place when you're with someone who really knows it. There's a place for everything . . . the best jazz, the best cheesecake, the best fish and chips, the best bookstore, the best shoe store . . ."

"When you got off the plane, I could tell you had visited the

91

shoe store." I grinned.

"More than once, alas. By the way, Noel sends his best."

"And I send mine whenever you talk with him." Noel was one of the actors who had been here for the really unusual production of *Hamlet* a few weeks back. During the preceding weeks of rehearsal, he and Mom met and fell in . . . something. Love, lust, friendship, all of the above? Mom never quite said, and nobody quite dared ask. She went into New York to spend a couple of weeks and be with him for the Broadway opening of the show. And that's really all I know . . .

Except. "Mom that's a beautiful opal ring. Does it mean what I think it does?"

"I doubt it. I admired it, and Noel bought it. However, we are not getting married, now or possibly ever. I am not moving to New York. Obviously he is not moving to Provincetown." She sipped her tea. "I don't know whether we are in love or confusion, but whatever it is, it's very nice."

"Then go for it. Whichever it is, you deserve it. Is he coming up soon?"

"No, his contract runs through March—if the play does, which I no longer find so hard to believe."

"The *New York Times* had nice things to say. That's the only paper I saw," I qualified, "but I guess it's the one that counts."

"The production has stirred up a lot of interest, thanks to the Provincetown production, not to mention the audience participation. I'll probably go down a time or two to see Noel. Then we may travel a bit or go to his place in New Hampshire. We don't know right now." She shrugged.

"But you're happy," I said. "Both of you."

"Very much so. I miss him already. But I missed you and Sonny before the plane even took off when I left. I love being with Noel, and I'm glad I'm home." She fluttered her hands in the air. "Perhaps I really am certifiable. You and Sonny may have to put me away."

"I think we'll have more fun watching you do it your way."

"Whatever that might be." She smiled. "You know, darling, this entire . . . situation . . . with Noel is something I never dreamed of. I feel more alive than I have since you and Sonny were little, and everyday was brand-new—for you, and consequently me. All I know is: we are both enjoying it tremendously, as of today."

I couldn't resist asking. "And tomorrow?"

She extended her hands, palms up. "Tomorrow? You know as much as I do. I'm reminded of an old saying my grandmother used to say a lot. Something like, if you burn your candle at both ends, it won't last through the night. But, ah, my dear, it will cast such a beautiful light. She used to be quite a scamp in her day, I think. So I shall enjoy the lovely light. If it goes out before dawn, I shall mourn the dark, but remember the light . . . and smile."

Then she patted my hand matter-of-factly and asked what had been going on with Sonny and me. I started to give her a rundown about our latest excitement and our efforts to bring it to a desirable close, but I could tell she was getting tired, so I cut it short. It would wait.

I hugged her again and left her to settle back into her Provincetown life where room service consisted of making yourself a sandwich and cup of coffee and taking it into the living room to watch TV.

Chapter 12

Walking into the house, I was still grinning until I saw Sonny and Cindy at the table with solemn faces and Cindy actually drinking a highball along with Sonny. I wasn't sure from this distance, but I thought her eyes looked red, and there was a rumpled tissue in her hand.

In something under ten seconds, I ran down a list of what could be wrong with someone I loved. Not Cindy or Sonny, they were right here and each looked okay. Mom was fine five minutes ago. Fargo was leaning against my leg, and Cindy was casually holding Wells. Aunt Mae? Cassie? Oh my God, a crash on takeoff? Then more logically, Zoe? Probably Zoe.

Cindy put Wells on the floor and got up to hug me. Sonny spoke first.

"Got a lousy one, Sis. I didn't want you somehow to hear it at the Wharf Rat or somebody on the phone or maybe the TV news." He only called me Sis when he was very upset or excited.

"Zoe's dead?" I asked reluctantly.

"Not that we know of. Still silence on that front."

"Then Aunt Mae . . . Cassie?"

"It's Charlotte Cohane, Alex. It looks as if she committed suicide." His voice was flat, as if he were reading off an address.

"Oh, Sonny." I suddenly felt weary and irritable. And I had had enough drama in the past month to last me a lifetime.

"Somebody has got to be mistaken or playing nasty tricks. Charlie Cohane wouldn't commit suicide. If the world were coming to an end at midnight, she'd still be dancing."

"I'm sorry, Alex, but it's no mistake. It happened at the Tellman Art Gallery where she works—worked, and the people who found her obviously recognized her. Also, Charlie had ID in her wallet. Anyway, Jeanine was the uniform that answered the first call and she knows her personally."

"How did she presumably do that?" I still couldn't admit it was true. I was grasping for anything that made it an untruth.

Sonny obviously didn't want to answer me. Finally he said, "All the indications are she shot herself . . . in the head. I'm sorry, Alex."

"Ellen. Does Ellen Hall know?" She and Charlotte had been together for years. They had a stable, easygoing rapport. They had no financial problems. Ellen was one of the town's more successful real estate agents. I imagined Charlie did well at Tellman's. She had been with them for years as office manager and sometime salesperson, and she loved her job. Suicide made no sense. I could only think of one thing that might make her pull a trigger.

"Sonny, was she terminally ill or something like that?"

"I have no idea. We aren't nearly that far along. Captain Anders and Jeanine are at Ellen's now with the news. Believe it or not, Anders is actually good at that sort of thing, and Jeanine could comfort a bear with a sore paw."

Sonny handed me a dark highball. I didn't complain. "I'm glad Anders is good at something. Five will get you ten that by nightfall he says she was murdered by a transient thief."

"Alex," Cindy chided gently. "That's terrible. You're just upset. Why would he say that?"

"Because," Sonny laughed shortly, "he says that every crime committed in Ptown is done by a transient thief, or transient killer, or transient rapist, or transient whatever. I'm sure he plans to run for selectman next year when he retires, and he doesn't want to accuse any local resident of criminal activity. If you're in jail, then you can't vote."

"You're awful, both of you."

"I guess we are," I said. "And I guess I'd better finish this and get over to Ellen's." I lifted my drink. "She shouldn't be alone. Has anyone called Charlie's mother?" They each looked blank, and I said I'd wait until I saw Ellen, then call on Mrs. Cohane if she hadn't already been notified.

I was glad I had put on good clothes to meet my mother. I wouldn't waste time changing. A brief encounter with a toothbrush and a comb would suffice.

"I'll go with you. I like Ellen. Maybe there is something I can do for her," Cindy offered, and I nodded my agreement and thanks.

"Uh," Sonny shifted uneasily in his chair. "Cindy, maybe you could run along over to Ellen's and let Alex come a little later. There are a couple of things I need to ask her . . . just background stuff that would only bore you."

Cindy looked at him keenly. "Of course. I'll just freshen up a bit." She went toward the bedroom.

Sonny dropped the subject of the Cohane death to ask, "Did Mom get home okay? Did she have a good time? Her cards all sounded like she was enjoying every minute of the big city."

"Happy as a lark, complete with a new hairdo and a wardrobe you won't find at Marshall's. Not to mention an opal ring in white gold surrounded by seed pearls. It's too bad this disaster de jour will put a damper on her happy return. She knew Charlie as a kid, and she's a close friend of Mrs. Cohane."

"Are Mom and Noel getting married?"

"No. They're enjoying the honeymoon too much."

"Good for them." Sonny laughed, as Cindy came back into the room, looking rather put out.

"Thanks for this, Cindy. I owe you one," Sonny called as she started out the door without a good-bye.

"You're welcome, I'm sure. I just hope my afternoon turns out to be as pleasant as yours seems to be." The back door closed firmly.

"Thanks a bunch, Big Bro. Cindy pissed off is about all I need to finish my day."

"Sorry about that." He leaned back on two legs of the chair—a habit of his that makes me absolutely livid.

I got up and walked around to him and pushed the front of the chair down. "If you only need two legs, then you can bloody well stand up. Now what is so secret you have to chase Cindy out of her own house? You find one of her brothers standing beside Charlie holding a smoking pistol because Tellman's started using a different shipping company?"

"Not quite. Now come on. We've got a situation we don't want spread around. Alex, I need some help."

"You sure pick a diplomatic way to get it," I snapped.

"What we don't want all over town yet is that money is missing from the safe in the same room where Charlie worked . . . where she was found collapsed over her desk. A fair amount of money is missing. Twenty to twenty-eight thousand dollars. They won't be sure till they check the books."

"Why don't they check them now?" I sat back down and sipped my drink.

"Ah, it's a little confused. You see, Jan and Betsy Tellman are in Philadelphia, meeting with some woman whose art they want to peddle. They'll be back in the morning."

He reached for my cigarettes and lit one. "And, ah, actually it was Emily Bartles who found the body."

"Emily Bartles? What the hell was she doing in a top-shelf art gallery? Shopping for refrigerator magnets?"

"She works there part-time. Does a little office work, fills in as a salesperson, especially if one or both Tellmans have to be away. So did Charlie . . . work when needed as a salesperson, I mean? Bartles said she was a great help with people who were undecided and better than any of them—sometimes even the Tellmans—at moving the really expensive stuff."

I grabbed the cigarette pack back and shook one out. It may have been my sixth for the day. Naughty. "I wouldn't be surprised if Ms. Bartles was good at moving expensive stuff . . . out the back door and onto a truck. So Charlie was their best salesperson. Now there's a good reason for offing yourself. By the way, do you know whose pistol it is?"

"Yes, it's Charlie's. Properly registered with us. Nacho remembers her getting it three or so years ago. That's when the gallery started handling more expensive art, so they began to have considerable cash there, and of course, there were trips to the bank."

Nacho "ran" the headquarters of the Provincetown Police Department. She had a memory that made tacks look dull. She could coax anything from any computer. She never forgot a face, and she was always munching on some snack or other. Hence, the nickname. And she was so nice and helpful, it was impossible to hate her, even though she had beautiful teeth and wore a size eight dress despite all the fattening snacks.

Sonny pulled a small notebook and pen from his pocket. I guess he was serious that I might know something helpful about this. Certainly I had struck out on the kidnapping.

"Alex, have you any reason to think Charlie was having an affair with Dana Portman?"

"I doubt it. Dana is—or shortly will be—eighteen. Charlie is early thirties. That's not an impossible stretch, but improbable. Anyway, I doubt Charlie was cheating with anyone. To my knowledge, she and Ellen were rock solid. Why would you pair up Charlie and Dana anyway? Do they even know each other?"

"According to Emily, they knew each other 'quite well.' Bartles said fairly often Dana would come around and go into the office, and Charlie would close the door. There's a couch in there. And Charlie left a note that didn't exactly sound as if she and Ellen were even tissue paper solid."

He reached in his pocket and pulled out a folded paper. He slid it across the table to me as he added, "This is a copy of what was on her computer."

I unfolded it and read:

My darling Ellen—

By the time you read this, it will all be over, both my troubles and

the agony and shame I have brought onto us.

Deeply as I cared for you, I let young, sexy appeal, desire and

wealth run me astray.

I have stolen from friends so I could keep up with my freewheeling lover, and they are bound to find out soon.

I cannot live with such dishonor and disgrace. I must end it so that you can start life anew. Try to forgive me. I do this for love.

Charlotte

I looked at Sonny, uncertain whether to laugh or cry. "Are you teasing me? That note sounds like something out of a Victorian novel, except for the parts that sound barely literate. The whole note is crazy. It sounds like a combination romantic novel and a note left by the trash collector. If—and that's a big if—any of this nonsense is true and Charlie felt she must kill herself over it, the note would have been more like 'Ellen, I've really fucked up all the way around. I can't face you or myself. I'm sorry. Love you, Charlie.' First and foremost, she would never sign it Charlotte. She used that only on legal stuff." I shook my head, perhaps to clear it, perhaps to deny all I was hearing.

Then I asked, "But if she were cheating, why did you pick

Dana? And how would Bartles know they were acquainted if she was only there part-time?"

Sonny giggled. He giggled when he was embarrassed. "Oh, they knew each other, all right. Dana was there pretty often, I guess."

I got up and freshened my drink. I didn't offer one to Sonny. He didn't need it. "I suppose, Sonny, your next revelation will be that Merrilou tended the flower beds at the gallery and Harry Maddock mowed the lawn.

"Could be." He poured some of my drink into his glass. "The way things are going, I wouldn't be surprised if they were all in on the kidnapping and killed Charlie because she stole the ransom."

I had a sane thought and tapped my finger on the paper. "Was there a printout with a signature? Or was everything just typed?"

Sonny looked chastened. "Just typed. Actually, it wasn't even printed out at all, it was left on the screen. I didn't like that either. And there's something else I don't like. Arlene Glover, our forensics guru, found something when she checked the keyboard for fingerprints."

"What's that?" I reached for my glass, decided that my getting drunk wouldn't bring Charlie back, and put some coffee on to brew. "Arlene's pretty sharp. She was on the ball with that bunch of lunatic thespians last summer. You want a drink or coffee?" He opted for coffee, so I got out a couple of mugs. "What did she find?"

"Most of the keys were just blurred smudges, like whoever used the computer last—to write this note, we presume—may have worn gloves. But most of the letters that were not used in the note—like q, k, j, x, z, plus the majority of numerals and control keys had partial or complete fingerprints on them. We're betting they turn out to be Charlie's."

I poured our coffee. "So Charlie didn't type the note. Someone else wrote this poetic beauty. I knew it. They didn't leave prints on the keyboard, and they couldn't print it out and sign it because they couldn't duplicate her signature."

"Always a red flag." Sonny sipped his coffee. "Good stuff. Thanks."

I took a sip of my own. I knew I needed to know more details, but God, how it hurt to ask.

"Sonny, how was it done physically . . . you know, how was she found and all?"

Sonny sighed. "That part seems kosher for doing it herself. She was in her office, armchair pushed back from the desk with both her arms thrown out to the side and then falling limp and dangling. The pistol was dropped in about the right spot. The wound looked about right. But I did question the angle a bit. I asked the medical examiner to look closely at it."

"What do you mean?" I lit the next uncounted cigarette and didn't even scowl when Sonny helped himself.

He didn't answer me directly. "Look, suppose you were going to shoot yourself in the head, how would you do it?"

I made a pistol out of my fist, with pointed forefinger and cocked thumb, lifted the forefinger to that little indentation in front of your ear, dipped my thumb and said, "Bang."

Sonny was staring at me strangely. "You used your right hand just now. Why? You are left-handed."

I shook my head. "Not really. I'm a mixed dominant . . . like Charlie. We both eat and write with our left hands, and I sometimes use a paintbrush or scraper with my left hand. But I play golf, throw a ball, use a screwdriver and shoot with my right hand. So did she. We played golf together, occasionally went to the firing range and a couple of times we shot skeet. Right-handed all the way. Both of us. I've always been like that. Ask Mom."

"Shit." Sonny set his mug down hard. "Charlie used her left hand to kill herself, or somebody used it for her. And there's something else I asked several people to do. It ain't scientific, but it's indicative."

"What's that?"

"You and four or five others 'shot' yourselves the same way. Forefinger aimed toward your temple. Charlie was shot in the forehead, which of course is possible, but not very easy. And she used her forefinger to pull the trigger, which is quite awkward. Using the thumb to pull the trigger is less of a strain on the wrist and digit. Especially, I would think, if she's using the wrong hand for some reason. I want to see some statistics on this."

"I don't think you have to, Sonny. I think you know. Charlie was murdered."

Chapter 13

The sun looked as if someone had turned its rheostat up to extra bright that day. The sky was a delicate, depthless, early autumn blue. The puffy little clouds sprinted and dipped sassily along, moved by some high-altitude breeze that reached down from time to time to give the trees a gentle stir. It seemed as if some callous, cruel hand had added another crime against Charlotte Cohane, burying her on a day when she would have so loved to be alive.

Thus far, the only good thing I had managed to glean from the day was that Episcopal funerals are brief and dignified. I love the Prayer Book, basically unchanged since Cranmer's sixteenth century writing of it. It seems hard to think of it as a product of Henry the Eighth's raucous reign, but its beauty and hope and promise have an assurance I personally would find difficult to write today. I'm glad he got it done before television and rap.

We went the whole nine yards: to the church, to the cemetery, finally to Ellen's house. I was exhausted and could only imagine what Aunt Mae must be feeling. She was white as a sheet and very shaky. After a stay just long enough to be polite, I simply told her and Mom they were leaving. I would drive them home in Mom's car. Cindy would follow in hers to take me home. They didn't argue.

Once home, I headed directly for the shower, and shortly discovered I had company. Strangely, given the strenuous day we had put in—and why—we began to play. We splashed, we gently pulled hair, we snapped washcloths, we ducked each other, we aimed the water stream at various parts of various anatomies. And of course, we made love. Awkward. Slippy-slidey. Laughing. Bury us tomorrow. Today we are lovers. We are blessed. And by God, we are alive.

Funeral, sadness and fatigue notwithstanding, I think I was more relaxed that evening than I had been in weeks. I know I was more hungry. Mom had made fried chicken and potato salad to take to Ellen's. Aunt Mae had made a peach and almond pie. It was old-fashioned, but it was the way things were still done in Provincetown, and I thought it very kind. Fortunately, they had made extra for us. Fortunately, they had made large extras, for Sonny arrived, looking strained and tired and handsome in his dark gray suit with white shirt and regimental tie. He had been at the church, but went back to work after that.

Not liking coincidence anymore than I did, Sonny apparently felt we were getting too many of the same people involved, albeit peripherally, in one too many crimes.

Sonny had drawn a blank with John Frost and Trish regarding Reed and Merrilou's prenuptial agreement. They both said they were sorry, but claimed client privilege.

Sonny was certain Emily Bartles would probably know the details and would be at Ellen's after the funeral. She would almost have to attend, their having worked together at Tellman's

Gallery. So Sonny called on the Rev. Lawrence Bartles, hoping to find him alone. The questions were: had his wife confided in Larry about the agreements and would he talk about them if she did?

Sonny said that for openers he used the excuse of asking Larry how the Catlett family was holding up under the strain of Zoe's disappearance. Larry thought they were doing pretty well, considering. His main concern was about Marie, because of her age. The ongoing nervous tension wasn't helping, naturally, but he felt Reed was a pillar of strength.

When Sonny told him of Reed's verbal threats to Sonny, and physical threat to me, Bartles was flabbergasted. Then Sonny said he told Bartles of Merrilou's weird behavior all along. By now, Bartles was thoroughly rocked.

Then Sonny said he casually added, "Of course, Merrilou could be behind the whole thing, feeling she needs to stash away every dollar she can."

Bartles looked confused, "Reed is rich, isn't he? Merrilou should have no money worries."

"Except one." Sonny drank some of the iced tea Larry had poured for them, and looked meaningfully over the rim of his glass to watch Larry turn pale, as Sonny opined, "I don't understand why the prenuptial agreement was worded that way, it was worse than insulting, it made her sound like a whore. And I don't understand why she accepted those terms. Do you?" Sonny said he just kept staring at him.

Finally, Bartles gave in. "Look, Sonny, I shouldn't talk about this, but maybe it will help you understand Merrilou a little better. Her actions may be a little cold and self-serving, but I cannot believe she is criminally involved."

He stood and put his glass in the sink, then leaned back against the counter as he explained to Sonny, "Merrilou comes from a lower middle-class family. By gosh and by darn she managed to get herself through college. While there, she met a young man who became a minister, and they married. We all thought it was a mistake to begin with, but what can you do? Nobody who thinks he's in love is going to listen to friends warning him about his fiancée. Bob was assigned to a small church in a rather wealthy community on Lookout Mountain, just outside Chattanooga."

"Did she know Bob was going into the church when she married him?" Sonny had asked.

"Sure, he was already ordained. Anyway, Merrilou kind of put on airs around the ladies of the parish. Spending way too much money on clothes in order to 'keep up,' suggesting the church give Bob and her a complimentary membership to the golf club, a new car every three years. I don't know what all. I know there was some bad feeling, including the general opinion that she had a lot to learn to be a preacher's wife. Then the other rumors started."

"Like what?" As if my beloved brother wouldn't have already guessed.

"Men. Or at least, the golf pro. Maybe Merrilou figured it was okay, now that they were members." Sonny said that Larry actually gave a man-to-man grin, along with the surprising remark.

Then he looked genuinely pained as he continued. "One of the church ladies saw them come out of the motel where the pro lived for the summer. Merrilou always swore they had just stopped by to pick up some clubs needed for her lesson. I don't know what was true. But divorce was the result, and I'm sure she got no alimony."

I couldn't resist adding my bit to the gentlemen's gossip hour. "Helluva lot of clubs they picked up if she had to go in and help the pro carry them out," I put in.

Sonny nodded and went back to his drumstick.

"Well," Cindy added, "she's apparently scared to death of finding herself penniless for the second time, poor woman. Even if you don't like her—and I don't either—you can't blame her for wanting some kind of nest egg. Right or wrong, she came out of one marriage without a cent. She wouldn't want it to happen again. She should never have accepted that last prenuptial clause from Reed."

"How could she not?" I grinned. "Should she have said, 'Darling, you know I would never cheat on you, but if you should catch me in the act, I want more than a lousy ten thou'?"

Cindy stuck to her guns. "She had a reasonable need of money, even if she took unreasonable steps to get it." She moved to another point in the discussion. "Do you suppose Emily Bartles knew the combination to the safe or knew the hour at which it would be open?"

"Presumably not." Sonny answered. "It was a confused morning all around at Tellman's. The two owners left around seven o'clock that morning. Cassie flew them over to pick up a Philadelphia flight out of Boston. Emily Bartles and Charlie opened the gallery at nine thirty as usual. Emily got there first by a few minutes and had to wait outside for Charlie. Charlie arrived by cab, and mentioned to Emily that her car battery had gone bad overnight." Sonny loosened his tie and collar and looked happier.

Then he continued, "Emily does not have keys, according to her. Oh, yes, Dana was supposed help out part of the day, but had to drive her grandmother to an eye doctor's appointment in Hyannis. And with the Tellmans away, Emily and Charlie would both have to work a full day."

I began to put the remaining food away. "I didn't know Dana spent so much time there. Did Emily Bartles hear a shot? Is that how Charlie was found?"

"Apparently Dana fills in from time to time. After all, she is the Tellmans' niece." Sonny stretched. "Nice meal, thanks. No, Emily did not hear any gunshot, and the morning went smoothly in general. Around ten, Charlie told Emily she'd better take her lunch hour from twelve to one. Charlie had a tooth bothering her. It was getting worse, and she had managed to get a one thirty dentist's appointment. She thought it might run a little long."

"Did she really have an appointment?" Cindy asked.

"Yep. Emily left at twelve and returned about ten of one, to find the front of the gallery wide open. She was surprised Charlie wasn't working at the front desk, which someone always covered when the gallery was open. Otherwise, anyone could have strolled in and carted out pictures and statuary or whatever. Emily shrugged it off, figured Charlie may have been in pain and nervous about the dentist, and assumed Emily would be back shortly. So Emily just began her work of dusting and straightening, taking care of the few potential customers who dropped in and answering the phone. When Charlie wasn't back by three, Emily called the dentist to see if she was all right. She thought maybe Charlie hadn't felt well, had gone home, and the dentist was supposed to have called the gallery."

"But Charlie had never been there," I guessed.

"Right. When Charlie was twenty minutes late for her appointment, they had marked her off as a no-show. It had happened before. After they explained this to Emily, she then walked down the hall to the back of the building and into the office and ran out screaming . . . called 911 . . . and was in the parking lot sobbing when the uniforms got there."

I lit a cigarette and didn't even pretend to count. "So if she did know the combination, or if Charlie had the safe open for some reason when she was shot, Emily could have emptied it and put the money in her car, or called Merrilou to meet her in the lot and given it to her before she even called the cops."

"Yes, but think, Alex. Did Charlie just sit there quietly while Emily or Emily and cohort robbed the safe, took her gun out of the desk and shot her with it?" Sonny gave me a wry grin.

"Maybe Merrilou lured Charlie out into the gallery on some pretext while Emily swiped the gun—she probably knew where it was kept—and shot Charlie when she returned to her desk. And the safe was already open for some reason. Maybe Charlie planned to combine the dentist with the bank. And that suicide note sounds like Emily."

I held my hands spread in front of me in a won't-that-work?

gesture.

Sonny shrugged. "It could be. By the way, Larry Bartles sent you his best. He also said to keep your eye out for Catlett. Larry now thinks there may be more there than just stress. And it could be violent."

"Swell. Did Larry have any specific information?"

"Apparently not. He didn't elucidate."

"Thanks."

"Any time."

"You two are not funny," Cindy snapped. "Is Alex in danger or not?"

"Oh, I doubt it," I said. "The entire family has been strange from the start. I mean, who wants to be a forensic geologist—playing with bones a thousand years old? And why would the wimpy little kid want to place himself in with a bunch of Marines who would have him for lunch and spit out the seeds? Why would Reed and Merrilou send Grandma out to get someone she knew as a nine-year-old kid to investigate Zoe's disappearance? And Zoe herself sounds a bit wacky. I think they all just need a good psychiatrist."

"Sounds like the all-American family to me," Sonny stated and left.

Chapter 14

Thursday Sonny stopped by to update me on Charlie and Zoe. What update? No news was not good news.

He had asked me to stop by his office this morning and let him swear me in as a deputy. He wanted the Tellman sisters to be interviewed as soon as possible and thought I might have more rapport with them than Jeanine or Mitch or even Sonny himself.

When I asked why, he said that A. I was female, as was Jeanine, but B. I was interested in art—an artist myself of sorts, and C. I could, if I tried hard, be more subtle than his other detectives. There was no point in antagonizing the women at this stage. After all, they had been miles away when the murder happened. It was a matter of what or whom they might know or suspect. But he did want me to be able to say I represented the police, not that I was simply Lieutenant Peres's curious sister.

It was quickly done, right hand raised, brief oath repeated, badge in its carry case slipped into my pocket. We had both done this before. And I was soon out and on my official way.

I realized it was a bit early to call on the Misses Tellman, so I swung by Mom's to see how she was faring after her happy-turned-sad homecoming. As I pulled into the driveway, I had a great view of two jean-clad bottoms in the air. Mom and Aunt Mae were catching up on the weeding. They seemed quite content to take a break, so Mom and I sat on the wall, while Aunt Mae pulled up a lawn chair.

"Where are you going at nine a.m., dressed so nicely and wearing makeup? Surely you didn't go to all that trouble just to avoid pulling a few weeds." Aunt Mae grinned. Then she turned serious. "I hope to heaven no one else has died."

"So do I. As it is, I am on my way to interview the ladies Tellman about this mess, and I thought perhaps I should forego the jeans and sweatshirt. I wouldn't want to upset the butler."

Mom laughed and brushed an errant strand of hair off her cheek. "Betsy and Jan Tellman may be aristocratic and just a teeny bit artsy, but they are basically quite nice and down-to-earth, and there hasn't been a butler since their father finally passed to the other side."

"I'm surprised the other side didn't pass him right back." Aunt Mae chuckled. "He was one miserable character. Forever doing 'the right thing,' but talking about it so endlessly and egotistically, it was much worse than if he had done the wrong thing and had to keep it a secret."

I smiled at Aunt Mae's gentle character assassination, and then noted that my mother was looking thoughtfully into space.

"You still with us, Mom?"

"Hmm? Oh, yes, I was just thinking. I've always assumed that Jan and Betsy were lovers."

"Mom." I leaned around to look at her and waved my hand in front of her face. "Hello, this is Earth calling. The Tellman sisters are . . . are . . . sisters," I finished lamely.

Aunt Mae shook an admonitory finger. "Legally, yes.

Physically, no. If they were a man and a woman, they could marry with no comments about consanguinity at all, and not worry about their children having no chins. They are actually very distant cousins."

"My God, are you sure? How did they get to be sisters?"

"Not complicated, really. Mr. and Mrs. Tellman had two daughters, Betsy and another girl several years younger, named Margo. One year their cousin Jan, who was about Betsy's age, came to stay with them for the school year. Jan's parents were going to the Philippines as missionaries, and they thought it better to leave their daughter in the States. They were concerned about the volatile political situation and various tropical diseases, as well as available schooling. So the Tellmans volunteered to keep Jan with them."

"Because it was 'the right thing?'" I teased.

Mother gave me a dirty look and Aunt Mae went blithely on. "Most probably. At any rate, her parents were both killed in some accident over there. Was it a plane crash, Jeanne?"

"No." My mother shook her head. "I think it was one of those crowded inter-island ferries that are forever going down in the slightest bad weather. Whatever it was, poor Jan was suddenly an orphan. And the Tellmans adopted her."

"Because it was the right thing," Aunt Mae and I chorused.

"If you both insist." Mom shrugged and smiled dryly. "But when you look at the Tellman family, I sometimes wonder if they didn't inspire that comment: no good deed goes unpunished."

"Why do you say that?" I wiggled into a new position. The wall was getting hard.

"A few years later the three girls were out horseback riding. Margo especially loved horses, and Betsy liked them, too, but Jan wasn't very good at riding. Her mount shied at a piece of blowing paper or something and threw her. For one thing, Jan was a lightweight. For another, the saddle may not have been properly maintained. Whatever the problem was, the emergency stirrup release didn't work. The horse panicked and ran away, dragging Jan by the leg."

"My God." I could picture the accident in my mind, and it was a horror.

"Margo was the youngest, but she was very brave and quick-witted and an excellent horsewoman," Aunt Mae put in. "She managed to catch up with Jan's horse, somehow reached over and got the reins and managed to stop him. Even so, Jan's leg and hip were appallingly damaged."

"I can imagine," I said. "She's lucky to be walking . . . even to be alive. Her adoptive parents must have been shattered. First the poor kid loses her family, then she almost dies herself."

"Her mother was heartbroken." My mother nodded. "Her father managed to be quite stoic as I recall. Of course, it was only right that he send her to some famous hospital that specialized in that type of rehabilitation. For months, they were afraid she would lose the leg, but they managed to save it, and as you know, she now has only a slight limp."

"Again, she's lucky." I lit a cigarette and Aunt Mae frowned. "You'd think Jan would have fallen for the brave Margo, not Betsy," I mused.

"Margo was considerably younger." Mom stood and propped her foot on the wall. "Jan and Betsy were about the same age. And of course, before too long, Margo had her own troubles."

"Yes." Aunt Mae crossed her legs comfortably. "A year or so later, Margo had the difficult job of telling her parents she was pregnant . . . with no potential husband in sight. And single mothers were not so casually looked upon in those days."

"How did you know? About the pregnancy, I mean." I asked, startled. "Were you two pals?"

"No, not really close. I had just married your Uncle Frank, and he was then a sales rep for a pharmaceutical company. Margo came to me, hoping I might be able quietly to get some drug through Frank that would cause a miscarriage. I didn't even know if the company made such a drug, but I knew darn well Frank wouldn't hand any out without medical supervision. It could have been dangerous to Margo—and to Frank—if anyone found out he was suddenly in the abortion business."

I had to laugh. "This sounds like a serial on the women's cable channel."

"It wasn't funny," my aunt snapped. "Margo's mother was adamant against abortion. Her father wouldn't consider letting her keep the baby, and Margo would not agree to give it up. She finally told them who the guilty man was. I don't know what kind of pressure the old man used, but shortly, there was a quiet wedding, and about six months later Dana Portman was born."

"Dana. So Dana is Betsy's and sort of Jan's niece."

"Yes, and they've been great to her. Old man Tellman disowned Margo and Dana, although I don't see how he reconciled blaming a baby for anything. Dan later divorced Margo and got custody of Dana on some trumped up morality charge against Margo." Aunt Mae yawned. "I'm going to go heat up the coffee. Excuse me for a moment."

I was confused and turned to my mother. "I don't get it. How could Dan Portman divorce Margo on a morals charge when it was him she'd been sleeping with, and Dana was his kid?"

Mom shook her hands from side to side. "It wasn't that way. Dan traveled almost constantly on business. Margo's only real companion day after day was Dana—barely potty trained and speaking about three understandable words. Margo naturally got bored, probably feeling trapped by the baby, even though she loved her. Dan was no fun when he was home. He either worked or slept, according to Margo. She started drinking quite a bit and going to parties with her old gang. At some point Dan came down with the flu and took an early plane home. The nanny told him Margo was at a neighborhood party, and for some reason Dan waited up for her. It was unfortunate, of all the nights he usually went to bed at nine, he picked that one to stay up."

Mom shook her head rather sadly. "Margo came in late that night, much the worse for booze, and she had obviously been with a man. She never would tell Dan who it had been, because she didn't want to hurt the man's wife. She told a friend it was the only time she had slept with Reed, and it only happened because he got her drunk and more or less date raped her."

"Reed Catlett," I said flatly. "Here we are with all the same people involved in some sort of disgraceful tangle again. And how do you know all this?" I gave her a raised eyebrow look.

She looked at me for a long moment. Finally, she answered. "Your aunt. Don't let her bifocals and apple pie fool you. When she and Frank were first married, they traveled at a pretty high speed."

She grinned. "For my peace and quiet, however, I would appreciate it if you didn't mention this. Yes, it was Reed. He was quite the young stallion, and Margo had a weakness for them, you know."

"Yeah. He ain't doing too bad now, either."

Mother gave a dismissive head shake. "I doubt it will last. Reed marries class and sleeps with sexpots. Only this time, he seems to have got it backward. He's married to Merrilou and making a big play for Martha Meyer, since her husband died suddenly."

Aunt Mae came out of the house bearing a coffee tray and muttering, "No, no, no! Martha will never give Reed Catlett the time of day. Her pedigree is so perfect, she could be registered with the AKC. Reed just ain't in it for her. Coffee, Alex?" She began to pour a cup.

"No, thanks. I've got to get over to the palace and interview the queen and princess. If you don't hear from me, I'm in the tower. Enjoy your gardening. Sorry I can't stay and help." I smiled winningly.

They both gave me knowing looks and I left.

The tale Mom and Aunt Mae had unfurled this morning reminded me of something I had read in school—not in fact, but in style. Then I got it, that F. Scott Fitzgerald story about Jay Gatsby, where the fellow says, the rich are unlike the rest of us.

It made me worry a little. Charlie Cohane wasn't rich. She was financially okay, but that wasn't rich. Had she gotten in over her head some way with one or more of her wealthy friends in the art world? Was she trying to keep up with the Gulfstream set? Did she know something she shouldn't? Could Dan have been smuggling in art from abroad? Did the Tellmans deal in fakes? Did Charlie somehow find out and threaten to report them? Or blackmail them? That was hard to believe, but a great reason for murder.

Was the note really true, just strangely composed under terrible stress? Who could have hated the good-natured Charlie enough to kill her? Or was it more than one person? Or was it really Charlie herself, perhaps painfully ill, and muddying the waters so her mother and Ellen wouldn't have to deal with the shame of suicide as well as death?

There were definitely two or more people involved in Zoe's disappearance. But that had no bearing on Charlie, had it? That was mostly a crime against Reed—who had a long list of non-admirers. The Bartles, the Tellmans, the Portmans, his own children and very possibly his wife. And, if you got right down to it, the kidnappers. Surely they could have gotten it all together by now. You'd think a quarter of a million would be a sufficient ransom. Who was stalling—Reed or the perps?

But now for the Tellmans. I turned into the drive of their imposing edifice and parked. As I walked toward the front door, I deeply hoped I wouldn't find one sister standing over the bleeding body of the other with a smoking pistol, while Zoe Catlett stood nearby and said fervently, "At last, darling, you can be mine. All mine."

Chapter 15

I was admitted to their home by both sisters, who seemed to come from different directions and arrive simultaneously at the door, laughing at their synchronized appearance. It was a pleasant way to begin an interview. I introduced myself. They followed suit, insisting we use first names for simplicity, and escorted me to a warm sunporch overlooking the marshes and tidal inlets and, farther out, the deep blue of the Atlantic Ocean. As we sat down, I noticed a definite family resemblance between the two. Not enough to be blood sisters perhaps, but definitely there. Certainly both were attractive still. I placed them in their mid-fifties, but lithe, with young-looking complexions and smartly styled dark brown hair. And not a gray root in sight.

Mom was right. There was no Jeeves the butler in evidence, but a maid appeared in answer to a bell I neither heard nor saw anyone ring. Jan asked for breakfast tea, Betsy opted for cocoa, and I followed her lead. It sounded refreshingly different from the gallons of coffee I had been drinking lately and would be—I was willing to bet—well made.

As we had walked through the house to the sunporch, it looked as if they were planning to move. Draperies were missing, light spots on walls showed where paintings had hung, furniture was out of place, and rugs were rolled up against walls. I wondered where they were going and why?

Betsy must have sensed my curiosity and explained, "We were planning to get just about everything into storage and then paint and make some minor repairs. After that, we intended to put the house and barn on the market. Now, with Charlie . . . gone . . . we're not sure exactly where we are."

"I'm not sure I understand," I replied. I wondered if they were running from something. Like maybe the cops.

"Nom of course you don't." Jan smiled. "Betsy, we have to go back a bit here."

She sipped her tea and turned back to me. "New England winters are getting a bit much, especially for me. We decided to sell the property, breaking it up so the house and barn go together and the gallery goes separately. I might add that the house was getting to be a bit much also."

When she paused, Betsy took up the explanation. "We've loved the Caribbean and especially St. Lucie for years, and last winter while we were there we bought a marvelous house—just the right size to have some company, but not much—and the master suite is on the ground floor. Oh, happy day." They looked at each other, and I could see they couldn't help grinning like two kids. They were obviously delighted with their future home.

"So what is your problem?" I asked.

Betsy ticked off on her fingers. "First of all, we don't wish to appear uncaring of Charlie's memory. We loved her, too, and would prefer to put everything on ice for a few months. But we can't. At this point, too many things are already in the works for us to call a halt."

She held up the second finger. "The gallery is already sold.

118

We are having our final gala reception there next week, hoping to move most of the remaining inventory as our guests belt down the free champagne. Then we have to clear out of that building. We would postpone, but we can't. Too many agreements made, all the invitations sent out, caterers hired from Boston, et cetera."

I nodded my understanding and sipped my cocoa. Superb. I was sure I had a mustache, didn't care and licked it off. "I think people will understand. Ellen Hall is a businesswoman herself. She knows you have to stick to certain schedules. And I imagine Mrs. Cohane is a reasonable lady. My mother is a friend of hers, and Mom doesn't usually go for the hysterical types. And who else matters, really?" I shrugged. "Especially if you're leaving the country."

Jan chortled, "I like your style. The only other big problem is the house and barn. Charlie was going to oversee the repairs, the touching up, et cetera. Now we have to find a handyman who's capable and honest and will simply do what's needed without someone standing over him. Then painting contractors will come in, and who will oversee them? We had planned to leave as soon as the gallery was cleared. Ellen, of course, was going to handle the sale of the house. Do you know her well? Do you think she will still wish to represent us? She's the best broker in town for high-end property."

I thought for a minute. "Ellen is a friend, although I was always closer to Charlie. My lover Cindy actually knows Ellen better. But, yes, I think so. Just explain your situation. I'll talk to Cindy and ask her if she has any relevant thoughts. I know a handyman who might be suitable if the job is fairly straightforward. Certainly he is honest. I'll ask him to call you. His name is Harmon."

Both women uttered their thanks for my suggestions. "I have a question, just pure curiosity, do you figure your new owner will actually use that beautiful old barn to stable horses, or turn it into a boutique? Or both?"

Betsy laughed and put her hands out, palms up. "In Ptown, who the hell knows? There's room for about six horses on the ground level, although none are stabled there now. The top level is a very plain, spartan apartment and a studio with great northern lighting. It could be made quite luxurious, but I'm not sure who would want to live on top of six horses."

We all laughed, and Betsy concluded, "So I would imagine the new owner would convert it into two or three condos and make a mint, once they got a hundred years of horse manure shoveled out of the bottom floor." She got another laugh.

"Is it rented now?" I asked.

"Not exactly," Jan explained. "Every year we let a couple of young artists use it in exchange for doing some simple work around the property—mowing the lawn, keeping the parking lot clean, trimming the hedge, painting the fences—the sort of thing young men or women can handle fairly easily, without trouble. And still have time for their own artistic endeavors."

"How generous."

"Sometimes we luck out," Jan said. "This year we have two young men. One of them is quite talented. We should have wanted a show from him someday soon, had we been here. We still will, in a way. We have an interest in a small gallery in Soho, as well as some other arrangements in the works. The other lad better stick to repairing fences, I think, although he does pleasant seascapes that sell well."

At that point, the phone rang. Betsy reached around and picked it up.

"Hello. Yes, this is she. Oh, no." There was a pause while she grimaced at Jan. I felt embarrassed to be listening, but couldn't really think of what else to do, and tried staring into space as if I were deaf.

Betsy went on. "Well, what about the Mercury? That, too, I see. There seems to be nothing we can do about it today. We'll expect them both tomorrow mid-morning, then. Thank you for calling."

She replaced the receiver. "Damn, damn, damn! That was the garage. The man who delivers the auto parts from Hyannis had some sort of accident en route this morning. The parts for the Lincoln and the Mercury, as well as various other people's vehicles are spread somewhere all over Route Six. We will have neither car until tomorrow. Isn't that just great?"

"Simply lovely," Jan said. "Especially since we have an appointment with Choate Ellis in an hour, and I really don't want to postpone it. I want some answers today."

Betsy shrugged. "We can always rattle up in our stylish truck."

"No, we can't," Jan replied rather testily. "I sent the boys off in it to do some errands. And it is not a truck, it—"

Betsy waved her hands airily. "Whatever. We'll just have to reschedule. We'll all manage to live."

"I'll be glad to give you a lift into town. It's the least I can do to repay you for the best hot chocolate I've had since I was eight. And I'm sure Choate Ellis will see that you get home. Most likely in grand style."

"I'm sure you're right. And how generous of you. Let's have a refill. We have a little time to spare."

We had the second cup and spent the spare time with me asking the standard police questions I should have asked to start with.

Had they noticed any strangers lurking about? Did they or Charlie have any known enemies? Did anyone have a grudge against the gallery itself . . . perhaps a past employee or disgruntled customer? Did Charlie have money troubles they knew of? Had she been depressed? Did anyone owe them a large sum of money? Had they noticed anything at all unusual recently?

One or both of the Tellman sisters answered no to every question.

Dropping the two of them off at the bank, I turned toward Ellen and Charlie's house. I really had put this off too long, but God, how I dreaded it.

121

From the parking space, I could see through the window that Ellen was in the office attached to the house, so that's where I went. She stood up as I entered and we embraced silently, tears very near the surface for both of us.

Finally, I managed to get my voice under control. "How are you doing, honey? Is there anything you need? Anything I can do?"

She sighed. "No. Sometimes I handle it pretty well. Others, I don't. I guess I'll get better at it."

I looked around the office. "Where's your secretary?"

"Over at the town hall registering some deed changes and looking up some tax assessments. Life goes on. Why?"

"Well, there are some things Sonny really needs to know, but he thought it might be easier if you and I just talked."

"About Charlie. I honestly don't know if she was killed or if she . . . killed herself. I change my mind almost every hour. None of it makes any sense to me. A year ago, I would have said suicide for Charlie was entirely out of the question. Now, I'm not so sure about it."

Her eyes teared up, but I pretended I didn't notice. "In what way?"

"It's been developing over the last year," she said dreamily. "Sometimes she was my sweet Charlie. Sometimes she seemed cold, and angry at the world. And angry with me. It was all so stupid. Nothing needed to change. We had never thought much about money. Suddenly—for her—it became everything."

I wasn't following her very well, but said nothing, as she continued. "As you know, my business has really done well of late. Yes, I spend a lot of time and energy at it. No, I'm probably not the sweet, naïve young girl Charlie fell in love with. But we aren't kids anymore, and things change."

Her expression was bleak and her voice had a bitter twang, and I wasn't sure what to make of it.

"At first, Charlie was as happy as I was at our increased income. Then, oh, at least a year ago she began making little snide remarks. Calling me Donella Trump and Jill Gates. Asking me if I could spare five dollars so she could buy a cup of coffee. My wardrobe expenses came under discussion. Alex, I'm not beautiful, but I do try to make a good impression on clients. I go to the hairdresser every week, and I have nice-quality clothes."

I had to admit to myself that Charlie—like me—was not the greatest American model. With us, cleanliness was next to all that mattered. Ellen was still enumerating their problems, and I switched my attention back.

"She really blew when I bought the new station wagon, but hell, Alex, it was for the business. I have to cart prospective big spenders around, and it makes a better impression to have a good-looking, comfortable car than an old milk cart. You can show a piece of prime property easier from a Chrysler than a beat-up Kia."

I offered her a cigarette, which she accepted. I lit hers and mine and asked, "Didn't she do pretty well financially at Tellman's? I know they thought highly of her. Didn't they pay her well?"

"Very well, plus all sorts of commissions and perks, and I'll tell you how much they valued her. You know how a business will take out a life insurance policy on a partner or an important employee to make up for how much they feel that employee's death would cost the company in lost revenue and good will?" I nodded. "They have one for a hundred thousand on Charlie."

"Good grief. You don't suppose they killed her?" I blurted. "Or had her killed, I guess?"

Ellen actually laughed. "No way. They'd have killed the Easter Bunny first. No. You can forget them."

She became serious again. "Alex, I have thought about this to distraction. I think Charlie had some sort of nervous breakdown. We never used to argue about money. If I had more available, well, I paid for some of our vacations, some household improvements. You know how it is. The bills get paid. That's all that really matters. I thought everything was for us. Charlie began to act as if we were no longer us, but you and me. We were definitely drifting apart. I don't know if it was just a bad patch in our lives together—you know, they do happen from time to time in any relationship—or the beginning of the end."

She picked up a pen and began to doodle on an envelope. I waited. "Last winter we went out to Aspen for a week. I paid for the business-class airline tickets and hotel—a good one. We had both been working hard. I thought we deserved a little luxurious coddling. It was my . . . my pleasure to be able to do it for us, Alex. You do understand, don't you?"

She looked actually in pain. "Of course I understand, Ellen. Last summer I had the deck redone on Aunt Mae's cottage that Cindy and I use. I got a real kick out of watching their faces light up when they saw it. Little thing or big, it's fun to do something nice for someone you love."

"Exactly." She nodded emphatically. "On the flight Charlie kept urging me to have more wine, more canapés, more coffee. She kept saying loudly that as I'd paid for it, I might as well enjoy it. By then I wasn't enjoying any of it. Later, at the hotel, Charlie went into this act of ordering the cheapest dish on the menu. Then, she tipped the room service waiter about five percent and complained every day about the cost of using the ski lift. It was awful."

She took a deep breath and went on. "Then this spring we went to Ireland. Charlie insisted we split the cost down the middle, and she made all the travel arrangements. It was a horror. Flying is bad enough nowadays, even if you can afford to upgrade, and at this point in life, thank God we can. But we didn't. We flew tourist, and I can tell you, it was grim from start to finish. Stale peanuts and all. Once there, we stayed in third-rate B and Bs. In one place, we had to share a bathroom with two other people. Instead of renting a car, we took tour buses. Ireland is supposed to be lovely, but unfortunately, all I remember is an upset stomach, uncomfortable seats, lumpy beds and rusty pipes. And every bit of it unnecessary."

I couldn't believe what I was hearing. This was like some hysterical woman in a bad movie. It sure wasn't the Charlie I had known so well. But Ellen wasn't finished with her saga.

"After a year of riding me about being Ms. Millionaire, while she never spent a penny on herself, a few weeks ago she suddenly went completely the other way. She bought herself a whole new wardrobe, and I must say she looked great. Then one night she came home in a new car . . . just whirled up the driveway in a new Accord and called to me, how did I like the color."

"Wowee. Had she hit the lottery or something?"

"Not that I know of. But she was very up. Almost manic. I asked her why she had suddenly bought such expensive wheels. She laughed and said almost exactly what I had said about my new station wagon: when you are in business you need to have a decent car and clothing."

"Was she going into some business or had she invested in one?" I asked.

Ellen spread her hands helplessly. "You tell me. She wouldn't. She just kept saying everything was great and that we would soon be on an even keel. Whatever that meant, and I would be proud of her."

I moved on to another subject. "You read her note, of course."

"Many times." Ellen stubbed her cigarette out and stared at it for a moment. "I can't start those again. Yes, I have put every possible interpretation on it from murder to suicide to an accident to a bad joke that somehow went terribly wrong. Obviously, it was completely unlike Charlie. She never spoke like that, and I never saw her write a letter like that. Bad Victorian prose wasn't her cup of tea. And there was nothing wobbly about her grammar. Oh, hell, Alex, give me a cigarette."

I complied and Ellen continued. "I assumed, however, that very few murderers would write like that, either, unless she was killed by a half-educated ghost left over from eighteen-fifty. I finally decided that she wrote it, and it really was suicide, although it nearly killed me to admit to myself she preferred death to being with me. Her mother isn't doing very well around that aspect, either." Her voice broke.

"Ellen, sweetie, you know that's not it. She short-circuited somewhere. I know how much she loved you. She told me often enough. I just wish I could have helped. But I never even knew anything was wrong. She never said a word to me about money. Nor about cars or trips or new clothes. I hadn't seen her in several weeks. The summer was such a nutty mix-up. I feel terrible about that. Maybe she had trouble with your success, thought it might lessen her in your eyes or something. Maybe if she had just talked to someone, she wouldn't have done this. Could she have developed some serious medical problems?"

Ellen simply shrugged. "I have no idea, Alex. At this point," she added sourly, "I wouldn't bet on anything. Don't talk yourself into a guilt complex over this. If she had wanted to talk to you, she certainly knew where to find you. And I'm sure she knew you would always find time to meet with her."

Startled at her hostility, I changed the subject, braced myself for an explosion and asked, "Do you think she could have been having an affair?"

Ellen shook her head and smiled wryly. "Quite possibly. Look, Alex, we were together nearly fifteen years. I'm pretty sure Charlie had a couple of brief flings. Maybe she was having one now, though I can't prove it. And I have to admit my trips to realtors' conventions were not always celibate."

I'm sure my mouth was open in surprise. "But, Ellen, I thought you guys were rock solid."

"So did I, Alex. I figured as long as we were both discreet, and as long as they were just little detours down our path together, what the hell? And that could still be true. Or maybe there was someone else who had become my replacement. Maybe not. But to get back to your most important question, I think that whole note was designed to be so unlike her that we would all think it was written by her killer. So we wouldn't think suicide. So her family and I would be spared that, at least. But, honestly? I think she killed herself."

And that about said it. I invited her to lunch and got the turndown I expected.

Chapter 16

So I treated myself.

The Wharf Rat Bar felt like a safe, cozy cocoon after my late-morning conversation. A few people at the bar, a few more at the tables, and mostly familiar faces. The weekday tourists were definitely thinning with every degree the thermometer dropped.

The large round front table was once again populated with some part-time fishermen who gathered most off-season days to bemoan the paucity of fish, the government quotas on the fish there were, the infringement of foreign fishermen on sacred fishing grounds, and the cost of fuel to get to the fishing grounds in the first place. Joe the bartender had dubbed them the Blues Brothers, and the name had stuck.

Harmon was one of the group, and interrupted the cantata to ask me, "Hey, Alex, how you guys doin' on Charlie Cohane's murder?"

"Actually, Harmon, we don't know yet that it is murder. Our information is still pretty thin. There's no conclusive answer yet." I was damned if I was going to broadcast what little we did know to the entire Blues Brothers contingent.

"Too bad, whichever it was." He shook his head. "Charlie was a good 'un. Well, I'm still lookin' for that van. I reckon they're layin' low now that lots of people have left town. You know when I'll find 'em? The first cold, rainy day. Everybody will be decked out in raincoats and hoods, and it's hard to tell people apart, that's when they'll be out and trading."

It took me a minute to remember that Harmon was referring to drug trades as usual, real or imagined. But I found his point about raincoats interesting. I had never thought of it. It made a strange kind of sense.

"Good thinking, Harmon. That rainy day idea really has merit."

He gave me a knowing nod. "There's more things than philosophizers dream up, Alex."

Harmon quoting—in his own style—Hamlet! Maybe I should have ordered a straight shot. The world was definitely askew. Actually, I ordered a pastrami with fries and half a sour pickle. I needed comfort food. Really, it was quite healthy: meat, grain, veggie and green. I felt rather pure.

Joe asked me if anything was new in the Zoe Catlett situation, and it pained me to answer in the negative. I certainly wasn't being of much help to Sonny. And, more importantly, to Zoe.

"I hope they find the girl soon," Joe mused. "Reed ain't going to stand up forever under that kind of strain. I went most all the way through school with him. He was the brainiest kid in the class, but he wasn't wired all that tight. And he sure didn't like to be crossed."

"Really." I was more interested in my lunch than Reed at the moment.

"Yeah." Joe gave the area an unthinking swipe with his bar towel. "I remember. A girl in our class turned him down for the prom or some other dance, and she said it pretty loud, so several of us heard it and started laughing at him. You know kids. They love anybody else's embarrassment. Well, Reed, he upped and slapped the girl—hard! Right there in front of everybody."

"My God. Talk about overreacting."

"Yep. If you were smart, you didn't cross Reed 'less you were bigger than him. But then he could turn around and be really nice. One time when we were in high school, when classes let out, the ice cream truck was in the parking lot. A bunch of us had all lined up to get something, and I noticed this little girl about ten or so from the grammar school across the way, standing off to the side and looking real sad at all of us having a treat. Next thing you know, there's Reed, handing her a cone he'd bought for her. I remember he even took her books and walked along with her, so she could handle the cone easier."

"How nice," I mumbled through a bite of sandwich. Why were loud bells going off in my head? Older boys could be nice to young girls. Some of Sonny's friends had been generous with me, especially after our father died. I just had a dirty mind.

Then I had another thought. Why had Marie Catlett agreed to have Zoe come live with her and her lover? Marie was retired. She had finally realized she was a lesbian and apparently met a woman to share her life. It was a time of life when she and her lover deserved quiet happiness. Maybe some travel, theater, gardening, the beach, whatever they wanted. And why would they want a rather difficult seventeen-year-old girl? Unless she felt the girl badly needed her.

Surely, Merrilou would have calmed down about Zoe being gay. Zoe wouldn't have the stress of changing schools in her senior year. She and Dana would have frequent weekends, if that relationship held up. It looked as if Larry Bartles might even be a backroom ally in keeping Merrilou from too many efforts to get Zoe into the Baptist equivalent of a nunnery.

At least Merrilou was up front in her feelings about Zoe's lifestyle and friends. Reed seemed to be going in circles, with

Zoe alternately his sweet baby girl and his cross to bear. And he didn't seem particularly close with either of his sons. Maybe he was just one of those people who find affection hard to express.

It came to me with a bite of french fries—so many brilliant thoughts did. If anyone really knew the Catlett family, it would be Mrs. Hengel, their long-time housekeeper and nanny. Recently termed redundant by the new Mrs. Catlett, she should be happy to disgorge any family secrets.

"Say, Joe, do you have a phone book handy?"

He reached under the bar and plopped one onto the countertop near me. "It may be last year's."

"I don't think that will matter," I said. "Thanks."

As I absently straightened some half-torn pages in the book, I remembered another family I hadn't followed up on—Harry Maddock's. I hoped Mrs. Maddock might possibly know something about Zoe, her family or her relationship with Harry that would be of help. It wasn't very likely, but I looked up their number. There was only one Maddock, and I jotted their address and number in my little green book.

I found three listings under Hengel: Martin Hengel, Martin Hengel, Jr. and D. Hengel. My bet was on the last one. Lots of women used an initial rather than a feminine name, which I thought advertised, rather than concealed the fact that they were women living alone.

The Maddock house was closest, so I started there. The doorbell was promptly answered by an attractive woman I placed in her early forties. She was wearing jeans and T-shirt, plus an oven mitt on her right hand.

"Mrs. Maddock?"

"Yes, may I help you?"

I explained who I was and why I hoped she might be of assistance.

"I doubt I know anything of interest to you, but come on in . . . in the kitchen if you don't mind. I've got cookies in the oven."

That explained the mitt. And the fragrance from the kitchen

made me hungry all over again. As we walked through the living room and a small dining area, I noticed that the furniture was not expensive, but was clean and in good taste. On the wall were pictures that were obviously prints of famous paintings, but they were attractive and tasteful. Evidently, Mrs. Maddock made the best of what must be a rather limited income.

She offered iced tea, poured it and then removed a large sheet of Toll house cookies from the stove. She seemed to keep turning her back to me, and I noticed her dabbing her eyes once or twice. Had she been crying? I hoped Harry hadn't joined the missing. I'd try to find out.

"Does Harry happen to be around?"

"No, he's working this summer at the Happy Hot Dog, and his shift ends around four. Then he usually hangs out at Mickey's till around dinnertime. Unless his father has chores lined up for him, and even then . . ." she trailed off with a grin. I guessed I had been wrong. Probably the heat from the oven bothered her eyes.

"We can try the cookies in a minute or so," she said with a smile. Had I looked that eager?

While we sat at the kitchen table and waited, I asked, "Mrs. Maddock, did Zoe by any chance spend the night here recently?"

"Please," she said. "My name is Karen. When someone says Mrs. Maddock, I think of my mother-in-law, and I try to do that as seldom as possible."

I laughed. "Okay, and I'm Alex." I repeated my question.

"No," she answered slowly. "I can only think of one time she stayed over. One of those fast ice storms came up last winter while she was here doing homework with Harry. We didn't want her to drive in it, so she stayed in the guest room. I called her father, of course, to tell him where she was."

She placed two cookies on a small plate and set it in front of me. "I see. Does she come by often, just to visit?"

Karen shook her head. "Not all that often. Once in a while,

they do homework together. Sometimes she gives him a ride somewhere. My husband Mark is quite strict about letting him use the car. Says if a bike was good enough for him, it's good enough for Harry until he can buy his own car. Actually, I think Mark would be happier if Harry had more male friends, rather than being quite close with Zoe and Dana Portman. I think he feels male bonding is more important than being friends with two nice girls. I tell him it will all balance out, but I think Mark still regards it as a bit sissy. Although when you see Harry on the ice, sissy definitely does not come to mind." She gave a barely visible, tight little smile.

"These cookies are to die for," I said with a mouthful. "But Harry and Zoe are good friends?"

"Oh, yes, I would say so. I don't think it's a sweetheart thing, but friends, yes. They talk about going to college together, but with Harry wanting to be the new Bobby Orr, and Zoe planning to be another Katharine Hepburn, and Dana all set for Yale, that seems a bit remote."

We both laughed. Then Karen frowned. "If we can get Harry to college at all. It costs so much nowadays, we're going to need a dozen student loans and an athletic scholarship to boot. I just hope his grades are good enough. His father doesn't encourage him. Mark doesn't feel college is all that important. I do. I think it's usually the difference between a career and a job."

I agreed it was a problem these days and then asked, "Has Harry seemed upset or worried lately?"

"As I think of it, he has been edgy of late. Naturally, anyone would be with a friend missing. I wonder why he didn't tell us? We had no idea."

I finished the second cookie and covered for Harry with a quibble. "I imagine he was asked by her father to keep it quiet. I think Reed feels it's safer for Zoe, the fewer people who know. The police think just the opposite: the more people who are aware, the more likely someone will see or hear something. But Reed Catlett is quite adamant on the privacy issue."

"That's too bad. I'd be shouting it from the treetops if it were my child, asking help from the entire town. So, I'm afraid I've not helped you. I hope it all works out well for her. She's a nice girl. Even my husband is fond of her, and he's not big on teenagers in general."

"Karen, I don't usually toss this kind of information around. I don't think it's up to me to do so, but we really are desperate for any kind of lead in this case. Did you know Zoe is a lesbian?"

She turned pure white. "My God, no. Don't ever tell that to Mark."

"Why not?" I was startled at her overreaction.

"Oh, I'm making too much of it." She waved her hand as if erasing a blackboard. "It's just that he doesn't especially like gays."

And there were the incipient tears again. What the hell was going on here?

"He picked a damn strange town to live in."

She shrugged. "He was born here. It's nothing really. He just had a bad experience in school." She stopped.

I wasn't about to leave it there. "What do you mean by 'bad'?"

She sighed. "When Mark was in his teens, he was slender, with big blue eyes and blond curly hair." She rolled her own eyes. "I thought he was gorgeous. So did some of the gay boys, and one or two of them came on to him. Nothing serious, and certainly not violent, but some of his own friends, who knew he wasn't gay, teased him about it. I guess it just sort of soured him on gays. You know, kids can be sensitive about that sort of thing. Actually, I don't know why he still lets it bother him."

I had a pretty good idea, but I wasn't about to delve into Mark's psychological pottage. "I see. And you don't know anyone else who might have some hard feelings about Zoe?"

"No." Karen smiled. "Zoe would be hard to dislike. She's bright, funny, nice . . . and her sexual orientation is her own business as far as I'm concerned."

"Thank you for talking with me and for the great cookies."

"Sorry I wasn't of more help. May I tell Harry you were here?"

"Oh, sure. And remind him if he's thought of anything or heard anything, be sure to let us know."

I thanked her again for the cookies, assuming it would be impolite to ask her to sell me the batch.

Moving right along, I reached the Hengel residence.

The doorbell played a couple of bars from "Home, Sweet Home," and the last few notes were accompanied by the heavy tread of someone approaching the door. It opened to reveal a corpulent woman with thinning white hair and still-bright blue eyes that looked at me warily.

"Yes?"

"Good afternoon Ms. Hengel. I'm Alex Peres, and I—"

"You must be Jeanne's girl. You look just like her." Now a smile played tentatively around the corners of her mouth.

"Yes, I am, and thanks for the compliment."

"Come on in." She got that wary look again. "You aren't selling anything, are you?"

"Nope. Not since I quit peddling Girl Scout cookies. You're safe." I grinned.

We went into a bright living room with chintz-covered, over-stuffed furniture and blond wood tables, probably avant-garde in 1950. Mrs. Hengel pointed me to a seat on the couch, into which I sank, and from which I doubted I would ever rise. She settled herself in a less enveloping chair across from me, wiggling into a comfortable position rather like a dog settling tail-first into his bed.

"Mrs. Hengel, I'm a deputy police officer. I don't know if you've heard, but Zoe Catlett has gone missing, and—"

"Yes." Her face had lost its cheery look. "Rob came and told me. Didn't want me to hear it as gossip and be shocked. My heart, you know. He's such a sweet boy. Don't tell me you've got bad news." She raised her right hand to her left breast in what I thought was a gesture of long habit, designed to warn bearers of bad news to tread gently around her sensitive heart.

"Not at all," I assured her quickly. "That's part of the problem. We don't have much news at all." I quibbled a bit as I went on. "My brother, Lieutenant Peres, thought that you might have some background information on the family that would be helpful. I know Marie slightly, but otherwise we don't really know any of them. Sonny would have come himself, of course, but he felt that perhaps it would be easier for you to talk to another woman, rather than a policeman marching up to your door in a uniform." Not that Sonny often wore a uniform, but it sounded good.

"Now isn't that thoughtful." She preened a bit, feeling special. "I don't know what I can tell you. The three children—they all have their mother's temperament, thank God. Frances was one of the kindest, nicest people you could ever meet. Now Reed, he was a cold, withdrawn man most of the time. Oh, once in a while he'd warm up, but mostly he just seemed to live for his work."

She closed her mouth firmly and leaned back in her chair as if she'd provided all the news she intended to.

"Am I right that you worked for the Catlett family part-time until Frances died and then, full-time?"

"Yes. Marie convinced me to. She had stayed with them quite a while after Frances died, but she wanted to get back to her own home, naturally. We all felt the children needed someone to be there for them. I mean, other than the day help, fine though they were," she added.

Mrs. Hengel frowned and continued. "God knows Reed was no help. He'd either call home in the late afternoon and say he was staying late at the office, or come home from work, have his dinner, go into his home office and work some more there for most of the evening. Weekends, he was always off on some social affair."

She shook her head and looked bemused. "I hardly saw him

or talked to him. He even put my check on the kitchen table when I wasn't around. I actually had the feeling he disliked my being in his house, and I've no idea why. My quarters were up on the third floor, so I certainly was no bother to him when I wasn't working."

Simply because, like Everest, you were there, my dear. What would you have found downstairs if you got the midnight munchies and went to the kitchen, or thought you smelled smoke and went to check? Would you have found a lady of the evening tiptoeing out? Or maybe his best friend's wife?

I trolled a bit. "Did you ever see any signs that he abused Frances physically? How about the kids . . . physically, sexually?"

She shook her head. "Depends on what you call abuse. I never saw any marks or anything on Frances, and she wasn't afraid of him. And the kids only had the normal kind of cuts and bruises that all kids get. I certainly saw nothing that made me think he molested them. Frances would have figured that out, and wouldn't have stood still for one minute. Now if you mean was he sarcastic and enjoyed being critical, that's another ball of wax."

"Frances died in a car accident, didn't she?" I asked.

"That was what the police report said," she answered shortly.

"You mean there was some doubt?"

"It was in the car wreck, all right, but I've never been all that sure it was an accident. I think that car was tampered with."

My eyebrows arched. "By whom?"

"I'd rather not say," she answered primly.

"Mrs. Hengel," I reminded her gently, "you have just accused someone of murder. You can't just shrug that off like you don't want to gossip about a neighbor who doesn't starch her pillowcases."

"All right." She sat up straight and looked me in the eye. "I've always thought it was Reed. So there."

"Why?"

"Alex." She cocked her head at me. "You keep reaching for

your pocket. For heaven's sake, smoke. There's an ashtray right in front of you."

Guilty, but relieved, I lit a cigarette. "Go ahead." I gestured. "Why would Reed have killed Frances?"

"Because he couldn't keep his zipper up." She snapped the words out in a heartbeat.

She looked embarrassed, and I smothered a grin. "So Reed was a womanizer," I said. "Was Frances aware of it?"

She nodded and continued. "After a while. You know, the wife is always the last to know. Some friend finally told her he had all but raped Margo Portman one night at a neighborhood party, when Dan Portman was out of town and Frances had taken the kids down to their place in Pennsylvania for a weekend. It was one of the few times I ever heard Frances raise her voice. I could hear them quarreling all the way from their bedroom up to mine."

"What was the result of her confrontation?" I asked.

She twisted her mouth with disgust. "Oh, typical man. He swore it was because somebody spiked his drinks and Margo came on to him, and he promised it would never happen again. I guess he was good—or at least careful—for a time. Of course, it finally started up again. Then Frances made her mistake."

"What do you mean?" I leaned forward.

"I was upstairs in my quarters and I heard them start talking loud again. I could tell from the tone that they were arguing, though I couldn't understand the words over the sound on my TV. I really didn't want to hear, but soon they got even louder. Just plain yelling, and one of them—I'm sure it was Reed—threw something that broke. I'm not sure if he was aiming for Frances or not, but I guess he missed."

Mrs. Hengel pulled a tissue from her skirt pocket and blew her nose vigorously.

Her voice was shaky as she continued. "Finally, I heard Frances say she'd had all she could take. She was going see her lawyer the next day. Then she was moving with the kids to their country place and he would never see them again. Oh, and she was going to take his last penny with her."

I lit another cigarette, number six for the day, I thought, and mentally said naughty Alex.

Aloud I said, "Those were pretty strong words for her to use, even under the circumstances."

She tucked the tissue away and steadied her voice. "Well, yes, for Frances that was like somebody else using every swear word you can imagine. But she was just beside herself, I'm sure. I knew her from a child. I worked sometimes for her mother when I was a girl. Frances would never have denied him seeing his kids, and she would never have gouged him for money. She was just hurting and raving on a little bit. We all do that sometimes."

"Yes, we do." I nodded. "But Reed must have believed her."

"I guess he did. I can't prove it, of course, but I'd bet my last penny he went out in the middle of the night and did something to that van."

"How did the wreck occur? And where?" Surely not a fatality on Provincetown's clogged, narrow streets.

"The day after the fight, Frances was on the way to her lawyer's up in Orleans. In fact, she had asked me to pick up Marvin at school in case she didn't get back in time." She sniffed, and the soggy tissue reappeared.

"Down just this side of the traffic circle she supposedly lost control of the van and hit a tree. Frances was a good driver. She could handle a vehicle in any weather on any kind of road. The cops said she was going well over sixty. Maybe so, but she didn't lose control of it in broad daylight on a dry road. By the time they got her to the hospital, she was gone."

Mrs. Hengel gulped and continued her sad tale. "The Eastham Police called the house, looking for Reed. All they would tell me was that there'd been an accident. I gave them his office number. He went to the hospital, I guess. I was never sure. I picked up Marvin. Soon the other kids came home. I had to tell them there'd been an accident. They could tell from me and the maid and the cook. We were all worried sick. It got later and later. Finally, Reed crawled in, about half in the bag, red-eyed and weepy. Right in front of the children he asked me, 'Did you tell the kids their mother got killed?' I damn near killed him."

I shook my head, speechless. All I could visualize was an accident happening to Mom when Sonny and I were children, Aunt Mae there and trying to keep us calm, and our father coming in drunk and asking, "Mae, did you tell the kids Jeanne is dead?" It would have been the perfect scenario.

I pulled myself back to reality and asked, "The police found nothing suspicious in the crash? Did you tell them about their fight?"

"I told them. They said they would check the van again. They found nothing—if they looked. They just said she was going too fast for the road."

Mrs. Hengel looked pale and spent.

I felt bad at bringing all this up again. The woman had obviously suffered, both for herself and for the children.

"Just a couple more questions and I'll move along. I know this is tiring. You stayed on several years after the, uh, accident?"

"Yes, I couldn't leave the children. Marie came up often to see them, but they needed someone full-time. But I tell you frankly, while I'm not in love with that made-up southern belle of Reed's, I'm not sorry she gave me the pink slip, either. It was hard, being polite around her and Reed, and I don't suppose she likes me any better than I like her. I'm getting older and so are the kids, and they'll all just have to get along and live their lives as best they can. Frances ain't coming back, and Reed ain't going to change, and the kids ain't gonna bow and curtsy to their step mama. Miss Belle o' the Ball hasn't figured all that out yet."

"I understand. Any ideas about this kidnapping?"

She pursed her lips and gave her head a curt shake. "Nope. But I imagine the belle may be right about it being a trick. Reed was getting cheaper by the day. Spending all his money on the belle, I reckon. And while he may put on a good face, I can tell you he's not thrilled at Zoe announcing she's gay. He's got a lot of clients who may think it reflects on him. Zoe may figure it's a way to get some money and get back at him and just get out. I can tell you, those two boys won't be there one day longer than they have to be."

"You think he'll pay the ransom? He seems to be stalling."

"Eventually. You see, he also has quite a few gay clients he won't want to look bad in front of, either." She laughed. "You've heard about that rock and the hard place? He's right there betwixt and between and it serves him right." She stood.

So did I, after a struggle. I thanked her and took my leave.

Chapter 17

I drove home in some sort of fog. I couldn't get over Ellen saying she and Charlie accepted casual affairs as normal after being together a number of years. Charlie had been my close friend, yet she had never said a word to me about that aspect of her life. Did she think I would repeat it? No, she knew me better than that. Did she think I was that stiff-necked? God knows I had had enough affairs earlier in my own life. I just managed to have them pretty much one at a time. Did she think I would have been judgmental? Would I have been? Possibly, I had to admit. I know Ellen's comments had not set well with me.

And all this jazz about money problems. Why would Charlie make them up where they didn't exist? Ellen was teetering on what people euphemistically called "quite comfortable." Spelled r-i-c-h. Charlie apparently made good money at Tellman's, and I'm sure she kicked in all she could reasonably be expected to. So if Ellen liked a little lace on the curtains, she was apparently happy to pay for it. What made Charlie so unhappy about that? I knew Charlie would never freeload, and I was virtually certain Ellen wouldn't be bitchy about a few extra bucks spent in their mutual behalf. I couldn't think of any couples I knew—gay or straight—where each person made the exact same money as the other.

Cindy made more than I did. It had caused no problems about that for us, as far as I knew. And I thought I would. Cindy had teased me in the beginning that I brought some pre-Cindy assets to the relationship—already owning a house with a low mortgage rate, and the very reasonable rent Aunt Mae charged for the cottage we used as a sort of local getaway. Cindy had been gung ho on getting me set up with a SEP plan for retirement, and watched over it like a hawk. We both contributed to a household account. I don't know. I wasn't all that involved with our money, but things seemed fine. As Ellen had phrased it, "the bills got paid." We were putting some away for our dotage. Once in a while we took a weekend in Boston or Maine. And we were thinking of a longer vacation next spring.

Should I inquire regarding our mutual finances? I thought for a minute. Not on your life.

I shut the door on money and moved on to Zoe's situation. Which of course was also about money. I knew that Sonny had advised Reed, as I had, to tell the kidnappers that two hundred thousand dollars was the absolute maximum amount of cash he could raise. They, in turn, were sure to knock at least some amount off the million. Then it became simply a bargaining session.

Say they all finally agreed on four hundred thousand. I knew Choate Ellis could have that in Reed's hands in an hour. At least some of it would be marked bills, and I would bet the sum would also include some doctored bearer bonds that could be easily tracked as well.

Then all that remained would be to set up a meeting time and point of exchange. If the kidnappers felt it too dangerous to bring Zoe along to the exchange, they could tell Reed when and possibly the general area where she would be released. Simple. Zoe is loose, and quite possibly the perps are not.

The only problem was, at this point, nobody knew when Reed was speaking to the kidnappers, or what he said to them. If he were speaking to them at all. Once the prepaid cell phones had got into the act, the calls were pretty untraceable. I found myself fearful that Reed had stalled so stubbornly for so long that the captors had by now simply killed Zoe—or worse, left her tied up someplace remote, where she would starve before she was found—and disappeared in disgust.

I pulled in the driveway and was not thrilled to see Harmon perched on the back steps. I was tired, mentally and physically. It seemed months since I had accomplished anything even vaguely productive. And I really just wanted to sit quietly and think. Or maybe just sulk. I did not feel up to hearing chapter three thousand and six of Harmon's personal encyclopedia of Ptown drug trades.

"Hiya, Harmon. I'll be right with you. Just let me get the animals out. Want a beer? You look hot."

"Sounds good," he answered and then explained, "I was in the sun, picking your ripe tomatoes and peppers before the squirrels got at 'em. I know you been busy with other things. I put them on the shelf in the garage." I thanked him, told him to be sure and take some later for himself and went in the house.

Fargo, Wells and I exchanged happy greetings before they remembered they were mad at me for leaving them all day. Then they went out and turned their attentions to Harmon, to let me know I was an unimportant blip on their busy radar.

I got Harmon's beer out of the fridge and concocted what I deemed a well-deserved bourbon Old Fashioned for myself.

Back outside I handed Harmon a paper bag to hold his produce later, motioned him around the side of the house to the tables and chairs, and made a fuss over the fur balls, who had once again decided to love me.

"What's up?" I asked.

"Sonny's in court, trying to get those home invasion kids who pistol-whipped that couple tried as adults."

"Yeah? I hope he succeeds. They may be young in years, but they're aged in meanness. Now, what else is on your agenda?"

"I stopped by his office a while ago. I got two important leads to give him in the Zoe case, and he ain't there. But now you're here."

"So I am." I laughed and sipped my drink. Already things looked better. "Okay, go ahead, what news have you got? We could use something juicy at this point. Clues have about dried up."

"This may be the most important," he stated firmly. "I saw them two women that was dealing drugs with that guy in the blue SUV out on the wharf a while back." He halted and sat back, as if he had completed some important news bulletin. Film at eleven, I supposed.

Finally the penny dropped. "Oh, you mean the women in the van."

"That's right." His face grew dramatically solemn. "You see, I repaired Ms. Hatcher's driveway gates right after lunch. Then I stopped by the bank to cash her check. Much as I hate to say it, as I went in, they was walking across the main floor with none other than Choate Ellis. Ellis, with all them fancy security guards watching everybody else, walkin' with drug dealers and patting one of them on the arm and telling her he was glad they had managed to account for most of their money. Choate Ellis of all the stuck-up people. I couldn't hardly believe it. I almost turned around and said something right then and there, but I didn't want to put them on the alert so they might disappear before Sonny could get to them."

I managed not to laugh. I could just see the expression on Choate Ellis's face if Harmon had accused him of drug dealing in the lobby of his own bank.

"Good thinking. What did the women look like?" I asked the question not from any real interest, but Harmon did try so hard to corral drug dealers, I figured the least I could do was react positively to his attempts.

"Oh, they was definitely from the New York connection. Tall, too skinny for my taste, dark hair all cough-ured. They was wearing pants, but they looked like they were expensive, maybe tailor-made. I don't think they were even from Filene's."

This time I laughed aloud. "Nice going, Harmon, nobody could beat your observations."

He grinned like a shy boy, head down. "Well, a cute description is very important, Sonny says, so I try. Oh, by the way, Ellis called the one whose arm he was patting Bessie or maybe Betsy."

I closed my eyes for a moment. Wonderful. Harmon had tapped the super-wealthy, pillars of the town, Tellman sisters and Choate Ellis, president of the bank and vestryman of the Episcopal Church, as drug dealers. Sometimes I wondered how Sonny stood it.

Harmon was moving right along to his next triumph in crime solving. " . . . and I decided to have a beer at the Fisherman's Dock for a change."

I took a healthy sip of my drink and turned what was left of my attention back to our detective extraordinaire. "You're slumming, Harmon," I teased.

"Yeah," he agreed. "Don't tell Joe. But it was lucky I did. Mark Maddock was there. He'd already put away a couple, and he was layin' it on thick to all his buddies at the bar."

It took me a minute to realize he was referring to Harry Maddock's father and asked, "What do you mean, laying it on thick?"

Would this day ever end? Seemingly, it was set to run forever-amen, even though I was not.

"Mark was bragging that he had twenty thousand cool ones, and he said he well deserved them and then some after all the shit—I beg your pardon, Alex—that had been handed him all his life by folks who thought they's better than him. I put it aside as just the booze talking, but one of his friends took him up on it. He asked Mark if he'd robbed Fishermen's Bank lately. Now Mark, he looked kinda funny at first, like he might start a fight, but then he realized it was a joke and laughed and said he'd had some good luck at the track."

I was beginning to be intrigued. "Maddock must have had a heavy bet on the exacta or something to win that kind of money," I said. "You don't win twenty grand putting ten dollars on Speedo in the fourth." I stood up. "Hold on a minute and let me freshen these glasses."

I got no argument from Harmon.

When I returned, Harmon nodded his thanks, obviously thinking of something else. He looked up and nodded again. "Maddock wasn't at no track. I saw him and another guy today carrying a couch into that upholstery repair place he works at."

"Maybe he meant another day," I offered.

He wiped his mouth on his sleeve. "It didn't sound like it. Nope, I figure he has somehow got himself lined up with Choate Ellis and them two women. Maybe some nights he kinda borrows that big truck and goes into Boston or New York, lookin' all innocent with Upholstery Repair painted all over the truck. I'm telling you, this is big-time, Alex."

I nodded. I'd agree to anything to get some solitary quiet.

"The sad thing is, I think he's got his boy, Harry, involved with him. While he was rambling on, bragging about his windfall, he said something about Harry was going to be proud of him for coming up with the money. I really do hope Harry ain't in it. He is a nice boy."

"Yes, I hope so, too." I sipped my drink carefully. I was so tired, it wouldn't take much to put me right up there with Maddock. So how did the high roller leave it?"

"He set the bar up with free drinks. I asked him if he wasn't afraid he'd spend Harry's part of the money, buying us all drinks. He said he guessed he could spare a few drinks out of twenty thousand dollars. I said I guessed he could, too, and after my drink, I just left. It looked like the rest of them was settling in to get a lesson in picking winners." He chortled at his own wit.

"Do you think he was lying about having the money? If he wasn't, where do you think he really got it?"

"He had a wad on him, all right, and they looked to be mostly fifties and twenties. I'd figure at least a couple of hundred. More like three. He sure didn't have twenty grand on him. Of course, it could be at home or someplace else. He's got to be involved in drugs in a big way, Alex. That kind of money, maybe he brings it in hidden in the stuffing they use for upholstery. So if you see Sonny before I do, you be sure and tell him about these two new important connections in town."

"Oh, I will, Harmon. And I know he'll be grateful."

He stood and thanked me for the beers with his usual politeness and left, detouring obediently through the garage for his tomatoes and peppers.

I sighed. Two new drug connections. Thank you, Harmon. I wish they were all that easy.

I thought of how Sonny would love Harmon's latest discoveries in crime and smiled as I nibbled at the orange slice I had put in my drink. There were a couple of cherries in the glass, too. In fact, if it hadn't been embarrassing around others, I would have put in four or five. I loved them. Cindy had suggested I simply drain the juice off a bottle of them, soak them in bourbon and eat them flambé with a spoon for dessert. I was pretty sure she was kidding.

The story of the Tellman sisters and Choate Ellis was typically, outrageously Harmon. Although shipping drugs in bales of couch stuffing might not be a bad idea, at that. Occasionally our Harmon was quite creative. The rest of the Maddock story began to bother me.

For one thing, this was not a characteristic Harmon tale. Here, he had actually seen a sizeable amount of money. More than Maddock was likely to have normally at any one time. Was Maddock in some way connected to Zoe's disappearance? I wondered if he knew Reed from years back and was acting as some sort of go-between. Or had he perhaps seen something? Or did Harry Maddock know more than he was telling about something, and had he let it slip to Mark, who then blackmailed somebody for the big money?

I brought myself back to earth. Of course, flashing a few big bills in a bar was no proof Mark actually had twenty thousand dollars. And I wondered why he had bragged that he had twenty thousand dollars, when all the gallery records indicated that slightly over twenty-five was missing. Most people who boast about money tend to brag up not down. But I rather imagined he did have some sizable amount, for the simple reason that he hinted at Harry's college expenses.

It would have seemed more realistic to me if Mark had claimed he planned to buy a boat, a new car, even a new house or a trip. Most likely to bet it all on his lucky horse tomorrow, now that he was on a roll. And come out a millionaire . . . in his dreams. Right up to the moment when he lost the last hundred dollars. According to his wife, college was not high on Mark's list of important expenses, hardly to be bragged about to his bar friends unless he really had it. At least for today.

I munched a cherry. Maybe Mark had felt more guilt than he had admitted about not providing at least some assistance for Harry's education. Maybe Mark, Betsy, Jan and Choate were planning to run the Cali Cartel out of business.

I must have said the last sentence out loud, for I received a snappy reply.

"How long have you been in the sun? Or are you just drunk on cherries?"

"Not long and no. Harmon was just here. You know what that does to one's coherent thought process. Hello, darling."

Chapter 18

I had left a bevy of phone messages around town for Sonny. I wasn't the only one in the family who frequently ignored or misplaced their cell phone, and thus far, I'd had no reply.

Cindy and I were both tired and were quite happy to sit down to one of those tossed together dinners that sometimes seemed better than planned ones.

She was delighted to learn that Charlie's reputation was intact, even though a portion of money was still missing. Apparently, if Harmon had overheard Choate properly, the books balanced. The cash, of course, was still missing, but it made no sense to think that Charlie had anything to do with the theft. Other than be killed by the thief, of course.

I told Cindy about Harmon's latest drug cartel. She was almost rolling with laughter and teased me—I hoped she was teasing—that she was going to tell Choate first thing in the morning.

I bribed her into silence by telling her about Ellen's and

Charlie's casual infidelities.

"Somehow that doesn't surprise me," she said quietly. "It saddens me, but it doesn't surprise me."

"Why?" I popped the last bite of salad into my mouth. "They're no different from us, and we don't cheat."

"Yes, they are—were. They were together a long time, and some people don't handle continuity well. Even their careers were different from ours. I work for a bank, where every penny must be in the right slot, both for the bank and for the customer. You are out there every day, upholding the law and trying to catch the people who don't. And I'm not teasing you about that." She stood up and started to clear the table.

I looked up at her, confused. "But they were both honest. The bank just proved that Charlie was. And Ellen's reputation is pure as snow. I've never heard of her in a slimy deal."

Cindy nodded and began putting dishes in the washer. "I don't mean they were dishonest. I mean, they were both in wheeler-dealer jobs, where half the sales effort is social, where a lot of big money changes hands with a lot of little side deals thrown in. It's just a different milieu than yours or mine, where something is legal or it isn't, and at closing time the books must balance."

"I get you now." I leaned back in my chair and lit cigarette number eight. It had been that kind of day. "Maybe they felt their jobs were so continuously stressful, they had the right to a little additional recreation."

"Maybe. Haven't you ever been tempted?"

I took a slow drag on my cigarette to give myself some time to decide how to answer. Truth? Lie? Truth.

"Once."

Cindy returned to the table and took one of my cigarettes, a sure sign she was jumpy. "It was Maureen, wasn't it? She was bound and determined she was going to get you."

"Yes, but I figured out it was nothing to be flattered over. She just wanted another notch in her well-carved belt."

"Still, she was lovely to look at, and very sexy. No wonder you were tempted. What stopped you?"

I was getting uncomfortable. Why the hell had I started this?

"It's simple. One day she made a major pass at me, and I had immediate visions of a very exciting afternoon. Then my brain turned on and I knew I would spend days—maybe years—of regret and self-hatred. Regret at losing you and self-hatred for not living up to my agreement with myself."

Sonny never did return my phone call, but he picked that moment to walk through the back door. I was extremely happy to see him.

We retired from kitchen to living room. I felt the need for comfort. Sonny and I flopped on the couch, while Cindy remained upright in one of the wing chairs. Sonny had carried in the coffee tray and we all helped ourselves to some needed caffeine.

I gave him the report of my day, and he was impressed with my endurance if nothing else.

"The Tellman sisters and Choate Ellis," he mused. "I would bet Father Jameson will be Harmon's next victim. No one else is left. He's already tagged that lady who runs the day care center."

"There must be a bishop who visits occasionally. He could bring the drugs with him in that tall hat they wear," I supplied dreamily.

"Wake up, Alex. It isn't bedtime yet." Sonny handed me my mug of coffee from the coffee table. "Some of what you picked up today is very interesting. I'm just not sure where things all fit. In fact, I'm not especially sure where anything fits. Maybe it's all just a bunch of gossip and neurotic people. Or maybe it's a conspiracy to drive the Peres kids crazy."

Cindy lit another cigarette from my pack on the coffee table. I hoped she wasn't getting back into old habits. "I think you both need a vacation," she said. "Start with Reed. If he killed his wife, he'd hardly flinch at diddling around raising money for his daughter's ransom, hoping the price would go down. Or maybe he paid Mark Maddock twenty big ones to kill Zoe so she can't embarrass him anymore."

Sonny sat up. "You know, you could have a—"

"Be quiet. I'm not finished. Maybe Harmon got it backward about your Tellman saints. Maybe they were on the wharf, paying someone to kill Charlie because she discovered those two young men are up in the barn painting over stolen masterpieces, which Dan Portman flies in aboard his Gulfstream and Jan peddles in New York on those trips of hers."

"My God, Cindy!" I put my mug back on the coffee table. "We could spend years unraveling this mess. Painting over masterpieces. What a can of worms that opens up. And Dan Portman has a reputation of being as honest as Abe Lincoln . . ."

" . . . who slept with a young soldier when his wife wasn't around."

My lady was on a roll.

At that point, the phone rang. Cindy reached to the table beside her chair and picked it up. "Hello. Oh, yes. She's right here. Hold on."

She handed me the phone, whispering, "Jan Tellman."

"How timely. Should I ask her about the masterpieces?" I whispered back, and then aloud said, "Hi, Jan. This is Alex." I motioned for Cindy to push the speaker button.

"Alex, we've had two rather strange things happen today, and the more we thought about them, the more we thought we'd better see if you, too, felt they were important." She sounded tense.

"Sure, Jan, what happened?"

"Well, first of all, at the bank this morning, the forensic accountant Choate had called in, gave us his report. Going back several years, he finds no indication whatsoever that Charlie Cohane misappropriated a penny of the gallery funds. One or two very minor errors anyone might have made, but no evidence of theft, whatsoever. We were delighted. Of course, the money from the safe is still missing, and we may never find it, but we certainly don't think Charlie took it. We were so fond of Charlie. It had been terribly painful to have even the slightest suspicion she had taken any money that wasn't hers. We feel as if we're breathing normally again."

I didn't tell her we were already privy to that confidential information—courtesy of the town's beer-guzzling character. "God, what a relief!" I exclaimed dramatically. "Ellen and Charlie's mother will feel as if you took a ton of bricks off their shoulders—not to mention their hearts."

"Yes, we plan to call them both shortly. But first, there's a new mystery."

The three of us looked at each other and grimaced.

"Oh? What's that?" I managed to ask neutrally.

"A woman named Marie Santos called us earlier today. She had found a piece of paper with the gallery name on it, caught among some flowers in her front yard. She assumed someone had just tossed it carelessly away, or possibly that it had blown off a garbage truck or something of the sort, and she started simply to put it in her own trashcan. Then she noticed it was a bank deposit slip and thought it might be valuable, so she called us."

Jan paused, as if taking a sip of something. I certainly felt that I could use a sip of something at that point. She continued. "Betsy went over to her home on Medeiros Street and picked it up. Alex, it is a deposit slip for $25,130 cash, which is approximately what we found was missing from the safe. It was made out on the day Charlie died, and it was—as usual—signed by her. What on earth do you think?"

I thought that twenty-five thousand had been in more places than Jack Kennedy had been in beds. I took a deep breath. "Jan, I frankly don't know what to think just offhand. Let me talk to my brother about this. Hang on to that paper. Does anyone else know about this?"

"No."

"Keep it that way, and get the slip into a safe place. I, or a policeman, will pick it up in the morning. Thank you so much for calling. I'll be back to you, Jan."

"I understand. Good night, Alex, and thank you."

"Good night."

We all started talking at once, and then we all quit. "Will this day ever end?" I wailed. Hadn't I said that before? "All we ever get are more questions. We never get any answers."

Cindy was on her feet and headed for the highboy where we keep the booze. "Here." She handed out small splashes of brandy. "This will either wake us up or put us to sleep. I don't much care which. I'll make some fresh coffee."

Sonny spoke slowly. "The deposit slip is dated and presumably signed the day of Charlie's death. The gun was found on the floor beside her. The safe was open. The money was missing. How do we get them all back together?"

He sipped his brandy and went on. "Where's the money? It's not in her—I guess now I should say Ellen's—house. Charlie has no safety deposit box in any bank on this end of the Cape. It's not in her personal account at Fishermen's Bank. With their permission, we've searched Mrs. Cohane's place, Ellen and Charlie's premises, and the gallery. It's not at any of them. Either she gave it to an accomplice to hold, or somebody else stole it. Either way, Mark Maddock comes to mind."

I shook my head. "It's hard to see Mark Maddock and Charlie as cohorts. He drinks too much, he gambles and he is a blabbermouth. By tomorrow morning, the whole town will know Mark Maddock somehow came into a bundle. That's a bit dangerous if you're going to stash your stolen goods with him."

"Yeah, I suppose." Sonny yawned. "And you forgot to mention, Mark's dumber than dishwater. If he was selling drugs, he'd put them in a little bottle with his name and phone number, so you'd remember where to get your next stash."

I was too tired to laugh. "Anyway, Mark's wife says he ain't fond of gays. So Charlie doesn't seem a very likely chum for

154

him. In any case, if she gave it to an accomplice, why make out a deposit slip?"

"Maybe it was someone other than Mark as an accomplice. Maybe someone she did business with."

"Charlie was as close-mouthed as they come. I doubt she would have had anyone for a partner in crime, as it were." I set my coffee down with a bang. I was tired and getting irritable. "Surely, she didn't have a cooperative teller who would verify the deposit and then claim the bank lost it."

Cindy sipped her coffee. "Emily Bartles was there. She could be the accomplice. Motive and opportunity, right there." She sounded right out of *Law & Order*.

"Okay." I patted her hand. "Then I still say why make out a deposit slip?"

"Don't be condescending. Maybe she wanted someone to think she was going to the bank." Cindy sniffed.

"So she took the slip all the way over to Marie Santos's house and tucked it in her rosebush? Who did she think was going to find it? It's only luck Marie Santos saw it. It could have stayed lost in there forever."

Sonny held up his hand. "Try this. Charlie plans to make a bank deposit. She opens the safe, takes out the money, puts it on her desk and counts it. From her desk she takes out one of a supply of blank deposit slips we found in one of the desk drawers, fills it out and signs it. At the same time, she takes the gun out of her desk drawer to take with her to the bank. Someone comes in, sees the money and the gun, shoots Charlie and takes the money."

He drained his brandy, set down the glass and continued. "He hurries away from the gallery. Wherever he's going, his route takes him along Medeiros Street by the Santos house. He discovers he's accidentally picked up the slip along with the cash, and tosses it out the car window."

"Absolutely reasonable." Cindy topped off her coffee and put the carafe down on a tile. "Who was it?"

155

"I dunno."

Sonny stood up and stretched. "Good night, ladies. It's time for me to say farewell. Tomorrow I'll get Jeanine to have another go at Emily Bartles. I'll have a go at Maddock. Alex, please go and get that rose-scented deposit slip. Try not to handle it more than it's been handled, and drop it off with Nacho. Now I'm going to have a go at my nice bed." He gave the fur balls a cursory pet and left.

I helped Cindy clear the living room and took Wells and Fargo out for last patrol. As usual, the two black bodies immediately disappeared into the shadows. I hadn't turned the floods on, and I called them both, to no avail. I think they knew damn well I couldn't see them.

Finally, I said, "Okay, you miserable beasts, no bedtime goodies." I can't swear to the first part of the sentence, but the word goodies is definitely in their vocabularies. By the time I got to the door they were dutifully at my heels.

We all settled quickly into bed, even foregoing the news. I was just dozing off when Cindy emitted a loud, lengthy sigh.

"What's wrong?" I asked.

"Oh, nothing really. I was just thinking how nice and simple it would be if the Tellmans still had a butler."

"Good night, Cindy."

"Good night, Alex."

Chapter 19

Our breakfast, never a leisurely affair Monday through Friday, was downright hurried this morning. Which meant I spilled the orange juice and spent time wiping it up. Wells jumped into Cindy's lap with wet orange paws, which meant a complete and time-consuming change of costume. I thought we had a second quart of milk in the fridge and poured the last of one container onto my cereal. We did not have another container. So instead of cereal, although I had offered her mine, Cindy was eating toast, which she pronounced soggy, and drinking black coffee to the tune of many yuks and arghs.

Actually, the day had started extremely well. Cindy had awakened in an amorous mood, and I was rarely one to turn down an invitation. But our rapturous moments had made us run late in the morning preparations for the day. Cindy was nearly always punctual in getting to work, but I doubted the bank would have to close its doors and turn away depositors in the hundreds if she were a few minutes late. I made the mistake of voicing this opinion and got a rather lengthy soliloquy on the necessity of setting a good example to one's coworkers and subordinates—a problem I did not face, she explained sweetly to me, since my occupation was a solitary one, except for Fargo, of course. And since I rarely had to be at a certain place at a certain time, whereas banks, as one knew, were punctual to the minute.

I replied pleasantly that if she would figure out a way to schedule crimes between eight and four, Monday through Friday, I should be more than happy joining her at the proverbial time clock, carefully noting brief coffee breaks and taking lunches never to exceed one hour.

I felt guilty eating the cereal, so I put it on the floor, where Fargo picked this morning to growl when Wells tried to share. This earned me a dirty look as Cindy arose from her pale toast and dark coffee, and stroked the cat. "Be brave, darling, I'll bring you some milk on my lunch hour. I won't have time to stay and eat with you, but at least you will be fed."

"She's got a whole bowl of crunchies she hasn't touched." It was a weak defense.

"She needs liquid."

"She's got fresh water."

"I've got to run. See you."

"Yes."

As quarrels went, this one was hardly critical, and we would both be over it soon. Cindy, as soon as she got some decent coffee and turned to CNBC on the small TV she kept on her desk. Me, as soon as I stopped by the deli for coffee and a hunk of Portuguese fried bread and took Fargo to the beach. Still, it got the day hopping around on the wrong foot. Especially following such a lovely beginning. Oh, well.

I straightened the kitchen and made the bed, and Fargo and I got out of Dodge. The Atlantic was still there, the early sun promised brightness and later warmth, and the breeze held no gusty threats. A small gaggle of Canada geese were bobbing just beyond the light surf, still resting from their nightlong flight toward warmer climes. Fargo took an appraising look, but elected to leave them to relax a while longer. Instead, he raced down the beach, scattering a bunch of scavenging gulls, then pausing to leave his conquering spoor wherever they had been. As Ozymandias had said, "Look upon my deeds, oh ye mighty, and despair."

I laughed aloud and felt much better. On the way home, I stopped and bought two quarts of milk. I journeyed on to the florist, not yet open and trying to get her plants sprayed, but willing to make a quick sale. I purchased a large and somewhat tacky bouquet of colorful somethings.

As she wrapped the stems in paper for me to carry, I filled out a card: The quality of mercy is not strained. It falleth as the gentle milkshake from Heaven. Love, Alex. I slipped it into a tiny envelope, which the owner tied to one of the stems.

"You just never know, do you?" she opined more than asked.

"Uhmmn," I felt was a proper answer.

"I only bought four of these bouquets from my wholesaler this morning, figuring their style might be a little . . . ah, excessive. And this is the second one I've sold before I've even opened the shop."

I wondered what other guilt-ridden soul patrolled the mean streets of our Provincetown at this early hour of the morning. It was comforting to feel I was not alone.

Arriving home, I was surprised to see Cindy's car in the driveway. The way her day was going, someone at work had probably spilled toner all over her second dress—thus far—of the morning. I very nearly just kept going, brave heart that I am, but the thought that something really serious could have happened sent me inside, mouth dry, ready to duck and run.

I stopped in my tracks at the sight of Cindy trying to fit two quarts of milk into the crowded fridge, and the clone of my boisterous bouquet sitting jauntily on the kitchen table.

When we both stopped laughing, we hugged and I handed

her the milk I had bought, and she groaned but finally found a spot for it. The two bouquets now sat on either end of the highboy in the dining room.

"And the end of this sad tale," she said in almost a whisper, "is that there was another container of milk all along. It had gotten behind the iced tea and neither one of us saw it. I can't stay, darling. I really do hate to be late. I just couldn't leave us at odds and ends that way. What on earth can we do with five quarts of milk?"

"I think Aunt Mae has a great recipe for chocolate pudding. I'll check it out. That should use up some of it."

"Don't you try to make it," Cindy said quickly. "I mean, you'll be busy and I can do it easily this afternoon when I get home." She smiled sweetly and falsely. "Just get the recipe."

"Yes, dear, you are so thoughtful. I'm off to the Tellmans'. I love you."

And so I was finally beginning my work day, complete with the partner who kept my job from being solitary. The Tellmans were cordial, as usual, and welcomed Fargo with smiles and friendly pats, but I sensed a strain—not between the two of them necessarily, but in general. Thinking to relax the atmosphere a bit, I told them of Cindy's and my morning. At least it made them laugh. I don't think it did much for their overall dispositions.

Betsy handed me the deposit slip, and I took it by the corner. God knows how many people had handled it by now, but one went through the motions. You never knew, as the florist said. The paper had at some point been damp, either from morning dew or possibly from Mrs. Santos watering her yard, but everything was still quite legible, if a bit smeary. The date was clearly that of Charlie's death. The signature was definitely Charlie's, as far as I could tell. The amount to be deposited was $25,130, well within the window of what the Tellman sisters said it should have been. The paper had at some time been crumpled and was slightly torn

160

in a couple of spots.

It was impossible to guess whether it had been tossed from a moving vehicle or by a passing pedestrian. Provincetown was rarely without at least a mild breeze, which could have blown the slip anywhere any time.

I slid it into an envelope I had brought along for the purpose and put it in my jacket pocket.

"Well, I guess that does it." I patted my pocket. "I suggest if you plan any cash deposits between now and the time you leave, you call the police department and request an escort. They'll send someone in plainclothes if you wish to do it unobtrusively, but there's no point in taking chances."

"How very kind of you to think of that. We have been a bit nervous, rattling around in the mostly empty house. Maybe we should borrow this lovely boy of yours." Jan lightly touched Fargo's shoulder. "As a matter of fact, the only cash we probably will deal with before we steal quietly away—oops, no pun intended—is the night of the gala. We hope to sell a lot of art that night, so we don't have to crate it and send it over to the Boston gallery we have an interest in. Choate is sending over two guards to babysit the money and checks for the evening and take it to the bank for us."

Betsy spoke up, writing a note on a pad she took off the table. "Yes, but first we have to take a bit out to pay Dana. Oh, and we have to remember to sign the van registration so Harry can take it. So many details. We'll never get out of here, and if we do, there'll be a string of people running behind us waving things we've forgotten."

My head was spinning. I managed to break into Betsy's screed. "Did you mean Dana works for you?"

"Oh, yes." She spread her hands. "Not as an official employee, you understand. She simply lends a hand when we need her. She does whatever needs to be done, but mainly she's our frame repairperson. She can make a ratty gesso frame look like it was made yesterday. No trace at all of where she replaced the plaster, no matter how intricate the pattern. And we pay her—quite frankly—under the table, because we know where the money mostly goes. Please don't tell the IRS. We pay them quite enough, thank you."

"What do you mean you know where the money goes?" I felt like Alice in Wonderland as things got curiouser and curiouser.

Jan answered me. "Most of it goes to Dana's mother—our sister Margo. That bastard Dan Portman cut her off without a sou. She and her lover—a very sweet man who loves her dearly—are living on a shoestring in Spain. They won't take any money from Betsy and me. We've offered time and again."

"But Dana wanted to help and was sure her mother wouldn't accept it from her, either. So Charlie came up with a genius idea," Betsy interposed. "They send the fairly small amounts Dana earns, but anything helps. Charlie got Choate also involved in the conspiracy. The overseas transfer paperwork from the bank looks as if the money is a dividend from some obscure start-up company our father had invested in years ago, so Margo accepts it."

"I see." I sipped the cocoa the maid had placed beside me unasked and smiled my thanks. "And since Dana is your niece, I imagine you pay her well?"

"We try to be generous to all our employees," Jan said.

"And is Harry Maddock an employee? I assume that's the Harry who's bought your . . . van, is it? Does it by chance have a blue streak on the side?" I daintily wiped my mustache away with a soft linen napkin. Such luxury.

Jan raised her eyebrows and rolled her eyes. "It's the remains of a van. We're just giving it to Harry at Dana's suggestion. Lord knows we couldn't sell it for a dime. The dent in the door and the blue streak were the final blow. Some man in a blue SUV from Ohio, I think it was, backed right into us on the wharf. It was a nothing accident, and being from out of state, he didn't want to file a police report and go through his insurance company to repair the van. As if anyone could. So he gave us two hundred dollars in cash. We figured we were more than amply paid. I just hope Harry is as good at auto repairs as he says he is."

Betsy grinned. "If he isn't, he soon will be."

Since Jan was smoking, I felt free to do the same. She pushed an ashtray closer to me and asked, "How did you figure the old rattletrap had a blue stripe?"

"I stopped for coffee at Mickey's Pizza one afternoon and two young men driving the van joined some friends at one of the sidewalk tables," I said. "I just wondered if they were your two live-in artists. By the way, one of them seemed never to speak. He smiled, pointed, used body English, but no words. Does he have some sort of speech impairment?"

Both women laughed. "Hardly," Betsy chortled. "Unless you consider a very lower-class British accent an impairment, and I doubt he would even know what you meant if you asked. Believe me, he can talk a blue streak if you get him started. You must have the wrong lads."

"Probably." I let it go. I didn't have the wrong lads or the wrong van. "Well, let us allow you to work on down your list of chores. Oh, is Dana working today?"

They both looked blank. "I'm sorry," Jan said sadly. "Charlie always made out the work schedules. I don't even know. Her car will be in the lot if she's here."

"Okay. Not important. Bye-bye."

Chapter 20

Dana's car was indeed in the parking lot, along with the Bartles' ancient van, mottled but not blue streaked. I was glad to see that Emily was also at work. It meant I could get Dana off to herself and talk to her without phone calls, drop-ins or deliveries interrupting us. And we had plenty to talk about. I put Fargo on lead in honor of possible delicate artwork lying around, and we walked toward the gallery entrance.

I really wanted this Zoe situation sorted out soon. The tension level got higher by the day. The atmosphere in the Catlett home must be palpable with antagonism on the one hand and concern for Zoe on the other. Tweedledee and Tweedledum must break a sweat anytime they heard footsteps approaching. Dana and Harry were under pressure. Zoe must be in the worst shape of all. And when people got that tight, they made mistakes. They made decisions that could haunt them for life. They took actions that could be fatal.

It was definitely time to saddle up and sound the charge.

"Good morning, ladies." I smiled as I walked through the gallery and into the back room that served as office, storeroom and repair shop. Emily seemed to be bathing an oil painting in a mild detergent mix, rubbing it gently with a washcloth, while Dana was applying plaster to a large ornate frame using such interesting tools as a Popsicle stick and a nutpick.

"Emily, won't that smear the paint?"

"That was my first thought, too," she said, continuing her efforts. "But apparently, if you rub gently with a soft cloth and then rinse it lightly with clear water, you just take off the surface dirt and brighten it up. You don't disturb the basic paint, but the colors show bright and fresh, like it was done yesterday."

"Just make sure it wasn't done yesterday and the paint is well, well set." Dana laughed. "Otherwise you have Kindergarten one-oh-one and then some. The paint on that one is safely years old and hard as a rock."

"Say, Dana," I said casually, "could I see you for a couple of minutes?"

"Sure. Let me just smooth this out and close up the plaster and get it off my hands. Five minutes max."

"Okay." I nodded. "I'll be outside."

I went out and sat on one of the benches placed randomly in a grassy area along the side of the gallery. I didn't have long to enjoy the scenery. Dana was true to her timetable as she sat down beside me.

"What's up?"

"You've been lying start to finish on this kidnapping thing is what's up. You can start telling me the truth right now, or I can call my brother to take you down to police headquarters so you can think about it in a nice cozy cell. What'll it be?"

She covered her face with her hands and began to cry. "Oh, God, Alex, I've been so frightened. I am so frightened."

"Tears don't hack it, Dana, not at this point. It's gone on too long, with everybody playing innocent, and I don't think anybody is. First, is Zoe still alive?"

"Yes. Oh, yes, she's all right. That's the only thing that's right."

Her gaze drifted up the hill to the old barn. Bingo! Why hadn't I thought of that eons ago?

"Start at the beginning, Dana, and one lie from that mouth and you go out of here in cuffs."

She took a deep, shaky breath and began to speak. "It really did start as a game . . . a lark, whatever. You know that. And the two guys—Rick and Gerald—really did just volunteer to help us. Hell, they knew the gallery was closing. Their summer of painting and beaching and parties and sex was ending. They had little, if any, money to go back to New York, or maybe England, wherever. It would be a farewell. A farewell caper for them, and five thousand each would be mighty handy. It looked like a win-win for everyone."

Dana gave a short laugh. "One of them had read an article about someone who got kidnapped and thought he now was an expert on all aspects of kidnapping. For example, they would put Zoe in a tent inside the barn so no one could accidentally see her moving around through the openings in the barn. And no one could see a dim light at night. Also, it would give her some privacy. Remember, she was not a prisoner."

I was glad Dana said that. It was hard not to think of Zoe as a victim. However she might be feeling now, she had been the instigator.

Dana ran her hands through her hair distractedly. "I lied to you about showing a sketch of the guys around town, but you know that now. It was just to throw you off. They really didn't want me following them out here to be with her the night she was . . . taken. They were afraid Jan or Betsy might see my car and wonder what I was doing up at the barn at night."

I managed to get a question in. "Why did they take a chance of hurting you badly, tossing you out of the van?"

She crossed her legs, looked at her still swollen ankle and

shook her head.

"They didn't toss me out. I was never even in the van. They were just pulling away—fairly fast, yes—but I would have been okay if I hadn't tripped over a skateboard some idiot had left on the edge of the sidewalk. I'm lucky I didn't fall under the back wheels of the van. And they couldn't very well back up to see what happened. They had to go on, and they knew Harry was there to help me. They got Zoe settled in the barn. The next morning Rick came out to my house and called Zoe's home and got that crazy bitch her father married. And then it stopped being a game."

I stretched and lit a cigarette. "In what way?"

Dana's tears had stopped. Her face was taut with worry, lips pulled into a thin line. I wouldn't want to cross her when she was fifty.

"Gerald told us that the kidnapping article said you needed to keep the house of the kidnapee under surveillance, so you would know who was at home and when, and if there were cops around, et cetera. That made sense to us. We certainly didn't want to call and get the wicked witch again. But the guys were so stupid they just took the van and parked it up the block a little way where they could see the front door and the driveway. And they parked in the same place for two whole long days. How could they be so utterly dumb? I was still home nursing this ankle, or I would have warned them they were just asking to be found out."

I grinned and shrugged. Sonny always said your average crook was not overly smart, and our Anglo-American duo was inexperienced to boot.

"Who spotted them? Marvin?"

"No. Reed. They were parked in their usual spot, one of them presumably watching the house while the other one dozed or read. All of a sudden this male voice at the driver's window says, 'Good afternoon, gentlemen. As you can see, I am not in the house.' Gerald said Reed had the biggest pistol ever made pointed at his head. They were plain terrified."

"With good reason." I laughed. "It was once pointed at my head, too, and I thought it bore a strong resemblance to a cannon. How did the encounter end? Obviously he didn't shoot them."

"Reed told them to go out to Race Point or the amphitheater—I forget which—and meet him there in half an hour. He said if they weren't there, he'd give the police the plate number and their description . . . if he didn't decide to settle the matter himself. He smacked Gerald on the head with the gun and walked back to his house. Obviously, control of the situation had shifted. Whatever control we had had was now in Reed's hands. He could describe Rick and Gerald. He could describe the van, and he had a plate number. I was terribly frightened for Zoe. None of the others seemed to realize how serious this was. They were still thinking only of the money."

I was impressed with Dana's maturity and insight, but I was also stifling a grin. I thought I knew how the trip to the amphitheater ended.

Dana continued. "They went out to the amphitheater, all right, but for some reason the place was absolutely crawling with cops. The guys tried to act nonchalant and look innocent, but they were scared and took off in a minute or so. They thought Reed had screwed them, but apparently not. Nobody followed them. Meantime, Zoe was getting itchy. I snuck up to see her a couple of times when no one was around, and got her some clean clothes of mine. After the debacle with the cops, we waited a day or so and called the house again. Reed told the boys to meet him at an outdoor greasy spoon down on Route Six."

She gestured toward the highway and then continued. "There he gave them some one-time cell phones and the number of his own cell and told them to stop using his landline."

He was worried the cops had it tapped. Strange that he was the one worried about that, isn't it?

It was indeed. We had all thought the kidnappers had instigated that ploy. I was getting warm and thirsty. "Any cold drink machine around?"

"Heavens! Nothing so lowbrow as a drink machine, but there's soda in the fridge in the office. Is Diet Coke all right or would you like ginger ale?"

"Coke is fine."

As Dana walked away, my mind began to race. Why hadn't Reed simply driven down to the Tellman place and rescued his daughter? He must have realized, if the guys were driving a van registered to the Tellmans, Zoe just about had to be in the barn or somewhere in that mausoleum they called a house. If he didn't want to go it alone, their use of the van was certainly enough to get the cops a search warrant for the entire premises, even though the Tellmans were not involved. And money should no longer even be involved. It was a straight rescue operation.

I figured that while Reed hadn't been in on the so-called game from the beginning, he was definitely in it now. He was stalling, stalling, stalling. I wanted to know why, why, why?

Dana broke into my thoughts as she handed over a wonderfully cold can of soda. "Thanks, this is great." I took a long swallow and asked bluntly. "What is Reed's part in this plot? He's in it now, isn't he?"

"To his neck." She set her soda can on the bench between us. "He's . . . he's punishing her, I think."

"How? Why?" I rubbed my cigarette out on the end of the bench, fieldstripped it and put the filter in my pocket.

"Well, some of this may sound crazy, but think about it. In front of the family, he was at least neutral, if not supportive, about her being a lesbian. That night, he came to her room and tore her a new one. He called her a pervert and an ungrateful bitch. Said she would tarnish the family name. Who does he think they are, royalty or something? I mean, her grandmother is a sweetheart, but she's hardly a blue blood. Then he said she could hurt his business, swanning around with a bunch of rough dykes. As if you'd cancel building your house of dreams because your architect has a gay kid. It didn't stop Dick Cheney. And Merrilou's a lot more likely to ruin Reed socially than Zoe. He ended up slapping her and walking out."

"So he lost it. Any idea why?" I hoped she had one. I didn't.

"Well . . ." Dana paused. "This is where it gets murky. A few weeks ago, Zoe showed me a picture of her mother at age eighteen. Until I finally realized the hair and the clothes were wrong, I thought I was looking at a picture of Zoe. I think maybe Reed is mad at Frances for getting killed and mad at Zoe for looking like her. And who knows? Maybe wants to have her . . . you know, physically." She looked embarrassed but determined.

"Could be. I'd have to ask a shrink." I sipped my drink.

"As to how he's punishing her, that's easy. He won't let her come home, for one thing. He told the boys he has the money, that he will give each of them fifty thousand Saturday night at the gala. But not till then. Then he—Reed—will 'rescue' her from the barn. Obviously, there will be no money for Zoe or Harry. He told Rick and Gerald to take all her clothes away and not let her wash, much less really bathe. He told them to give her a bucket to use for a toilet. She could dump it once a day. Bread and water should be her diet, and there should be no lights for her, much less radio or TV. Oh, and no blanket at night. Let memories of her lover keep her warm despite the chill. I could happily kill the son of a bitch."

"I can hardly believe it. Her own father? Do you believe Gerald and Rick are telling the truth?" I lit cigarette number something, more to hide my horror than anything else.

"Yes. Alex, they aren't really bad guys. Remember, when they got into this, it was mostly for fun. Maybe wrong, and not nearly as funny as we thought it was. But fun. And I didn't tell you the worst suggestion he made. Reed laughed and told them if they didn't mind a little B.O., they should feel free to have sex with her as often as they wanted. He said probably all she needed to forget all this gay shit was to get laid by a couple of healthy, raunchy young men. Can you imagine any father saying that to two men?"

"No, I can't." And I couldn't. My feelings toward my own

father might not be exactly warm and fuzzy, but he would have killed any man who raped me. And rape was the proper word for what Reed had invited Rick and Gerald to do. "Did they take advantage of the offer?"

"Oh, no. Rick is gay, for one thing. But they are both decent fellows. They wouldn't do that. In fact, they haven't done any of the awful stuff Reed suggested. They know he wouldn't dare be seen going up to the barn to check if they did follow his instructions, so they're safe enough. Zoe is bored, sick of McDonald's food and getting frightened that it's dragging out so long, but she is basically okay. She doesn't even know what her bastard father said. We haven't wanted to add to her stress. I'll tell her about it afterward."

"Maybe you'd want to make sure her grandmother is with you when you do that. Zoe's going to be feeling pretty insecure for a while. It will be a lot for you to try to handle by yourself."

"I know. I've been worried about going away to school. I would like to stay home, but I just can't screw that up." Dana giggled and it was good to hear the girl that still lived inside. "My father would have somebody kidnap me if I went through everything I did to get into such a good school and then just casually decided to take a semester off before I even started."

"And so he should." I smiled at her. "Maybe Rick and Gerald could start a kidnapping business. Although they don't seem too adept at it. By the way, how do they plan to get away from here?"

"Reed got them two phony passports from some friend of his. I think he said down Cape someplace." She picked up our two empty cans and winged them neatly into a trashcan. "I saw them, and they certainly looked genuine to me. Reed says a rental car will be parked by the gate over there Saturday night. They will get away from the East Coast right away, driving some inland route down to Atlanta. From Atlanta they fly to Dublin and are on their own."

"Reed seems well versed in a life of crime," I remarked

sourly.

"I wondered about that." She turned to me quizzically. "Do you suppose he has a secret life of some sort?"

I ignored what I assumed was a facetious question, wanting to get us back on a cop/suspect role if I could. It was hard to think of any of them as anything but naughty children, who should be spanked and then hugged and forgiven. The only villain seemed to be the highly respected father.

"Dana, as far as I can tell, you have broken about a dozens laws. What I should do is take you down to headquarters and let my brother, Lieutenant Peres, decide what to do with you. I know he will at least want to talk with you, if not arrest you. He'll doubtless have questions I've missed. But I hate to see you walking into the police station, firmly escorted by a deputy police officer."

She turned pale. "Oh, please Alex, please don't do that. My grandmother might literally die of mortification. Is there any place else I could meet your brother? Any time, anywhere. I promise I would be there. Although I can't think of anything we've missed, I'll be glad to go over it again with him. I just have this feeling we should get Zoe out of there soon. Maybe your brother can think of something. The boys would like just to let her go now, but they really do need some money and especially the car."

"And," I added dryly, "there is a little matter of the various laws they have broken. Or did you think the police would stand by, calling 'Erin go bragh' as they drive down Route Six?"

"Oh, oh, yes, of course."

"Give me your cell phone number and I'll have Sonny call you."

She wrote it in my little notebook and handed it back to me.

"And don't pull a disappearing act on me, Dana. I would be seriously irritated if you did that."

"Don't worry."

She walked back toward the gallery. I hoped to God her next stop wasn't the Costa del Sol.

Chapter 21

I watched her walk away and had to smile to myself. To Dana, to the two young men and Harry, perhaps even to Zoe, this whole mess was still simply a practical joke that hadn't worked out as planned. Reed had not slipped on their banana peel. I found myself half-wishing that he had, and that all of the kids had gotten away scot-free with a fistful of his money. I could join the chorus myself, with no trouble at all, as they all trundled away singing, "We're Off to See the Wizard."

I took a final drag on my cigarette and stood up. That was not exactly the attitude a deputy police officer should entertain. I went through the field-stripping ceremony again, fished the other filter out of my pocket and tossed them both in the trash, as Fargo and I walked to the car.

Driving back into town I decided to drop off the wilted deposit slip and see if Sonny were free for lunch. I could tell him what I knew, and he could decide how he wanted to approach

Dana. And when and where. I knew he didn't like the way Reed had handled any of this, including pointing a loaded gun at his sister. I imagined he might be as lenient as he could be with the kidnappers and try to convince the town prosecutor to be the same.

I, on the other hand, was considering rethinking my decision not to prosecute Reed for bursting into my house and scaring me half to death. Not to mention my pets. I could certainly go after him for trespass and reckless endangerment. Possibly even assault with a deadly weapon.

Or maybe I could use it as leverage against Reed. I wouldn't prosecute him if he didn't prosecute the kids. That was a thought. It might also be blackmail. But perhaps not if tactfully presented by the town prosecutor.

As I turned onto Bradford Street, there was a sudden tingling in my left breast, which startled the hell out of me until I realized it was my cell phone, buzzing away in my shirt pocket. Somehow it had gotten switched from ring to vibrate. What the hell, they used cell phones for everything else nowadays, why not that? I could hear the late night ads now. How I really hated that damn thing. I fished it out of my pocket and answered irritably as I pulled over to the side of the road.

"Yes, hello."

"Alex, it's Cindy."

"Hi. What's wrong? Are you all right?" I knew she wouldn't be calling to discuss the dinner menu.

"I'm fine, but I don't think Karen Maddock is."

"Who is . . . oh, yeah. What's wrong with her?"

"I decided to come home for lunch. I thought I'd have a sandwich and a nice big glass of milk."

We both gave the obligatory laugh and she continued. "She was on the answering machine, crying so hard I could hardly understand her. Something about there being a lot of money somewhere that it shouldn't be and she couldn't find her husband. I swear she said she was afraid he was on the rack. How could he be on a rack this day and age? And could you come at once, as she had no one else to call. Does this make sense to you?"

I shook my head as if she could see me. "Only the last sentence. Did she leave a number?"

"No."

"Okay, I'm in the car now, not too far from her house. I guess that's where she is. If she calls back, tell her I'm on the way and try to get a number. Thanks, honey. I'll see you later."

"Glad to be of service, ma'am. Be careful, and don't forget the chocolate pudding recipe. 'Bye."

It took me until I had driven several blocks to realize that Cindy was not sending me to get a pudding recipe from a hysterical Karen Maddock, but from my Aunt Mae. God, when would I have time to do that?

Common sense finally prevailed. Surely if anything were critically wrong, if the roof were smoldering or someone was bleeding in the driveway, Karen would have had the brains to call the firemen or the EMTs. If not, she could wait five more minutes. I pulled over to the side of the road again—law-abiding citizen that I am—and dialed Aunt Mae's number, hoping very much she would be home. She was.

I recounted to her how we came to have a plethora of milk and explained my scramble at trying to help Sonny. I asked if she could call the house and read the recipe for her chocolate pudding to the answering machine. She would be happy to do so, she assured me, and I left her laughing at our mixed-up morning.

While I was parked, I called police headquarters and told Nacho I had the deposit slip, which looked legitimate, if battered, and would get it to her at some point. Not to worry, it was safe. I patted my pocket and panicked at its emptiness until I remembered I had locked it in the glove compartment. Sonny wasn't there, so I left a truncated account of why he should see Dana ASAP.

I drove on and swung into the Maddock driveway. There was

only Karen's car in the drive, but the garage door was closed. Another car could be in there. I hoped Karen was home. I would have no idea where else to look for her.

I left Fargo in the car until I could make sure just what was awry in the Maddock household, and rang the doorbell. There was no answer, and after three rings, I walked around to the back and tried the kitchen bell. There was no answer there either, but I thought I saw a curtain flutter. In a moment, the door flew open and Karen launched herself into my arms.

It would not have ordinarily been an unpleasant sensation, but she was crying heavily and snuffling mightily, and I was praying urgently that the moisture on my neck came only from her tears. I patted her back, said, "There, there," about a hundred times, and finally sort of waltzed her out of the doorway away from the gaze of any nosy neighbors, across the kitchen and into the living room. Pushing her gently onto the couch, I then went back in the kitchen and grabbed a couple of paper towels. The situation seemed far beyond the capabilities of a tissue.

I asked her where they kept the liquor, and she waved abstractedly toward the kitchen. I made another trip there and found it in the third cabinet I tried. I got out two glasses—do you blame me?—and put together two stiff vodkas with 7UP, some dried up lemon I found in the fridge and ice. A couple of sips reduced Karen's sobs to mere sniffs and gulps, and in another minute or so, I felt relatively safe in asking what was the matter. I had been a little ahead of myself in expecting a sensible answer.

"I found eighteen thousand dollars in the freezer, and I think Mark cleaned out our savings account and I can't find him and his boss can't either. Or the passbook, or his pal Richard."

A new freshet of sobs and tears resulted from this befuddled screed, and I'd had about enough. Enough with missing money and missing kids and missing husbands and missing pals and bastard fathers, not to mention murder. And finally, having been unable to find any bourbon, I was drinking cheap vodka, which I didn't really like, even when it was expensive. Got that?

"For God's sake, Karen, get a grip. I can't help you if you don't make sense." Something in my voice apparently got through to her. She blew her nose and straightened up.

"We have a freezer in the garage where we keep extra stuff. I do a little catering on the side and keep extra dough and other things in it, plus we use it for food that won't go in the freezer in the kitchen. I went out a while ago to take out some pastry dough, and the freezer was a total mess."

She sipped at her drink and took a deep breath. "I assumed Harry had been looking for some special flavor of ice cream or something and had messed it up. I started taking things out so I could put them back in proper order. About halfway down I found this canvas bag."

She pointed to a table in the small adjacent dining area. I recognized what the bag was as soon as I saw it. It was like several others I had seen at Fishermen's Bank, looking rather like large school lunch bags, and used by people who dealt in sizable amounts of cash for deposit or withdrawal. I was sure it would have Fishermen's Bank stamped on one side.

"Did you check what was in it?" Stupid question, but it got her in gear again.

"Oh, yes. I saw right away it was money, so I brought it out here and dumped it on the table."

The voice broke and tears began again, but a schoolmarm's look from me got her back on track. "The bills—they're mostly fifties and twenties and a few hundreds—had gotten a little damp and were hard to count. I did it twice. Once I got a little over eighteen thousand, once I got nineteen."

She was talking freely now, and my mind wandered for a moment or so. Eighteen or nineteen thousand . . . somewhat under what was missing from the gallery, if Karen had counted correctly, between damp bills and doubtless shaking fingers. The track! Karen would have been afraid her husband had gone to the track. That took care of torture on the rack.

On the other hand, Harry Maddock was in dire need of

money, and he hung around the gallery, at least sometimes. Had he somehow opened the safe, or seen the money on Charlie's desk? Had mild-mannered Harry killed her? Even though he was counting on a share of the kidnap ransom? Stranger things had happened. Maybe he just happened to walk into the office and couldn't resist all that lovely money.

I pulled myself back to Karen's tale. Something about a maiden aunt, with no other relatives, had died and left Karen plus two distant cousins all the poor dear had on this orb. Karen had gotten a letter from her aunt's attorney up in Sandwich, where the aunt had lived, telling her to come to his office with ID and pick up her third of the money. At least I think that's what she said.

"So," she continued, "my cousin Ruthie and I decided to drive down together to each pick up our portion. Then Ruthie suggested asking the third cousin to ride down with us. No use taking two cars when we all lived in Provincetown. I agreed and asked Ruthie who it was. Ruthie said she knew her slightly and her name was Charlotte Cohane. I had heard of her, but had no idea she was kin. So that's what we did. We called and invited her to ride with us. She was delighted and I was glad we did. She was so nice."

Karen babbled on. "I looked forward to knowing her better, and then of course she—died. And I think that may be why Mark stole the money."

I was staring at her, speechless. She was Charlie's cousin. And she had just found nearly twenty thousand dollars in her freezer. And her homophobe husband was missing. I had that Alice in Wonderland feeling again.

I was falling . . . falling . . .

My hands were shaking in time with Karen's when I lifted the glass to my lips. I took a sip, cleared my throat and tried to speak normally.

"Let me get this straight. Your aunt died and left her three nieces about twenty thousand apiece—you, Ruthie and Charlie Cohane? Right?"

That would explain Charlie's spending spree. I wondered if it would explain her telling Ellen that she needed a more respectable car than her old VW because she, too, was going into business?

"Yes," Karen replied. "Aunt Jane never married. She was a nurse and lived with another nurse for a number of years. I figured them as lovers, but maybe they were just friends. Doesn't matter. They were very close. Aunt Jane's partner died several years back, and Jane was never really well after that. Ruthie used to take the twins to see her once in a while. And sometimes I took Harry. Aunt Jane loved him from the time he was a baby. Said he looked just like her father." Her voice got wobbly again and she sipped her drink.

"I wish we had seen more of her, especially after her friend died," Karen continued. "But you know, Sandwich is a long drive for just a casual visit. Ruthie and Charlie both said they saw her sometimes, too, but we all felt bad it wasn't more. Especially lately."

"Yes, I'm sure," I said abruptly. I wanted to get past the sentiment and into how Charlie fit into this sudden gaggle of relatives.

"Did you say you think Charlie was the reason your husband may have taken the money you got from Aunt Jane? How could that be?" I asked.

"Let's see . . . on the way home we three girls stopped for lunch, to celebrate our good fortune and to drink a toast to Aunt Jane. We got to talking about what each of us would do with the money. We giggled about silly things we would never do, like go to Paris in April, buy a red sports car, get a new wardrobe and an 'escort' to squire us around New York. Just having fun, you know?"

"Indeed," I answered patiently. "Then what?"

"Then . . . I guess it was Ruthie who said she and I should start

179

the catering business we had always wanted. She's a fabulous cook, and I do real well with canapés and desserts. Then we sighed and got back to reality and said we guessed we'd spend it on the kids' college expenses. Ruthie and Carl are a bit better off than Mark and I, but they also have twin kids who will be in college at the same time, so they are really in a bind."

"Did Charlie say what she might do with her twenty thousand?"

Karen's face lit up, and she was very nearly beautiful, red nose and all. "This is what was so great!" she exclaimed. "Charlie said to me, 'If you spend twenty thousand on Harry for college, in one year—possibly two—you'll be broke again, and he still will have two or three years to go. If you and Ruthie go into your catering business, you can both help Harry every year, and then you can both help the twins when they get to college age, and still be making money.'" I was beginning to feel like a member of the family, listening to the plans for all the kinder.

I was also ready to scream at Karen's seeming inability to give me a straight answer. "Karen, that's wonderful advice to you and Ruthie. God knows this town needs a first-class caterer. The ones we have all think a spiral cut ham, potato salad and cole slaw plus ice cream with strawberry sauce is perfect for all occasions. If you can better that, you should have our yuppie set beating your door down. But what did Charlie plan to do? She certainly couldn't cater a party of starving explorers. The only thing I ever had that she cooked was a TV dinner, and that was still cold in the middle."

Karen managed to delay things further by making herself another drink. I declined. I was confused enough as it was.

Finally, she returned and continued. "Charlie was going to run the business end of things. She said she would handle the advertising and sales promotion. She said the Tellmans swore she could sell ice cubes to Eskimos. And she said she could keep the books and inventory items we always had to have on hand, and that way you got the best prices from vendors. She would figure profit margins, too. Honestly, Alex, she actually knew more about it than we did. It was perfect. All Ruthie and I had to do was cook. And that we can do."

It was sad to see her face fall as she realized these dreams would never be. I patted her hand. "Maybe you could find some other third person," I suggested weakly.

She just looked at me.

Well, at least now I knew what Charlie had been so excited about. She'd found an outlet for her many business aptitudes. And a family, to boot. I wished I'd known. I would like to have told her we'd book their first party. What a waste. What an effing stupid waste of her talents and enthusiasm. The only good thing I could think of was at least Charlie's mother and Ellen would be relieved she hadn't suffered some sort of mental breakdown.

I realized Karen was looking at me quizzically and shook my head.

"Sorry, I was daydreaming."

She smiled sympathetically. "Yes, I've done a lot of that lately. Anyway, to finish this soap opera, we all parted that day on cloud nine. I couldn't wait to tell Harry and Mark. I made a special dinner and bought a bottle of champagne. Over dinner, I told them my good news. I was all excited. I kept laughing, saying who could guess that we could all go head over heels. That I just fell in love with Charlie in minutes. And she even knew a well-equipped little place we could rent, at least for a start."

She lifted her glass of vodka as in a toast. "Harry was so happy, he actually almost cried for a moment. Mark was furious."

"Did you say furious?" I thought I heard wrong.

"Yes. I had mentioned what Charlie had said about running the business and the promotional end of things, and he yelled that he wouldn't have me turning Aunt Jane's money over to some queer and catering queer parties just because they had more money to burn than the rest of us." She looked down for a moment, embarrassed.

"Then, right in front of Harry, he screamed that the way I

had acted in bed the past few years he shouldn't be surprised if I had become queer myself and had some dyke on the side. Alex, I thought I would faint."

"I don't doubt it." I stubbed out my cigarette in the ashtray, wishing it were Mark's nose.

"I was hurt and angry," she went on. "If Mark thought our sex life was lousy, he was right, but he forgot how many times he came to bed so drunk sex just didn't work. Anyway, he stormed out and didn't come home that night. I imagine he stayed with a young man he'd gotten friendly with at work. I don't think Mark has a girlfriend. Frankly, I don't know who would have him."

Possibly the young man from work, I answered silently. Aloud, I said, "And you think he took the money out of the bank so you couldn't invest it along with Ruth and Charlie?"

"Yes. I had deposited the check from Aunt Jane immediately in our savings account. There's a thousand or so missing from the check I put in the bank, and I can't find the bankbook. The account's in both names, worse luck. When I found the money in the freezer, I called Mark at work."

She sighed and shook her head. "Nothing was going right. On the phone, I got his boss, who was really seeing red. This is a busy time of year for them, and both Mark and the young fellow—Richard somebody—had called in sick this morning. The boss says he's going to fire them both. I don't know if he means it. I hope not. But we agree on one thing—we'd both be willing to place our own bets that Mark and Richard are at the racetrack." She slammed her glass on the coffee table so hard, I was very glad it was plastic.

I put the coda on this sonata by asking, "The bankbook is missing, you said?"

"Yes. I've looked everywhere."

"Let me call the bank. We may be able to make certain of your balance without the book."

I called Cindy's direct number, and wonder of wonders, she picked up. "Cindy Hart, may I help you?"

"I hope so, honey, we have a bit of a situation here. Karen Maddock's husband has disappeared, possibly having cleaned out their savings account. Karen can't find the bankbook, but she did find eighteen thousand or so in cash in the freezer, where Mark may have hidden it. She wants to know if it's part or all that remains of the savings account. Is there any way you can help us?"

I could almost hear her shrug. "If they want to be helpful downstairs I can. Hold on a minute."

I heard a click and then was treated to "Tales from the Vienna Woods," which I rather like. Karen was watching me like a mongoose eyes a cobra, so I didn't dare whistle along with the orchestra.

"Alex, are you still there?"

"Yes, darling. I am here."

"Okay. The husband may be gone, but the family fortune seems intact. There is a balance of $23,405.05. No recent withdrawals. When Mrs. Maddock made the latest deposit—of $19,994.65—she left the bankbook along with the check. The teller assumed she wanted the bank to hold the book. They have it safely in a drawer somewhere. She can pick it up anytime. So can the husband."

"Thanks a million, honey. Mrs. Maddock will be greatly relieved. By the way, she thinks Mark may be at the track, though I don't doubt she would prefer he was on the rack. Oh, and please advise the teller to check first with Ptown Police if anyone tries to make a withdrawal or get the book. Tell Choate the police will officially freeze the checking and savings accounts shortly. See you tonight."

"Yep. Gotta run, other phone." She clicked off.

I leaned back in my chair and grinned. "Your fortune totals something over $23,400. There have been no recent withdrawals. When you deposited Aunt Jane's check, you left the bankbook with the teller. You were a little excited, maybe? They have it safely stowed."

"Oh, thank God!" Karen had one or two tears left, but not many. "Oh, I feel ten years younger. I wonder where all this other money came from? Could he possibly have won that much at the track, or maybe on the numbers? I can't believe it. Mark has never been lucky at that sort of thing. And he certainly hasn't been acting elated the last week or so."

I stood up and stretched. I was beginning to feel numb in spots. "What do mean?"

"Was he depressed?"

"Not exactly," she demurred. "More edgy and short-tempered. He wasn't sleeping well. I'd wake up and he'd be over by the window looking out. If I asked what was wrong he'd just snap at me to go back to sleep. And Harry got accepted at Northern Connecticut College. At the dinner table I said we'd better ask them about a scholarship. Mark blew up and said just have faith in him for once. We wouldn't need any scholarship." She shook her head. Sad? Bewildered? I didn't know.

Then she asked, "And why did you freeze our bank accounts? Do you have a legal right to do that?" She was ready to display a little righteous anger now.

"I don't. I'm a mere deputy, and temporary at that. That's why I need to call Sonny right now." I picked up the phone again.

"Who is Sonny?"

"My brother, Lieutenant Edward J. Peres of the Provincetown Police. You see, your bank account still has all your money in it." I gestured toward the dining table. "But over there sits a lot of money that did not come out of your account. Where did it come from? I don't know, but it is worrisomely near the amount that was stolen from the Tellman Art Gallery the day Charlie was killed."

Karen dropped her glass. But at least it didn't break.

Chapter 22

At police headquarters, Nacho worked her usual magic, chased Sonny down at some carefully undisclosed location and patched him through to me—sounding thoroughly irritated.

"I'm busy as hell, Alex. You're beginning to remind me of Harmon."

"And you remind me of Captain Anders. What are you so involved with? A blonde or the *Wall Street Journal?*"

"Neither. If you must know, I'm interviewing Dana Portman." He went on to tell me how surprised he was at her maturity . . . what insight she had into Reed's warped personality . . . what a keen perception of the problems the police department faced, having never been officially involved in what might not be a kidnapping in the true legal sense anyway . . .

"Goodness, Sonny, I told you she was a charmer, but I didn't recognize she had such deep intellectual powers. When are you announcing your engagement?" I could tell that Dana was in no danger of being subject to police brutality, especially since I could hear restaurant sounds in the background.

"Don't be an idiot, Alex. She's all of eighteen."

"Wonderful. You won't have that nasty ol' problem of statutory rape."

"Alex," his voice was dangerously soft. "Why did you call me?"

I told him, as briefly as possible. His reply sounded more like the Sonny I knew and sometimes loved.

"Shit."

"Indeed," I agreed with a nod. "What do I do if Mark walks through the door as we speak?"

"Don't let him get your gun. You do have it with you? Are there any other firearms in the house?" He was suddenly all business.

"I have mine, yes. I don't know if there are others in the house. Hold on." I looked at Karen, who was studying the lemon in her drink. "Karen, are there any guns in the house?"

Wherever she was, she brought herself back with difficulty. "Guns? Harry used to have a bunch of cap pistols. Oh, and he had a BB rifle."

"Karen," I said gently, "real guns."

"Oh." She frowned thoughtfully. "Mark has a shotgun—maybe two. He goes duck hunting once in a while. And I think maybe a pistol, I'm not sure."

"Will you please get the shotguns now, and see if you can find the handgun. Bring them down here pronto. And be careful, he may have left them loaded." I turned back to the phone. "Did you hear that, Sonny?"

"Uh-huh. I'll stay on the line until you have them. Look, no funny remarks, please. I really need to finish talking to Dana. We have to get that kid Zoe out of there soon, but we also want to nail everyone involved. I probably include Reed in that list, and it may take a little time to set it all up." I heard him sip something that was probably better than what I had. He cleared his throat and went on.

"So I'm tied up here for the next few hours. I'm sending Jeanine out to you. She's the only person I have available except Officer Mendes, who is still learning how to extract his pistol from its holster without endangering himself and everyone else within a one hundred and eighty degree arc. Can you and she handle Maddock if he shows up drunk? He can be pretty obnoxious."

I took the last swallow of my watery drink with its slight aftertaste of kerosene. "Jeanine could handle a Bengal tiger by herself. We'll be okay. What shall we do with him if he shows?"

"Ask him sweetly where he got the money. He's going to be very upset when he sees it laid out wherever you've got it. Be careful with this guy."

"Yeah. Oh, here's Karen bringing all three guns. Jesus, Karen, watch where the hell you point them. Sonny, I've got to go. Quick, tell me, do I get into the Charlie thing with Mark?"

"Sure, you and Jeanine can put him into a good sweat. Bring him in for more questioning if you want, or if you get enough, arrest him. If you really need Mendes, call Nacho. Okay? See you later."

I said good-bye to a dead line and turned carefully to relieve Karen of two shotguns and a revolver. I broke the shotguns and found both empty. The revolver was loaded, but dirty, and didn't smell as if it had been fired lately. I dumped the cartridges in Karen's hand and suggested she put them in a baggie somewhere obscure.

I took all three weapons out and locked them in the trunk of my car and let an anxious Fargo out to trot for the nearest tree. Output taken care of, we turned to input, and he had a drink from his little bowl and the thermos of water I keep in the car. About this time I spotted Jeanine walking up the sidewalk, wearing jeans and a sweatshirt, looking most unlike a policewoman. She had parked her unmarked car around the corner so Mark wouldn't be suspicious at two strange cars in his yard.

187

I looked pointedly at her garb and mine and remarked that Mark would probably think we were both lesbians, on our weekly visits to various homes, handing out literature recommending the lifestyle.

We turned toward the house and she laughed. "Maybe we should tell him we're members of a twelve-step program to help make conversion easy. I told my husband if he gets me pregnant one more time, I'm turning gay."

I smiled and shook my finger at her. "Be careful of the promises you make. You could end up with no husband and four kids."

I took Fargo in with us, mainly because the car was getting a little warm to leave him and partly because he makes an impressive appearance.

We spent a long, boring, nerve-wracking afternoon waiting for Mark—and possibly his pal Richard—to show up. Jeanine and I carefully counted the money and finally got the same total: $19,050. If this were indeed the money from the Tellman Gallery, it was some $6,000 short of what it should be. Between what he spent on drinks for his barfly buddies last evening and what he took to the track today, surely even Mark wouldn't have gone through that much money. I wondered where it was.

Then the lightbulb went on above my head. No, Mark wouldn't have spent six grand on drinks for the house, but he might have given a generous present to his 'pal.' Especially if that friend had been with him when he robbed Tellman's . . . and probably shot Charlie. I didn't say this to Jeanine because Karen was nearby futzing with something in the kitchen.

I did get up, take my 9 mm Glock out of my purse and stick it in the rear pocket of my jeans, pulling my shirttail out to cover it. Jeanine raised her eyebrows. "You just had a thought?"

"Yeah," I answered. "That there may have been some help from the junior partner."

She thought a minute and then got it. "So if the partner is

here, too, we might have two to take in?"

"Yup."

"That could get interesting. Do you have cuffs?"

"Yeah, I got them out of the car earlier, just in case Mark beat you here and got rambunctious."

The day dragged on. Karen gave us coffee and cheesecake, for which I was duly grateful, having missed my lunch.

We sat around the dining room table and tried to chat—three women with little in common. If they talked about kids, that left me out. If Jeanine and I talked about cops, it left Karen out. If Karen and I talked of looking for a third catering partner, it left Jeanine out. Finally, of course, we got to the weather and wrung it dry. We started with today's autumn loveliness and worked all the way back to the myths we had heard about the hurricane of 1938.

We almost missed the sound of a motor in the driveway. Karen jumped up and peeked out the window. I wondered for a moment if she were about to dash out and tell Mark to run for it, but she came back and sat down.

"It's Richard's truck. I guess he brought Mark home."

"Will he come in, too?" Jeanine asked.

Karen shook her head. "I doubt it. If they have been drinking and didn't go to work, he knows I'll be well and truly pissed."

A car door slammed. We waited a few seconds and there was no second door. I think we all let out a breath. Mark was enough to handle. Richard could wait. Jeanine was on her radio, advising headquarters Mark was here at last, and that Richard drove a green Ford pickup approximately three years old, plates unseen.

Mark entered the front door, crossed the living room and came into the dining room with a tentative smile for the three women seated innocently at his dining room table. Then he spotted the money neatly stacked in the middle of it.

"What's going on here? Who the hell are you? Karen, where did you get that money? Answer me!"

Karen seemed as frozen as her cookie dough, so I answered for her. "She found it in the garage freezer, where you hid it, Mark. I'm Deputy Officer Peres, and this is Officer Marcus. We'd like to know where you got the money. Sit down, Mark, and tell us how the horses have been treating you."

"Oh," he laughed a little too loudly. "Horses're like women. You never know, one minute to th' next. You jus' got to hope for the best." You could smell the booze, and he was slurring slightly, but he was far from dead drunk. I wasn't sure if I was glad or sorry.

"How did you fare today? Were they good to you?" I hoped they had been. Mark in an expansive mood might be more likely to talk. He still hadn't sat down.

"Fared fine, fine. Woulda had a real good day if my last pick hadn't stumbled comin' outa the gate. Stupid jockey's fault." He shook his head in disgust. "But I'm on a real roll here. Got the system beat all to hell and back. Gonna double my money in a month or less."

Karen found her tongue and produced a truly wifely statement. "You'd better more than double it. Your boss says you're fired. You and that Richard calling in sick on the same day! You think Mr. Ambrosio is such an idiot that he wouldn't know? And now you've got the police involved saying you stole the money from Tellman's Art Gallery. Are you really that big a fool? Did you actually rob them? I can't believe you would do such a thing."

Mark turned pale and leaned both hands to steady himself against the table. But his mouth was hard-set now and his tone no longer jocular. "Jesus, Karen, you stupid cow. What have you been telling people? I knew once you got mixed up with them queers, you'd be less than worthless. Now you're callin' your own husband a crook and a thief. You know that money came from our savings account. I never stole a penny from anybody. Karen, go get me a beer."

He swung his index finger back and forth, pointing at Jeanine and me, swaying slightly. "Now you two dykes got no business coming into my house, trying to influence my wife and insult me. So you can just get the hell out and right now!" He gestured grandly toward the front door.

Karen set a can of beer on the table and scampered for the kitchen.

Jeanine does not suffer fools lightly. With her around, I would greatly prefer to be on the side of the law. She stood, reached across the table and grabbed the front of his shirt, pulling him toward her. "Dykes is not a friendly word, cowboy. If you use it once more, you may be talking with a cute little baby boy lisp because your front teeth are missing."

She pushed him and he sat down so hard that the chair beneath him gave an ominous crack. Jeanine sat herself down more gently and continued. "Now everybody knows you saw that twenty-five thousand dollars all neatly stacked up on Charlie Cohane's desk, and it was just too pretty to pass by. You might as well admit it, Mark. We can prove it."

"I'm admitting nothing, and you're not proving nothing." He crossed his arms and smirked. "Now, I am telling you nicely to get the fuck out of my house before I throw you out."

Before Jeanine could make him try to prove that he could, I said, "Look, Mark, you are in trouble, and it will cause hardship on your family. About twenty-five thousand worth. We have checked the bank. This money"—I waved my hand over the table—"did not come from your savings account. And the bank doesn't give out those little green canvas bags to every customer to pack his lunch. They go to a few really heavy hitters. And you ain't one of them. If you cooperate, things will be nicer for everyone involved, including you."

Jeanine took up the tale. "Yeah, Mark, you know, you weren't too clever leaving the bands around the bills. How much do you want to bet your fingerprints are all over them? I'd say the odds are approximately nine to one. Then there's the five grand missing from the Tellman deposit—and which we know you gave to your blond Adonis for all his help . . . one way or another. Just how long do you think he'll sit quietly when he gets pulled in as

191

an accessory to murder?"

I came back on the scene after a sip of coffee. Mark was swinging his head from one to the other of us like a stunned bull. But still a potentially dangerous one. "One other thing, Mark, the bank deposit slip you tossed into Marie Santos's yard. She found it and called the Tellmans. What would you say if it had your thumbprint right smack in the middle of it?"

I had no idea if it did or didn't, but it sounded good.

"You have no way of checking my fingerprints." Mark sneered. "I've never been arrested. Man, you dykes are dumb. You think I'd fall for that?"

"You don't have to fall for that. You left your fingerprints all over Charlie Cohane's desk."

"The hell I did!" he shouted. "We wiped that desk cleaner than a whistle. I didn't kill her!"

We all realized what he had said at about the same moment. Jeanine and I looked at each other and smiled. Karen let out a groan from wherever she was lurking in the kitchen. Mark, with upper arm strength, due no doubt to lifting sofas in and out of trucks, turned the dining table over. Glasses, cups, dirty dishes and money cascaded into Jeanine's and my laps, and the edge of the table itself pinned our upper legs to the chairs in which we sat.

Mark bolted through the kitchen toward the back door. Jeanine and I finally got a coordinated lift and got the table off us. She ran toward the kitchen door after Mark. Strangely, Fargo followed her, I suppose because that was the door he had come in. I went for the front door, assuming Mark was headed for the garage and his car.

I hoped to get there first and be standing by the door, gun in hand and saying sternly, "All right, Mark, hands against the garage, legs spread out, and don't move." Then Jeanine would cuff him, we would march him to the unmarked car, and away to the police station we would triumphantly go.

It didn't work out quite that way. My script bore little

resemblance to the performance. First of all, I seemed to be having some trouble extricating my weapon from my hip pocket. It seemed caught on some errant threads. Perhaps Officer Mendes and I should schedule a date to go to the firing range.

Secondly, where was Jeanine? Nowhere in sight.

Fargo came dashing around the corner of the garage—obviously ahead of everyone else—and jumped for my arms to tell me he would protect me. Trying to fend him off, I didn't see Mark careen around the corner, skidding on the long grass, and running headlong into Fargo and me. We all three went down in a messy heap, winded and confused.

Fargo recovered first and began to struggle to get out of the pile. I got my breath back and grabbed the dog's collar and held him tight. He hates being collared and complains bitterly with high-pitched whines and yelps and barks. He's only protesting, but most people think it is prelude to an attack. Mark obviously thought so, and began an effort to roll free.

I managed to prop on one elbow and said, "Don't move an inch or I'll let the dog loose, and he'll have your balls before you know they're gone." Mark laid his head slowly and carefully back on the grass. I had just begun to wonder how long the three of us could maintain this tableau, when Jeanine appeared.

She was moving at a crawl and limping heavily, face twisted in pain. But trouper that she was, she had her revolver out and cocked. We got Mark handcuffed. I couldn't stand Fargo's shrieks any more and let him loose. Unthinking, I swatted him lightly on the butt and said, "Oh, okay, Tiger, go ahead and kill."

Mark sank to his knees and wet his pants.

At that moment Officer Mendes pulled up, wheels squealing, siren dying away to a low whine, answering a neighborhood call that someone was torturing an animal.

Chapter 23

I recall last year, when Cindy's father had a mild heart attack, and she was frantically waiting for Cassie to return from a charter and fly her down to Connecticut. She cleaned the whole house, including windows, in just about two hours. I was very worried about him, too, of course, but I did the sensible thing. I quietly sat at the kitchen table, drank cup after cup of ever-stronger coffee, smoked half a pack of cigarettes, ate two or three doughnuts and worried.

Karen Maddock, it would seem, was of the Cindy ilk. I would never understand people like that. Anyway, while Jeanine and I had been questioning Mark in the dining room, she had begun to mop the kitchen floor. When Mark had run through the room he accidentally—or purposely—kicked the bucket of water over, and Jeanine slipped in it and twisted her ankle badly.

She needed a hospital. I needed another cop to ride with Mendes and Mark while I took Jeanine for medical care. Fargo needed a ride home. The unmarked police car needed a driver, and Mark needed a bath and clean clothes. Our Abbott and Costello act seemed destined for a long run.

Karen offered to pack some clean clothes and personal items for Mark and send them with us. Somehow, I did not want either Mendes or me walking into the station carrying the suitcase for a smelly murder suspect, more the bellboy than the dauntless law enforcer. I suggested she bring it down later.

Finally, finally! After standing around forever, we put Jeanine and Mark, sitting as far apart as possible, in the back of the police cruiser, driven by Mendes with all windows down—first to police headquarters to install Mark in a cell and get the money in a safe, then to the clinic to install Jeanine in a cast. I drove my car home, with Fargo now dozing in the front seat, weary of it all. The unmarked police car would doubtless be picked up sometime by someone.

Cindy met me at the door with a big hug and kiss, followed by a look at my clothes and a wrinkled nose. "I was getting a little worried. What on earth have you been doing? Rolling in a pasture? You're covered with dirt and grass stains and you smell of cat piss."

"Not cat piss," I sighed. "Mark Maddock got scared."

"What on earth scared him that badly?"

"I told him Fargo was going to bite off his balls."

She looked at me sharply to see if I were kidding. Realizing I was not, she burst into laughter.

"My sweet creampuff? Never! Oh, Fargo, such an insult! My poor baby, let me feed you. We can't have you reduced to cannibalism."

I wished she had offered to feed me, but I said meekly, "I guess I'll go take a shower." No one argued with me.

Resting my eyes. I was only resting my eyes as I listened to the TV. I was not asleep. I was listening to several people prove they were not smarter than a bunch of fifth graders. Neither was I, to my chagrin. Some of the science questions were not even understandable, much less answerable. Yet, the kids mostly just rattled them off, while the contestant stood looking humiliated. I opened my eyes to find my brother standing over me, smiling.

"A well-deserved nap. Sorry to wake you up." He looked worn out. I could almost feel sorry for him. Then I recalled that he had probably had a delicious lunch, whereas I had had none. And my dinner had consisted of a cold chicken leg, sliced tomato, a hunk of cheese and the end of a baguette.

"I was only resting my eyes."

"Whatever you say. I just wanted to let you know, tomorrow night is D-Day—well, D-Night . . . oh, hell, you know what I mean."

"Perhaps you need a well-deserved nap to perk you up," I said kindly. "Do you feel up to talking about it? D-Day, I mean?"

"Coffee should help." Cindy's smile was genuine as she brought in the tray and set it on the coffee table. "You both look like you need a good night's sleep and a day off."

Neither of us would admit to that, so we all took coffee and at least two of us tried not to gulp it down.

Sonny set his coffee mug down and rubbed his eyes with a sigh. "Okay, here we go. Dana just called me. She was at the barn for one last check on Zoe, when Reed Catlett phoned with the final instructions for Gerald and Rick. I'll give the kid credit, she has good timing. If it weren't for her, we'd still be pretty much in the dark."

Cindy shook her head. "I can hardly believe it. The father of the kidnapped girl is giving instructions to the two kidnappers, and they are prepared to follow them. That is absolutely absurd."

Sonny nodded. "The word I think I would use is obscene. Anyway, as you know, tomorrow night is the big farewell shindig at Tellman's Gallery, and Reed figured with a crowd milling around, it would be a good time for him to get the money to Gerald and Rick. They can make their getaway and Reed will gallantly rescue Zoe once the coast is safely clear."

Cindy snapped her fingers and stood up. "That reminds me." She reached up on the mantel. "Our invitation to the party came today. You can't get in without it, Sonny. Do you have one? We have two here for some reason."

"I'll have a dozen after I see the Tellmans tomorrow morning," he answered sarcastically. "First of all, I was told by Trish to get an invitation if I had to steal it. Second, I was told that I'd better be wearing a tux, or she would show up in her ratty old bathrobe. I ask you"—he looked at us with a shake of his head—"am I on duty, or am I escorting my girlfriend to some artsy-smartsy gala?"

"Both," we chorused.

Cindy added, "Trish and I will look after each other, mingle with the multimillionaire New York and Boston jet sets, get slightly tipsy on Krug champagne and have a wonderful time dancing the night away. We may even buy a picture or two. I know about how much I'll see of you, my love." She gave me a pursed-lip smile and spoke to Sonny. "But don't worry, she will be in her tuxedo also. And so, I imagine, will a great many other people."

"That's a great comfort." Sonny pulled out his little notebook. "Now here's how it will go down. You'd better take some notes, Alex, so you can go over it in your mind tomorrow."

I was aghast. "Sonny, I agreed to help you out for a day or so. Glad to do it. But enough is enough. I want to have some fun tomorrow night, too. Mom and Aunt Mae are going. Cassie and Lainey will be there, along with Walter and Billy and God knows who else. I do not intend to pass up champagne and caviar. And you want me to run around chasing kidnappers?"

"Now, Sis . . ." I knew I was in trouble. "You can have fun at the party. We hope most of the people there won't even know what is going on. And your little role will be—well, mostly—ah, supervisory. Let me explain the whole picture, so you can have a completely easy mind."

I waited for him to go on. He sounded so oily, I half expected him to offer me a beautiful nineteenth century bridge at a bargain price.

"First of all, Reed has arranged for a rental car, a light blue Toyota, for the two 'kidnappers' to escape in. It will arrive around seven and will be parked in the lot, near the front exit. The keys will be left in one of those magnetic holders under the right front fender. Even if one of the Tellmans should notice the car arriving early, they would think it belongs to one of the caterers or some of the security people who'll be watching the art all night, to make sure nobody wanders out with one of the smaller pieces—something they haven't bought."

I had a brilliant thought. "Sonny, couldn't some of the security people help you out better than I?"

"No. Reed and his lovely wife will arrive at eight, when the party is in full swing and it is fully dark. Reed will have a briefcase. He will walk with the lovely Merrilou to the bar and leave the briefcase on the floor at the end of the bar. It will contain one hundred thousand dollars, plus two plane tickets from Atlanta to Dublin, two driver's licenses and two credit cards, which will not be reported stolen until after the two young men have landed in Ireland and had time to move on."

Sonny reached for my pack of cigarettes on the table, and Cindy took advantage of the intermission to ask, "I wonder where a respectable man like Reed got those credit cards and all those false papers? I wouldn't have any idea in the world where you get a false passport."

"I think I can answer that question."

The three of us looked around, astonished to see Harmon and another man standing in the dining room door.

"Your kitchen doorbell ain't working, Alex. I'll check it out tomorrow and fix it for you or pick up a new one. We knocked, but you didn't hear us. I hope we didn't scare you ladies none."

"No, no, it's fine, Harmon," I reassured him. "You and your friend have a seat. Can I get you some coffee?"

The two men passed on coffee and sat down gingerly on the loveseat, which Sonny had vacated to sit by me on the couch. "What's up, Harmon?" Sonny asked. I knew he couldn't be any happier to see Harmon than I was. We really didn't need one of Harmon's drug-dealer fantasies. But we all had managed smiles of welcome. Cindy's was probably genuine. She was fond of Harmon and loved his theories on who was who in his imaginary Ptown drug cartel.

"Did you just say you could tell us where Reed got some phony ID papers and credit cards?"

"Yes, but first, Alex, thank you for recommending me to the Tellman ladies for that repair work on their house. It'll have me in work for quite a while. First thing I did was apologize to them for thinkin' they was drug dealers, and I told them they could tell Choate Ellis I wasn't watching him no more, neither. They said everyone should be so ass . . . ass . . . assidious in their civic duty. They thought that it was kind of funny, and they weren't mad at all at my mistake."

They weren't the only ones who found it funny. I, at least, found it absolutely delicious, visualizing stodgy Choate Ellis's reaction to learning he'd been tailed as a drug dealer by Provincetown's Character in Residence. Neither Sonny, Cindy nor I dared make eye contact.

"Now, this here"—Harmon pointed a thumb toward his companion—"is my brother-in-law, Clete, from Fall River. He's on vacation for a couple of weeks and is going to stay and help me with the outdoor repairs, so's we can finish them before it gets too cold."

We three nodded greetings to Clete, and Sonny remarked, "That's all good news, Harmon. But what's it got to do with Reed Catlett?"

"I'm getting there. I went down to Fall River to pick Clete up so he could leave their car with his wife—my sister Georgia. While I was there, Clete took me out to lunch at this place he claims has the best fried oysters on the whole East Coast. Well, I ain't so sure the Wharf Rat don't beat 'em, by a hair, but they was good." He cleared his throat several times. "My throat is a little dry. I wonder might I trouble you for a little something cold?"

I got up. We had all decided we were a little dry. Cindy actually requested a small glass of wine. The rest of us settled for beer.

Drinks served, Harmon finally cleared his throat and got to the core of his latest investigation.

"This restaurant Clete took us to, it was a workingman's place, plain and simple. A bar with a TV up at one end, some kinda rickety tables and chairs, a pool table. You didn't feel out of place in jeans or coveralls, 'cause that's what everybody had on. And the portions all looked to be what a man with a half-day's hard work still ahead of him would need." I had to admit Harmon was observant.

Here he turned to Clete. "I think you can tell this part better than me."

Clete nodded and began. "These two fellas come in and took the table next to us. Tables are fairly close together in there. The first guy, his name is Bill Slote. I know him to speak to, and we did. He had on khakis and a shirt with no tie, carried a hard hat, so he couldn't have got a table at the Ritz." He smiled at his humor and paused for a sip of his beer.

Then he went on. "This Slote—he's a contractor, got a reputation for being a tough guy and for hiring tough guys. He gets at least half of the jobs around Fall River that are plums. Mainly the county and state stuff. Well, the other contractors, they grumble, but they don't do nothing about it. Rumor says you cause trouble for Slote, and you won't even get the crumbs you do get, and you might find some of your large equipment breaking down kinda frequent. I don't know whether that's true or not. But it's what I hear."

He let us digest that for a minute and continued. "The guy having lunch with Slote stood out like a . . . well, he stood out.

He had on a suit that cost more than I make in a month, shoes all shined up like my little girl's Sunday school pumps and those thin, shiny socks with some kind of fancy stitching up the side. Actually had on a lavender shirt. Looked like silk. Probably a good thing he was with Slote. This dressy guy, he gave us both a real politician's greasy smile, like they give you whether you know them or not. I only know his last name. It's Cuniff. He works for the state, something to do with okaying bids for new construction. They had a drink, waitin' for their lunch."

Harmon took over again. "It was nearly two o'clock and pretty quiet in there, so you could hear what people was saying. Slote, he says to the other guy that Reed Catlett is getting to be a pain. He don't want to dummy up the specifications, but he still wants his cut. This Cuniff smiles, nasty-like, and says, 'I got a young architect that'll fit real nice right here,' and he patted his jacket pocket. 'You just carry on the best you can with Reed for now. Within a month or so, I'll have this young guy all sewed up, and Reed may find himself designing public bathrooms at the beach.' Then their lunch came and I didn't hear them anymore. But if I wanted a phony passport, I bet you Reed Catlett could get it for me."

Well, damn, I thought, Harmon has finally stumbled onto something that sounds real. Not only real, but much more far-reaching than the odd drug trade. God bless him, his ship has come in.

Sonny was more down to earth. "Have you mentioned this to anyone else?" Harmon and Clete both shook their heads. "Be sure you don't. Not only could you tip them off to start covering their tracks, but also, if what you say is correct, you could get hurt. I mean this. Don't you guys have a couple of beers and start bragging how clever you are."

"No, Sonny, we won't breathe a word." I hoped he meant it.

"Okay." Sonny smiled. "You've both done a great job. I know a guy in the state police down your way, Clete. I'll see what he knows about it. Now, you two, be patient, be careful, be quiet!"

Sonny stood up and shook hands with them both. They could hardly take it as anything but good night, and so they left.

And we once again addressed my briefing for tomorrow.

Cindy was literally drooping over her wineglass. I took it from her gently and pointed toward the bedroom. "Go."

She looked up at me with tired eyes. "You won't mind? I hate to do this. You both look as tired as I feel."

I pulled her upright and held her against me for a minute, then kissed her. "Now I feel fine," I said. And I did. "We won't be long." I looked meaningfully over her head at my brother.

"Absolutely not, just a few more small details. You run along." He patted her on the head as if her name were Fargo, which I thought would earn him a snappy retort. But she was too tired. She went.

"You got anymore beer?" Sonny watched her walk toward the bedroom with envy.

"Yeah, but it may put us both on the floor."

"Seriously, I won't be long."

He wasn't long getting the beer, either, and we started the action back at the Tellman's bar.

"After Reed and Merrilou get their drinks, she—who knows nothing of this, we are sure—will start to socialize. So will Reed, but he will be on the lookout for Gerald and Rick. They will have a similar briefcase, containing some newspapers to give it a little weight, and the key to the barn."

"Okay." I sipped the beer, if I passed out it wasn't my fault. "So when Reed sees the guys come in he goes and picks up the case with the key, and he goes and gets Zoe. Tweedledee and Tweedledum pick up the case with the money and go to the car. Which I assume will be under observation by Provincetown's finest."

"Yeah," Sonny replied. "Mitch will be back from vacation and will come in a day early. He and Pino and Dobis will cover the

Toyota and your two Tweedles. Mendes and Sanders will be in two cruisers up where the road turns onto Route Six, just in case Rick and Gerald get away somehow. Anybody in a blue Toyota is going to spend a lot of time talking to cops tomorrow night." He laughed. "We've even got the state guys alerted all the way up to the bridges just as a precaution."

I lit a cigarette and tossed the pack to Sonny. He was considerate. He carried his own lighter.

I sat up straight and tried to concentrate as he continued.

"Now comes the part that makes me hope Reed does spend some nice long prison time for doctoring design plans for a kickback and a few other things." His mouth turned down at the corners and his eyes were cold. "That son of a bitch told Rick and Gerald that Zoe is to be well sedated and entirely naked when he gets to her tomorrow night. He will 'rescue' her, put his suit jacket around her and carry her, otherwise naked, right down the hill and into the crowded gallery. And, doubtless with crocodile tears streaming down his face, he'll be yelling, 'Look here everyone, my darling daughter is back in her loving father's arms!'"

My cigarette tasted suddenly harsh and bitter. I stubbed it out. "Sonny, that cannot possibly be true!"

"Well," he admitted, "I don't know exactly what words he will be yelling, but you can bet it's something that makes him the loving, heroic father. And the drugged and naked part is true. But there is one good thing. Your Tweedle boys are getting smart, a little late in the game, but better than not at all. They taped the call and, according to Dana, will put it in the mail to me tomorrow morning." He actually smiled. "They don't realize they will all be here to tell a jury the details about it in person."

"What do you think you can charge Reed with?"

"At least two counts of reckless endangerment, endangering the safety of a juvenile—Zoe isn't eighteen yet—conspiracy to commit a rape, illegal restraint, bribery, illicit use of drugs and anything else we can come up with, like throwing a gum wrapper on the sidewalk." He grinned.

His grin faded and he slugged down a goodly portion of his beer. "I am not going to allow that girl to be publicly humiliated and terrified, being carted virtually unclothed into a crowd of a hundred people. They'll all be staring, yelling questions, cheering and pounding the valiant father on the back. And all the women will be making a fuss over her."

Sometimes I quite liked my brother. "You going to arrest him when he picks up the briefcase with the key?"

"No, he could explain that as just accidentally picking up a similar briefcase. I want him showing that he knows exactly where she is. First of all, there will be an ambulance with an EMT crew, parked behind the gallery. If anyone sees it, it will simply look like a precaution in case anyone faints in the crowd or whatever. But when the ambulance driver sees Reed reach the barn, he will quietly drive up the hill and park beside the entrance."

He turned to me and poked me rather hard on the leg. "This, dear sister, is where you come in."

"Ouch!" I didn't want to come in. I wanted to go to bed.

"When Reed leaves the gallery and starts up the hill, give him a fair lead and then follow him." Sonny had taken control of the cigarettes and helped himself. "He won't look back, I'm almost sure. He's got a one-track mind about this thing. And I want a witness. You follow him into the barn—if he sees you then—he does. What the hell, you are technically still on his payroll. Tell him you're just backing him up. But I still think he won't look behind him. He thinks he's righteous as hell, dealing with this disobedient, ungrateful, queer daughter. I don't want him to have a chance to rape Zoe himself, or to beat her up, later blaming it on the guys. When he carries Zoe downstairs, I want her put in that ambulance and taken to the clinic for a thorough checkup."

"And just how do I manage to accomplish that with this fanatic? What do I do, Sonny? Do I curtsy and say 'This way, your Grace, please put Zoe inside the pretty red and white vehicle?'"

Sonny shrugged. "Just flash your badge and your weapon at him. They are more convincing than a curtsy. If he argues, just shoot him in the foot." He stood, orders to the menials now complete.

"There is one small problem, sir. I'm not carrying a handbag tomorrow night, much less a Glock semi-automatic. There is no place to put it. My tux is a sleek fit, and I will not have a great bulge in my hip pocket, nor will I have my jacket dragging down below my knee from carrying it in a side pocket. And a shoulder holster is out. No gun, Son."

He lifted his hands helplessly. "Hit him with a rock. Seriously, you better have a weapon with you." He turned back toward the door as he said, "See you at the station about eight thirty in the morning. Coffee and doughnuts on me."

"What? Why? Are you crazy?"

"Mark Maddock. I didn't get a chance to talk to him. The minute he got a shower and some food, he passed out. When he wakes up, he'll be sober, with plenty of worrisome thoughts. I'm just as glad he did pass out. I had a lot to do."

"Oh, of course," I said. "You were running behind after your three-hour lunch with Dana? She's an infant and she's gay."

"I am aware of those two things, Ms. Morality Police. She is also a gutsy kid and our only reliable contact with Zoe and her keepers. You and Jeanine had Mark pretty well rattled. We should get a confession in no time. See you at eight thirty." He was gone.

I tossed my clothes on a chair and turned to the bed where Cindy lay, deep in dreamland. I didn't even bother shooing Wells and Fargo off my side of the bed. I merely curled up in the little space they had left me. It was just fine.

Chapter 24

The darling four-legged members of the family woke us early. I got up to let them out and wondered yet again where they found their energy. I stood in the doorway, watching them, my mind a virtual blank. I felt Cindy's head nestle between my shoulder blades and I asked, "Why are you up? You are the only sane one in the family. Go back to bed."

"We have time to take them to the beach before you have to leave," she answered. "I vaguely heard Sonny say something about eight thirty last night. Shall we take the little buggers for a romp?"

Cindy and Wells rarely joined Fargo and me for a beach trip, and I was pleased.

"Sure. That's a great idea."

We rapidly donned last night's clothes, called the kinder and left, with Fargo shifting around the backseat, complaining that he was supposed to ride in the front seat, and Wells, hissing quietly

206

when he crowded her. A typical family excursion.

I stopped at the Topsail and picked up Portuguese fried bread and two coffees. Cindy actually broke off a hunk of bread and tore into it like a hungry sailor. Not a typical family excursion.

We reached Race Point, and I parked right at the top of the paths down to the beach. There were only two other cars there, probably surf fishermen. Fargo scampered down with Wells in hot pursuit—and I had no camera.

Cindy and I followed more slowly.

When we got to sea level, I turned and looked out over the ocean to the horizon where the sun was just sending exploratory rays along the whitecaps, making them look like dainty, timeless gold antimacassars on the ocean's ample armrests.

"What's your forecast, Caleb? Fair weather?"

"Ayup," I answered in my best fisherman's accent. "She may blow a little toward evenin' but thar'll be no rain, lady. You c'n wear yore best boa t'night."

"I'm glad there'll be no rain, thank you, but I am not at all sure the world is ready for me in a boa."

We strolled on. Cindy laughed and pointed. Fargo had rousted a bunch of plovers and they flew away, low over Wells, who performed several athletic leaps and finally did a little jig on her hind feet, front feet waving ineffectually in the air where the birds had been. Fargo gave her a disgusted look and plunged into the water, managing to spray her rather thoroughly, which, of course, had been his purpose.

I shook my head. "Sometimes they are so human they almost frighten me."

"At least they are rarely vicious without a reason," Cindy said. "Rogue animals do happen, but few and far between. You can usually trace a bad animal to a bad human."

"Then no wonder ours are such paragons of virtue."

I popped my empty coffee cup into the bag our breakfast had come in. Cindy added hers and I took the breakfast detritus over to one of the trash barrels placed at intervals along the beach.

207

We walked slowly back to the car, holding hands and leaning slightly into each other. I turned to her and said, "I love you," just as she simultaneously said, "I love you."

Cindy tilted her head against my shoulder. "Isn't it nice we're in accord?"

"Yes. Yes, it is."

A soaking shower and second cup of coffee put a finishing touch on my morning's good humor, and I arrived at Sonny's office at eight thirty sharp, wide awake and smiling. Surprisingly, so was my brother. He handed me a cup of coffee and actually used a paper napkin to hand me a doughnut.

"Has Mark just given you an eight-page written confession?"

"No, he's still whining that he didn't do it. But one Richard Merrill arrived at the front desk a little while ago, announcing that he wants to clear his good name in the Charlotte Cohane matter. That probably means he intends to muddy Mark's." Sonny flashed his Great White Shark grin.

"Ah." I took a bite of the pastry—still warm! "I take it Merrill is Mark's coworker and buddy—well, used to be his buddy, anyway."

"Yep. He's in the interrogation room awaiting our pleasure. Shall we join him?"

"Oh, yes. I wouldn't miss this." I swiftly finished off the doughnut, wiped my mouth and followed Sonny down the hall, carrying my coffee.

The young man seated at the table was rather fresh-faced and pleasant looking, with dark brown curly hair and dark brown eyes that looked clear and warm. His posture was straight but not nervously stiff. I judged him to be around six feet tall. He actually rose when we entered the room.

"Good morning, Mr. Merrill, I am Lieutenant Peres and this—" He was stopped in midsentence by Merrill reaching across the table and extending his hand. Sonny was so startled, he took it. " . . . and this is my deputy," he finished weakly.

I suppressed a giggle, sat down and arranged my notebook and coffee several times until they straightened themselves out.

"Now, er, Richard. What's all this about clearing your name? Thus far, you have no police record in Ptown, or in the state as far as we can judge at this time. Not even a parking ticket. What is it you think may cause you a problem?" Sonny smiled his sweetest smile, offering Merrill all the rope he needed.

"Sir, I'm afraid if I don't straighten this out personally, you might somehow get the idea I was somehow involved with Ms. Cohane's death, and I wasn't, except maybe a little bit afterward, but nothing that would have helped her."

"I see." I was glad Sonny did. I wondered if Richard were kin to Billie at the Rat. "Would you like to start at the beginning, and would you mind if I taped this interview?"

"Not at all, sir, Lieutenant. Tape away. No confusion that way. I guess you could say it started when we got Mrs. Widman's sofa and chair loaded on the truck to be re-covered. Her house is maybe half a mile from the Tellman Gallery, and Mark said he'd like to stop by and tell Ms. Cohane he had no hard feelings. He and Karen had been considering a divorce anyway, he said, and he for one thought it was a fine idea. He'd been unhappy for years, but just stuck it out because of his son, Harry."

Sonny was clearly speechless. I managed to ask, "You mean Karen and Mark were considering a divorce, and Charlie Cohane was somehow involved in their decision?"

"Ms. Cohane was the reason for the divorce." Richard gave a short laugh. "Karen told Mark that the very day the two women met, they knew they were meant for each other, and they were even going into business together. Mark informed her he wasn't going to sit still while she got involved with some dyke and made him the town's laughingstock. Karen said, well, then he could sit still somewhere else. A divorce would be fine with her. She wasn't giving up her new business or her new, uh, friend."

Sonny finally found his voice. "You mean Mrs. Maddock and

Ms. Cohane had fallen in love with each other? Just like that?"

"Sir, it surely sounded that way to me."

Without thinking, I had lit a cigarette. I blew smoke toward the ceiling and said, "That romance is a little hard to believe, and Mark Maddock would never wish any two lesbians well. He hates all gays, and if his wife has discovered she is gay, that would put him right over the edge. If I had any doubts that Mark killed Charlie, I just lost them."

"I hate to disagree with you, ma'am, but you're wrong. Mark did not kill her. I'll tell you what happened. I parked the truck in the art gallery lot like Mark told me, and we went over to the gallery. There didn't seem to be anybody there, and we wondered if they'd all gone to lunch and somebody forgot to close the door. We were standing inside the main door, and Mark was telling me to stay there where I could see if anybody pulled into the lot or started down from the house. If anybody was coming, I should yell and tell him. He would be in the office if Ms. Cohane was there, and we would skedaddle."

By now Sonny had made the necessary hand motions to tell me he wanted a cigarette, and I slid the pack down the table as he asked, "Why were you going to run if someone came in if you weren't doing anything wrong?"

Richard looked unhappy at the smoke, but answered politely. "Mark said he didn't want to run into anyone he knew. He was afraid of getting teased about losing his wife to another woman. In fact, he said he might look for another job and move farther up Cape, so he didn't have to listen to it every time he went out for a beer."

"Okay, you were standing guard. Then what?" Sonny looked dubious.

"I was by the main door, as I said. Mark took two or three steps toward the office door, which was closed, and then there was a loud pop! Mark and I looked at each other, and then we ran for the office door. We banged on the door asking was everybody all right. When no one answered we opened the door."

He swallowed hard and continued. "I saw a lady running out the back door. She got in a car right outside the door and roared off. And then I saw another lady sort of slumped in an office chair kind of pushed back from the desk with a little bit of blood running down her forehead. Then I realized the back of the chair was a mess. I yelled for Mark and he came over. I picked up the desk phone to call nine-one-one, but he took it out of my hand. He felt her wrist and said she was a goner, which was what we had better be."

"Did you leave then?" I asked.

"No. I don't know when I first saw the money on the little table by the desk. God, it looked like a fortune all stacked up and neatly banded. Mark had already noticed it and had put some of it in a bag there on the table. Then he quit doing that and picked the gun up off the floor and wiped it with his handkerchief and put it in the lady's hand. It fell out, which Mark said it would have done if she'd shot herself. He said that we had to make it look like we had never been there and never saw a thing. You see, we didn't know if the tall lady had been so upset she ran away when Ms. Cohane shot herself, or whether she had shot Ms. Cohane and thrown the gun on the floor as she left."

"Did you know Ms. Cohane?" I asked.

"No, never met her."

"Did you notice the gun was on the floor to Cohane's left side, as if she used her left hand to shoot herself, or as if this other woman made it look as if she had?" Sonny followed up.

Richard looked down, as if he were somewhat ashamed. "I never even thought of it. You see, the money was beginning to look good to me, too. Mark saw my face and said, 'Help me get the rest of this in the bag, and five thousand is yours.' That would get me through another year of college with what I made this summer. And I said okay. It occurred to me somebody just driving by might see our truck with the name on the side. Not that we did a thing to that poor lady, but if we should be seen, and later questioned, it would be a lot better for us if she had some reason to have killed herself. Mark thought a minute, then laughed and agreed, so I did it."

"In what way?" Sonny's dubious look was fading.

"I saw some plastic gloves I guess they used handling some of the pictures and put them on. The computer was already on, and I wrote a suicide note."

Merrill frowned as I lit another cigarette, but didn't complain. Instead, he said, "I figured if this lady ran an art gallery, she was probably pretty arty herself, so that's the way I wrote the note. Mark said it was really good, so that's how we left it. Mark said now nobody would ever figure out whether Ms. Cohane killed herself and the other lady just found her, or the other lady killed her and phonied up the note. He said it was brilliant. Then he just made sure we left no prints on the telephone or anything, and we walked casually out with the bag. We hadn't seen a soul except the runaway lady."

"Didn't you see anything at all of what she looked like?" I asked.

"Not really. She had on slacks of some dark color and her hair was blond-ish and kind of long . . . well, not really long, just medium, I guess you'd say. Oh, she was really tall, I think. Almost as tall as me, a good five-ten."

"What about her car?"

"Yeah, it was a dark beige. Kia, or maybe a Saturn, I think. I'm not sure."

Sonny looked at me and breathed, "Jesus!"

I gave him a wink and turned to Merrill. "Do you happen to know a lady named Ellen Hall?"

He pondered a moment. "No, I think not."

"Now that's strange, Mr. Merrill. You just described her perfectly. But I believe you when you say you don't know her. You see, we have a lot of herring in this town, and Mark has given you a nice big red one to drag across the trail. And you fell for it. Perjury, if you testify to this in court, could be a real mistake. But if you want to stick with your story, we'll bring her

212

in for a lineup, and we'll check her alibi. It's up to you."

He pushed his chair back from the table and held up his hands, palm out, as if he were trying to stop a train. "Now hold on, ma'am. I'm not perjuring myself for anything or anybody. I don't know her. I never saw her in my life, and to tell the truth . . . she wasn't even there! Mark thought it would be a good idea to have a stranger there, so she could have killed Ms. Cohane and taken the money. He just told me what she looked like and what her car was like, and said we should both describe them the same way. Look, I want no part of any of this. I only took the money to help me through school. Here."

He reached into his hip pocket, and Sonny and I tensed, but he brought out a folded manila envelope, well filled. "It's the money. It's every bit there. I was going to give it back anyway. I figured it would be bad luck."

"And you don't know whom you were describing?"

"I do not. I figured it was just someone Mark dreamed up on the spur of the moment."

"The woman you so perfectly pictured, Ellen Hall, was Charlie Cohane's lover and housemate for fifteen years," I said. "The only place you went wrong was on the car. She traded the Kia for a Chrysler some months back."

"Oh, God. I'm fucked."

I could not help but agree.

Sonny and I looked at each other and smiled. "Now, Mr. Merrill, let me tell you what I think really happened. I think you stood at the front entrance, as you said. But I think you were alone. Mark had gone into the office for his little chat with Charlie. You heard the pop and ran into the office. There you saw Charlie with a bullet wound to the head and Mark holding a pistol. Right?"

Merrill was searching madly for innocence, and I had to admit that the not-too-bright young man had been led down the old garden path.

"Lieutenant, ma'am," he sputtered. "It was an accident. Mark swore it was. Then he thought up this lady and I stupidly went along with his idea, and—worse—I thought up the suicide note. I admit I did that and I shouldn't have. But that's all I did, and I am very sorry to have misled you. Can I go now?" He was pale and sweaty, and his hands were shaking.

Sonny gave him a pitying look. "Richard, I'm afraid you must be our guest for a while. How old are you? Do your parents live around here?"

"I'm nineteen. They live down in Rhode Island. Why?"

"I suggest you call them and tell them to get you a very sharp lawyer. You are under arrest as an accessory to murder, but a good lawyer may be able to cut that down to obstruction of justice."

"My mom's going to kill me."

"Yeah, well, better her than the state." Sonny pressed the intercom and Mendes came to escort Richard Merrill to a cell. "Book him for accessory to murder," Sonny instructed. "Then give us about ten minutes and bring Mark Maddock in here. Don't let the two of them see each other," he said. "Tell Nacho to let him call his mommy as soon as he's booked."

While we relaxed for a few minutes, Nacho brought us fresh coffee and Sonny actually produced a pack of his own cigarettes. Before he lit his, he lit one and handed it to me. I felt as if I were in an old Bette Davis film.

When Mark walked in, firmly gripped by Mendes, he looked very different from the last time I had seen him. He was sober and clean. His hair was combed, and he was recently shaven. The handsome young man he had been was still in there somewhere. He didn't know Richard Merrill had turned himself in and confessed all, however inadvertently, and I was sure Mark thought he was in the clear except for the money. And a sympathetic judge might be quite lenient about that if Mark pleaded that when he saw all that cash, his only thought was for his son's college tuition. He had an arrogant look about him that made me eager to puncture it for him.

Sonny courteously asked Mark to tell him what had happened

214

that day, and we listened without interruption. Mark's tale was almost verbatim to Richard Merrill's first story. He tried to make it that Richard had insisted on stealing the money and that he—Mark—reluctantly complied, but that was about the only real difference.

As for the person running out the back door, Mark said he was trying to see if Charlie was alive and could be helped, and all he saw was a tall woman with fairly long hair, wearing slacks, running out the door. Then he saw the blur of what he thought was a brown Kia leaving swiftly.

"Mark." I tapped my finger on the table. "You are lying through your teeth. You never went to Tellman's to have a friendly chat with Charlie! You couldn't have a friendly chat with anyone who's gay, much less someone you think is sleeping with your wife. I'll grant maybe you didn't go there to kill her. Maybe you just went there to try to frighten her into leaving Karen alone, probably to beat her up for good measure. But when you saw the gun on the table beside the money . . . bingo! Kill this wife-stealing, lesbian bitch and get a fistful of money to boot.

"Then you got the bright idea of putting another woman on the scene," I added. "You made her the spitting image of Ellen Hall, because you know when someone is murdered, a spouse or lover is always somewhat suspect. That gave you another laugh. Maybe Charlie's bitch lesbian lover knew of the Charlie/Karen affair and could go down for the shooting There never was a second woman in the room. You made her up and Richard swore to it. You do know Ellen, don't you?"

"No. I mean I know her when I see her. We redid her office furniture. She and her friend picked out the material."

"Nice going, Alex. Sounds good to me," Sonny said.

"Look, Sonny, I tell you I never killed her."

Obviously, Mark was not going to talk to me, a mere woman, and gay at that. "Yes, I was mad," Mark admitted. "Wouldn't you be? This crazy woman, Charlie—whoever named a woman Charlie?—comes on the scene and decides she's gonna start up

215

some hoity-toity catering business with my wife. And Karen's cousin Ruthie goes along with it! Her own cousin going into business with a dyke who's screwing my wife? What's the world coming to? Then Karen wants a divorce, she's so in love with this queer. A divorce, after we been married nearly twenty years. Okay, Karen hasn't been much of a wife lately, but she's not all that bad. I wouldn't never have left her."

He sounded as if he were describing an old lawnmower that wasn't cutting evenly but was still usable.

"So what were you going to do?" Sonny asked. "Rough her up?"

Mark looked up slowly. "Maybe, but no more than that. I just wanted her to back off. What would everybody think of me? What kind of man loses his wife to another woman? They'd be laughing all over town. And Harry. What would this do to him? Would he be laughing, too? I walked in the office and there she sat putting big stacks of money in a green bag. Looked like a million. She looked up and asked me—real tough-like—who I was and what did I want?"

He buried his face in his hands, his next words barely understandable. "I saw her hand inching across the desk and realized she was after a pistol, sort of half hid under some papers. I knew she'd shoot me. I could see it in her eyes. I was just some low-life thief come to take her money."

He was talking faster now, hands rubbing up and down his reddening cheeks.

"I grabbed her hand and tried to get the gun away from her or turn it away from me. I think her elbow slipped on the table and the gun went off and she kind of reared back in the chair with the back of her goddamn head blown all to hell. I didn't mean it, Sonny."

He began to cry. "I didn't mean it. It was an accident, I tell you. I didn't kill her! And then that fool Merrill comes thundering through the door yelling his head off, screaming we gotta make it look like suicide and get the money and get out before somebody comes back to the gallery. Then he was running around to the computer. It was like some of those crazy kids' cartoons."

"Did you know Charlie did some things left-handed, so you put the gun in her left hand and let it fall to her left side?" I asked.

His sobs grew heavier. "No, I never thought about that . . . I guess it was just the easiest way to do it with the way she was sitting. But I didn't mean it, Sonny. I wouldn't never have killed nobody! All I wanted was Karen and things back the way they was."

And I realized that in about five minutes, we had listened to the tale of a man's life—rather dull, but not really unhappy— disintegrating into a hell he would never leave. And along with him, he had taken his own family and Charlie's, plus Charlie's lover, and even, to a lesser degree, Richard Merrill's and Karen's cousin Ruthie and Charlie's many friends.

All because he didn't like the lifestyle of certain people.

Chapter 25

I was at home. I had told Sonny I simply couldn't take any more of Mark's—probably genuine, but still self-serving—remorse. If I were to be of any use to Sonny tonight, I had to get away from the whole mess and try to recoup some of my early morning sanity.

Cindy had listened with interest and sympathy to my account of Mark's and Richard's actions, and asked only one question: Why did Mark try to place Ellen at the scene?

I shrugged. "He hates all gays. If Ellen had no alibi for that time period, we would at least have had to give her some serious thought, especially since she and Charlie were going through some rough waters at the time." I lit my hundredth cigarette and cringed at the taste.

"Sonny won't question her, will he?"

"No, there's no reason. I hope she never even hears about Mark's tale. She's had enough."

She stood and came over to me and held me tight for a moment. I felt I could have stayed there forever, but she backed away slightly and put on her I-will-be-obeyed voice. "Now, darling, I want you to mix yourself one stiff drink and have it while I make you some scrambled eggs and toast. You have to eat something. And then take a nap. We are going to enjoy tonight, even if World War Three is announced on the six o'clock news."

It all sounded good to me, except—the way things were going—I thought we might skip the news.

Cindy woke me gently about five o'clock, whispering in my ear, "The two furballs are outside terrorizing the squirrels, and the phone is turned off."

I yawned. "What amazing good luck."

We took full advantage of our fortuitous privacy. By six, we were beginning our toilettes for the big night and had forgotten all about what might be on the news. In any event, it was a slow night, with the lead story about a boat chartered by the Loyal Order of the Moose that had managed to run aground near Plymouth, with no casualties. Even the weather was cooperative, the forecast calling for clear skies and a brisk, but not cold, breeze. Ayup!

Our sartorial efforts were not in vain. Cindy actually had her dark curls under some kind of control, piled atop her head, the better to display her long and graceful neck. Her off-white dress had a scoop neck and a rich red and gold sash just below the waist. Her only other touches of color were a sizeable single-ruby necklace of my mother's and red pumps with her signature stiletto heels, which I suggested should be registered as dangerous weapons.

I felt pretty sharp myself, in my tux with a single-button jacket and the traditional stripe down the trousers. Instead of a tie I wore a white shirt with a frilly jabot, so heavily starched I felt it would break before it would bend. My black slip-ons were

219

as brightly polished as Sonny's favorite boots.

I was not carrying a weapon, unless you counted the jabot. I figured, if I hugged somebody tight enough, I would probably stab them to death. Otherwise, I was pretty harmless, and the sleek lines of my tux were undisturbed. I even carried a slender cigarette case in the breast pocket.

Driving over to the Tellman Gallery, Cindy chattered happily about who would be there and how they might look. Her monologue required only the occasional "Umm," and "Oh?" for answers, which was just as well. I was going over Sonny's carefully detailed plan in my mind, and that was what worried me. Too many details, too much that might go awry.

What if the light blue Toyota wouldn't start and the rental company sent a black one? Would everyone realize only the color had changed? What if someone actually had a heart attack? The EMTs and their ambulance couldn't remain aloof, waiting for Zoe. What if Gerald and Rick looked in their briefcase to find that Reed had filled it with one-dollar bills? What if the key to the barn didn't work? What if they accidentally gave Zoe an overdose and killed her?

"What?"

"For the third time," Cindy said with some asperity, "Where do you want to park? It's seven o'clock, as your dear brother requested, and we certainly have a wide choice of spaces. I think he and Trish are the only others here, except the security people. Oh, no, there's one other car, and one next to it with Mitch and Pino getting out. They actually have on tuxes. Why do they still look like cops? I'll bet Sonny won't."

"Because they feel like cops disguised in tuxedos," I said. "Sonny simply feels gorgeous. Park by him. I don't want either of us anywhere near that Toyota."

"Why not?"

"It's the so-called getaway car. If there's going to be a screw up, that's probably where it will be."

"Okay."

As we walked across the parking lot, I noticed a few other cars coming up the road. I was glad. I didn't want to be conspicuous, glued to the bar, awaiting the switch of the briefcases. On the other hand, if I had to be stuck somewhere, the bar was certainly preferable to the entrance to the men's room.

Tendering our invitation to the security fellow at the door, we entered the main gallery, where Cindy was immediately cornered by a middle-aged couple I assumed were her customers at the bank.

Smiling vaguely, I continued toward the bar, stopping now and then to give a closer look to this or that painting. One large pastel caught my eye with favor. Three young women were in their garden, one clipping flowers, the other two holding out baskets to receive the bouquets.

The colors mere muted, lines indefinite, the costumes suggested rather than detailed Edwardian design. The overall effect was serene and innocent. I liked it and looked closer. Then I saw that one girl's hair was combed forward, partially to conceal the fact that she had no ears. A second figure lightly held her friend's arm, and her smiling face revealed no eyes. The third—by now I knew what I was looking for—was drawn with her face in shadow provided by a large, period straw hat, and of course, she had no mouth.

"You like it?" a high-pitched English voice asked. It was Tweedledum, alias Gerald.

"Very powerful," I said. "It's also lovely, and your moral is quite definite. You'd have to be blind or deaf these days not to hear evil, or to see it. And you'd have to be mute not to speak evil. We all do it from time to time, even though we may try not to. Yes, I like it. Is it your work?"

He actually blushed. "Yes. Not everyone understands. They just think it's freaky. I will make you a gift of it. I'm leaving anyway. I want someone who understands it to have it. What's your name and I will tell Betsy you will pick it up after tonight."

"That's very kind. It will be particularly meaningful after

tonight. Are you sure about this? It would probably sell easily."
My fingers reached out of their own accord and stroked one girl's
cheek.

"Very sure." He nodded. "Your name?"

"Now don't scream and go flying out." A waiter approached
with a tray of champagne glasses. I took two and handed one to
Gerald. "My name is Alex Peres, but I'm only here to watch out
for Zoe. Dana called me, and I don't want Reed to take advantage
of Zoe, or make himself out some hero to the crowd."

He swallowed half of his champagne in a gulp. "Good. Reed's
a rotter if I ever met one. I'm glad you'll be with her. Dana says
you're good stuff." He looked at his watch. "Reed should be here
in about ten minutes. When I see him I'll go in the office, ring
the barn, and Rick will come down with the briefcase for him."

I nodded, and we both set our glasses on a convenient table.
"We'd better separate. In case Reed is early, he shouldn't see us
together. Thank you again for the picture. I'll treasure it."

We shook hands and he walked away, leaving me feeling as if
I should model for a portrait of Judas. I had to resist an almost
overwhelmingly strong urge to go tell him to beware blue Toyotas
and have Cindy slip the keys to her red Civic into his pocket.

I checked my watch and walked a few feet from the bar,
ostentatiously studying a piece of statuary that looked to me
like the cornerstone of a building, or possibly the headstone of a
grave. Quickly dropping that thought, I looked over and saw my
mother, shackled as usual by Choate Ellis. She looked desperately
at me for help, but I simply smiled and waved and walked back to
the bar. I knew she would love that.

I took another glass of champagne. I nodded and smiled and
waved to various people and spoke to a few who came to the bar
for hard drinks or beer. But I didn't move. My mother looked
worried, and the last thing I needed was a parental visit to my
guard post.

I managed to catch Trish's eye and pointed at Mom. Trish
frowned, then her face cleared. She took Cindy and started

222

across the floor to assure my mother—I hoped—that I would not shortly be falling-down drunk.

I turned back to see Reed standing nearby, ordering a double Scotch straight up and placing a briefcase at the end of the bar. We nodded to each other, but apparently neither of us could think of anything to say, and I wandered back to my statuary, where I could keep an eye on him.

He finished his drink and ordered another one. I hoped it didn't make him nasty. About the same time, Rick sauntered up to the bar with his attaché case, placed it near Reed's and ordered a Perrier. Smart. Reed tossed off his second drink, picked up Rick's case and started for the door. I patted my marble mystery good-bye, set my glass on top of it, swiped a red and a green cherry from the bar and placed them artistically in the glass, to the amusement of the bartender, and went into my bloodhound act. I passed a smiling Rick as he picked up an obviously weighty case and sidled toward the back door.

Chapter 26

There was a quarter moon, which didn't provide much light, and as the wind picked up, it caused clouds to scud across the narrow crescent, making what light there was intermittent. The driveway up to the barn was not well maintained, with deep ruts and loose rocks that were giving me trouble in my leather-soled shoes. I stopped for a moment to catch my breath and heard the sound of shoes scraping along behind me.

Turning quickly, I was not happy to see Cindy and Trish hobbling in my wake, arms around each other's waist, making a rough go of it in their high heels.

"Go back," I called softly. "You're going to break your necks, and you're making a racket."

"You're not going up there by yourself!" Cindy hissed. "Did you see how much Reed was drinking?"

"Yes. I'll be okay if I don't break a leg getting there. Stay back, dammit." I turned and tried to go faster. Reed was almost at the barn.

I was not far behind him when he reached the door. I slowed and tried moving only when the moon was covered. Still, I wondered why he didn't hear me. In one fairly lengthy bright period, I realized he was bent in concentration over the door, apparently having trouble with the key. I was now only a few feet behind him, and even Cindy and Trish were making progress.

Just what we needed: the four of us standing around trying to look as if we always took a moonlight stroll up the Matterhorn, while Zoe awoke, dizzy from her Snow White sleep, and fell naked out the window.

Ah, now he had it open. Why didn't he turn on the interior lights? The switch was right inside the door. If I knew it from Dana, surely the guys had told him. I couldn't really see, but sensed he had gone through the dark door and was inside. I got to the door and felt for the switch, moving it up and down with no results. Probably as some last-minute attempt to make Reed's life more difficult, they had thrown the master switch, and God knows where that was. I took a step forward and stumbled over a bale of hay.

I wondered how the hell old it was, and then remembered Betsy had told me they had stabled two horses for the summer. A couple they knew just couldn't bear to leave their pets at home in New Jersey, pining for them. What was it Fitzgerald said? That the rich were different? Indeed they were.

Reed's feet clattered off to the left, telling me he had found the stairs leading to the apartment on the second floor. Hopefully now I could turn on the mini flashlight I carried on my key ring. It was strong for its size, and I immediately picked out the foot of the staircase.

As silently as possible, I ascended the stairs and crept through the guys' living room and the tiny hall toward the kitchen. I noticed a flickering light ahead of me. My God, instead of bringing a flashlight, Reed was using some kind of large cigarette lighter that he had for his pipe! An open flame in a barn full of straw and hay. Swell. I'd discourage that as soon as I caught up with him.

Betsy and Jan had told me that the barn apartment had a living room, bedroom, bath and kitchen. They had planned to add another bedroom and bath on the other side of the kitchen, but hadn't yet done so. Consequently, the end wall of the kitchen, really wasn't a wall at all, but several vertical two-by-fours with a sheet of canvas nailed over them and a thin plywood door opening onto the rest of the loft. It was here that Zoe was domiciled when the Tweedles weren't home, in case someone should come into their apartment.

Reed stopped in the kitchen, and I pulled up short in the small hallway that led into it. He removed his tux jacket, and I was not pleased to see the hilt of a pistol jammed into his trousers. I had some thin hope that it might go off and catch him in the . . . well, let's be generous and say foot. Next, he removed his tie and undid several shirt buttons. I was getting uneasy with all this making himself at home. He turned to the refrigerator, scrabbled around in it and actually came up with a can of beer.

As he walked toward the makeshift door, he popped the can and took a long swig from it before he crossed to where Zoe lay on what looked like piled-up straw covered by a clean blanket and pillow. She wore only a T-shirt and panties and had pulled a corner of the blanket up over her legs.

He knelt over her, patting her cheeks none too gently, saying, "Come on, Zoe, wake up! This damn game of yours is over. The cops have got your boyfriends, and if I have my way, they'll get Harry and Dana, too. God knows her father caused me enough trouble for a lifetime. Wake up! I'm sick of your tricks. You're just like your mother." He slapped her harder.

Zoe moved restlessly and murmured something unintelligible.

Obviously, it was time for me to make an entrance. I summoned up all the insouciance I could muster and leaned casually in the doorway.

"Hi, there, Reed. Looks like our girl is coming around. I can take it from here if you want to go down to the gallery and spread the good news."

He was like a baseball player who couldn't check his bat in mid-swing. He backhanded Zoe cruelly across her breast and certainly aided her in regaining consciousness.

She slurred, "Ouch! Quit it, Daddy. That hurt. What are you doing here?"

He started to hit her again, and she knocked his arm away. Unfortunately, in her still-groggy state she knocked the hand that held the lighter. It dropped to the straw-strewn floor and started a small blaze. Both Reed and I tried to step on it and succeeded only in jostling each other.

I dived for the lighter and got it and flipped the cap closed. I did my version of Cindy's tarantella on the little flames, but for every one I stamped out, another grew stronger. I could have used some help, but Zoe had dozed off again, and Reed had sprinted for the kitchen. At first I thought he had run for a fire extinguisher I had noticed beside the stove, but when he did not return, I finally realized he had simply scarpered.

Truth to tell, I doubt if the extinguisher would have done much good anyway. Between the straw all over the place, the old dry timbers of the barn and the draft that seemed to be turning into a gale, I realized that the only thing left was to try to get Zoe and me the hell out. Soon.

And she looked like about a hundred and ten pounds of dead weight. I hoped I could handle it. I sat her up and poured the last half of Reed's cold beer over her head and did a little cheek slapping of my own.

"Come on, get your arms around my neck and hang on unless you want to fry. This place is going up like a volcano. We gotta get out now!"

She tried. We both tried. We fell back onto her makeshift bed a couple of times, and finally found our balance at the same time. I started for the kitchen and the stairs, with some vague idea of getting the extinguisher and using it to cut us a path through the flames to the stairs. Just as we reached the door, the canvas wall went up with a frightening roar and unbearable heat.

We fell back, and I left Zoe sitting for a moment while I ran to the window and looked out. The ground, some fifteen feet below us, was rough and scattered with sizeable rocks. To jump would almost certainly mean permanent injury for one or both of us. Suddenly Trish was beneath the window, waving her arms and shouting something I couldn't hear over the truly terrifying roar of flames. I knew I'd only increase the draft if I broke the window, but I couldn't think of any other options. I kicked out the window.

"The other end of the loft!" Trish screamed. "A ladder. No flames yet. Hurry!"

I waved and got Zoe vertical again. We started for the east end of the barn, Zoe hanging on doggedly as I half dragged her behind me. It seemed to me we moved in some slow, drunken lockstep, and it was getting hard to see and harder still to breathe. We went on, although my legs were definitely wobbling. What the hell, I thought. We had nothing better to do.

Cool drops on my face and chest pulled me from my dreamy state. A thin stream of water like that from a garden hose was spouting up through a hole in the floor, with the top rung of a ladder sticking out. I had not seen the hole for the smoke, and we would have fallen through it in another two steps.

Cindy stood below us with the hose. Trish scrambled nearby, pushing bales of hay together around the bottom of the ladder. Suddenly there was a long, agonizing crack and then the crash of a rafter and section of the roof gave way in the west end of the barn. It cleared the smoke for a minute, though the roar—if it could—grew louder.

Cindy's dirty wonderful face appeared near the ladder top. "Get Zoe over the edge, and I'll put her feet on the ladder." She sank out of sight as I struggled to obey. "Okay," she said shortly, "We've got her. Let her go and come on. Don't linger!"

I swung my shaking legs over the edge and onto the shaky

old ladder. When my weight hit the second rung, it went flying, followed by the third, followed by my falling the rest of the way.

Don't ever let anyone tell you that baled hay is soft. It has all the give of an empty swimming pool. I knocked the breath out of myself, and even when I finally started to breathe again, it was simply too much trouble to move. I would just rest for a day or two and then move. Surely, no one would mind.

Someone did. I felt an icy stream of water move up and down my body, and I moved with an alacrity I thought was a lost art. "What the hell are you doing? That water is ice cold. I'll have pneumonia."

"Your clothes were smoldering," Cindy said casually. "Now will you get the hell out of here before it all comes down? Can you walk?"

I walked, Cindy behind me with her trusty stream pointed back at the disintegrating barn. We propped on the rim of a nearby water trough and smiled at each other.

"Aside from that, Mrs. Lincoln, how did you enjoy the play?" I asked.

"Terrible. The ingénue was at least fifty, and the champagne at the interval was flat. Are you hurt anywhere? You look awful."

"Have you looked in a mirror lately? I don't think I'm hurt. Did Reed get out?"

"Not that we have seen. Wasn't he with you?"

"Yes, he went into Zoe's room to wake her up. That's another story, but briefly, he was using a lighter for a flashlight and dropped it. When he saw the fire start to build, he ran. I don't know where. I thought he went to get a fire extinguisher, but he never came back."

At that point the fire engine arrived, groaning, lurching and spattering rocks behind it. They had had to lay hose for a long distance to a hydrant. Right behind it was the ambulance. Had they really been sitting behind the gallery all this time, waiting for a dim electric light to go on in the barn? Hanging tightly to the running board of the ambulance was my brother, looking worried. Hopping off, he looked around anxiously, found Cindy and me, then Trish and Zoe, and let out a breath audible even over the sound of the fire.

"Everybody okay here?"

"I'm fine," Cindy said. "Your heroic sister has a small burn on the back of her hand and one around where her pants cuff burned. But not serious, I think. Trish is fine. Zoe is stoned, but seems otherwise okay. Reed is missing. Bastard is probably down at the gallery slugging down champagne and telling everyone how he walked through fire to try to save his beloved child."

"Wherever he is, watch out," I said. "He's got a big automatic stuck in the waistband of his pants, and he's had a good half pint of Scotch to drink."

I stopped to cough. My throat felt raw when I talked. "He was working up to beating the hell out of Zoe. He is not in a happy mood. If he ever has been."

"Excuse me, folks." It was the fire chief, who had been standing quietly behind Sonny. "Sonny, who was the young lady you wanted taken to the clinic? And does anyone else need to go?"

"She goes." Sonny pointed at Zoe. "Please have the driver ask whoever's in charge to hold her overnight. She's drugged. We don't know with what or how much. And she goes." He pointed at me.

I started to protest and coughed instead.

The chief smiled. "You'd better come along, miss. You probably need some oxygen. We've got some in the ambulance to start you on. They'll probably release you later tonight."

He took my arm and then turned back to Sonny. "Is everybody out?"

This time, I managed to speak. "We don't know where Reed Catlett is. The last I saw he was running through the apartment toward the stairs. And he's armed and nasty."

The chief's mouth tightened. "No way can I send men in

there now, anyway. There's nothing holding the structure up but stubbornness. It will go anytime now. Maybe Catlett got out a window and just wandered off. He could easily be injured and disoriented."

At that point Reed solved the mystery for us. The firemen seemed to aim their hoses at one point in the roof and the flames momentarily grew small and harmless looking. And Reed cannonballed through a window, landing on a wet, grassy area, and rolling to his knees.

As he knelt there, probably getting his breath back, a section of the old tin roof slid to the ground with a crash and gave us a sad view of the remains of the apartment. I thought how easily Zoe and I could have been trapped there and began to shake in earnest. An EMT appeared, to put a blanket around my shoulders and handed me an oxygen cone.

I saw Reed get to his feet and turn toward the ambulance and our little group around the water trough. Above the noise of the fire, lessening some now, there came a light pop as if someone had pricked a balloon with a pin. And then another pop!

Almost simultaneously, I heard the old trough make a metallic noise, and a spate of dirty water shot out a small hole in the side. As I stared, there came a loud ping from the back bumper of the ambulance.

"Get down," I yelled. "Reed's got a gun. He's firing!"

We all hit the ground except Sonny, who was peering cautiously around the corner of the leaking trough. The area was well lit now, between floodlights and flames, with the exception of little smoke puffs that skittered along the ground before joining their larger companions drifting skyward.

"He's not shooting," Sonny called. "I can see him perfectly well and both hands are empty. He's just standing there. Who's still inside? Who else had a weapon?"

Another pop sent Sonny diving behind our leaky shelter." Oh, God," he cried. "I know what it is. I'll bet Reed dropped his automatic somewhere and the ammo is cooking off in the heat.

Stay down. The damn bullets could go anywhere."

Two more pops had issued forth as Sonny spoke. "Alex, you saw the gun. How many cartridges would it be if he had one in the chamber and a full clip?"

"Who do you think I am, the local gun dealer? I barely got a glimpse of the thing. It was big. Period. Maybe twelve, even fourteen cartridges. I don't know. Three more pops, that's seven. Sonny, Reed is lying on the ground."

"Probably finally woke up to what's happening and got to the ground. Another one, that's eight."

Then we all cringed at the sound of a small explosion. "That's it," Sonny sighed. "Thank God, the rest of them got hot enough to blow all at once. I don't think there will be anymore."

The chief got to his feet, his boots sucking in the now muddy area we inhabited.

"Okay, folks, party's over. Everyone okay?"

Apparently everyone was. Now that the barn was just a low-burning mess, with only the bereft looking chimney to hold a hundred years of history. The chief was busy sending some of his minions down the hill to help the beleaguered cops make sure the crowd stayed safely down by the gallery. The EMTs were getting the ambulance turned around, preparatory to boarding one sleepy and one reluctant passenger.

I was making sure Cindy would come as soon as she could to the clinic and bail me out, when I noticed something odd.

"Sonny," I called and pointed. "Reed isn't getting up."

Chapter 27

"Shit!" Sonny muttered. Things were getting back to normal.

He ran almost daintily across the slippery grass to where Reed lay on his stomach, one arm extended as if to have broken his fall. Sonny said something to him and shook his shoulder, getting no response I could see. Then Sonny squatted beside him and shined a flashlight on his neck and head. At that, Reed began to jerk his arm in small movements, and I thought I saw his lips move.

"Medic! Over here, please. Now!"

The medic grabbed his bag and ran, sliding to a halt at Sonny's side. First, he looked at Sonny with a tired man's disbelief. Then he donned plastic gloves and knelt beside Reed, ruffling through his hair. He stopped, pointed with his other hand, and Sonny nodded and stood, stretching. The medic yelled back to his cohort for a stretcher, and Sonny returned to us.

"He's alive . . . barely. He's got some really bad burns on his neck and back. But what will probably do him in is a gunshot wound." He flashed a sardonic smile. "You might say that Reed shot himself, or at least his own gun shot him. What's the saying—you can run, but you can't hide?"

"How ironic." I shook my head. "He didn't give a damn if his own daughter died, much less me, and then he's hit by a totally random shot from his own gun. I don't know whether to hope he lives or dies." I suddenly felt very tired.

"If you're feeling kindly, you'll hope he dies," the medic said, approaching Sonny with a pen and some form that required his signature. "That is a large caliber bullet rolling around his brain, fired at fairly low velocity I would guess. God knows what a merry mix-up has gone on in there. Much easier on his family to go to one funeral than to have Reed sitting around the house for years, a confabulating turnip. Thanks, Sonny. Can you spare one of your cars to take these ladies to the clinic? I really don't want them to ride with Reed."

"Sure, very thoughtful of you. Cindy can take them, or Trish."

"We'll each take one," Trish said. "I need your car anyway, Sonny. I need it to get home."

"Okay. One of the firemen will carry Zoe down. See you all later. I have a little matter to take up with the manager of Econo Car Rentals, if I can track him down, bloody idiot!"

"What did he do wrong? The blue Toyota was parked right by the gate when we came in." A small rainbow of hope began to shimmer in the back of my mind.

"So it was, and is, and ever shall be until Econo comes and gets it."

"I don't understand. When we came in Mitch and Pino we're lolling around two cars away, like they were just catching a smoke, all decked out in tuxedos. They couldn't have missed the Tweedles getting in the Toyota. Anyway, didn't Mitch take the keys out from under the fender?"

"Oh, yes." Sonny sighed. "What none of us thought about was that your Tweedle-not-so-Dumbs never intended to go near the blue Toyota. They went out the back door where they had parked a car they rented earlier from Econo and drove sedately out the back gate. The security guy back there says he remembers a car going out around seven thirty, but nobody had told him to stop cars using that gate, so he didn't. And all he remembers is a large, light-colored car. Wouldn't you think Econo might at least have mentioned bringing two cars instead of one?"

I managed not to cheer. Cindy and Trish also seemed to have developed coughs.

"Maybe you can stop them at the bridge," I said helpfully.

Sonny flashed an acid grin. "By now they're over the bridge and hell-bent for grandmother's house. If they're smart, they'll ditch the car at some all-night diner and go to Logan Airport where one of them will rent a car and drive to Toronto or Montreal for a flight to Europe. Or maybe Tokyo. The other will fly to Nova Scotia or maybe Pittsburgh and get an overseas flight from there. They won't go anywhere near their original itinerary."

"What about getting all that money out of the country?" Cindy asked.

Sonny shrugged. "Each one will have fifty thousand in large bills. A lot of it will fit in a wallet. The rest will roll up in dirty socks and underwear and shirts. Or in various folders in an attaché case. It doesn't take up that much room."

The ambulance passed us slowly, trying to avoid the worst of the ruts. We four managed to walk down, at least now able to see where we were going. Zoe was groggy, but able to walk with Cindy on one side and Trish on the other. I managed.

At the foot of the hill we got Mitch to run interference for us and drafted Pino to find my mom and tell her Sonny and I were fine.

The first person I saw in the clinic's emergency room was

Dr. Gloetzner. It didn't surprise me. I seemed to encounter him anytime I needed medical aid or information, or was accompanying someone who did, especially under unusual circumstances. My mom said he and I had a love-hate relationship. I think it was simpler. We had the same sense of humor, which was sometimes, under stress, quite out of the realm of proper behavior.

"Ah, Ms. Peres, I was afraid you weren't going to stop by. Yet I knew it was a night just made for us to meet."

"Sorry to be late, Doctor, but I like to be early at a fire sale."

He looked at my ruined and filthy finery, sniffed my obvious reek of smoke and nodded. "I hate fires. They are the most frightening kind of crisis—with the possible exception of a tsunami—which I've never experienced."

"I know. I guess it's that both of them are so inexorable. I was scared out of my wits tonight, I can tell you."

"I doubt it." He actually patted my back. "Scared, yes, witless, no. I understand you were the one who rescued young Zoe."

"Had plenty of help." I stopped short, coughing again, which inspired the good doctor to listen to my chest and back and pronounce minor smoke inhalation. I resisted an urge to inform him there had been nothing minor about it.

He called a nurse over and pointed to my arm and ankle, muttering something I didn't understand. It resulted in her spraying my arm and ankle with something that felt wonderful, and placing a light bandage on both areas.

"They may be a little sore tomorrow, but they aren't deep. Are you in some kind of minstrel show?" The nurse grinned.

"Bunch of wannabe comedians," I muttered. "I was practicing my Santa Claus act and somebody lit a fire in the fireplace. Any news on Zoe or Reed?"

"Zoe is sleeping it off. Her doctor thinks she was given a mild overdose of one of those sleeping pills they advertise with butterflies and soft music all over the TV. She'll be okay by tomorrow. Maybe hungover, but okay."

The nurse turned to Dr. Gloetzner. "Dr. Baylor said to tell

you the swelling in Mr. Catlett's brain is slowing. He is still with us, and the medevac chopper should be here in ten minutes."

Gloetzner nodded. "Thank you, nurse. I'll be right there." He turned to me. "I think you are basically okay, Ms. Peres, having come through still another of your perilous adventures. Your middle name isn't Pauline by any chance, is it?"

"No. It's bad enough, but not that bad. Can I go now?"

"In peace, my child, in peace. Sleep with an open window and none of those white, tube-like things until tomorrow soonest. Preferably never."

"Yeah, yeah. Thanks"

"Good night, Charlie Chaplin. I hear you done good."

I grinned. He always got the last word. Escaping into the waiting room, I spotted Cindy, holding hands with someone I really did not want to see. Marie Catlett sat upright and dry-eyed, her face gray with fatigue and grief.

"Alex!" She tried desperately to smile. "I am so glad you seem to have come through this terrible night with only minor wounds. I will thank you properly for my granddaughter's life in a day or so, when I get my wits about me."

"Please, Marie, don't even think of it." I spread my hands and moved them in a negating motion. "Anyway, Cindy and Trish did as much or more than I did."

"Then I shall thank them also. Alex, is there any news of Reed?"

The last thing I wanted to do was give her false hope. The other last thing I wanted to do was take away the hope she still nourished. Finally, I said, "He's definitely still with us, and one of the doctor's said the medevac chopper is now only about five minutes out."

"Thank God." For the first time, her voice sounded old. "They are letting me ride over and go to the Boston hospital with him, in case he should regain consciousness."

Fat chance, I figured. "Oh, fine. Should I fetch Rob or Merrilou to go with you?"

"No, I think this is a time for me alone. He is my only child, you know."

Before I could burst into tears, a nurse appeared in the door, motioning toward Marie. "Mrs. Catlett. We're ready to go now."

I vaguely remember the ride home, the shower and soft pajamas, the mug of tea lashed with rum and sugar. The chunk of chocolate cake. I finally realized Cindy was stoking me with sugar to counteract delayed shock. I felt dreamy and removed from all the chaos and danger and grief. Wells was in my lap, Fargo balanced with front paws on my leg and cheek against my arm. It was so sweet, I squeezed them both and told them I loved them. They didn't like being squeezed and moved away, and I cried a little at their departure.

The phone rang and Cindy picked up. She said "yes" and "oh" several times, added, "I guess I'll tell her," and hung up.

"Tell me what?"

"Reed died in the chopper. They turned around and came back."

"Did he regain consciousness?" I cried a little at the thought he might not have.

Cindy nodded. "Probably more or less. He took his mother's hand and said, 'You were always a wonderful woman.' Who knows whether he was talking to her or to Frances or a hooker in Boston?"

"Come on, it's bedtime," I was suddenly sleepy and assumed everyone else was.

"No lobster, no caviar." I noticed Cindy looked concerned as she tucked the quilt up around my chin. "I mean," she said, "The Tellmans were going to serve a buffet with cold lobster and deviled eggs with caviar. We didn't get any."

I must have looked bereft, for she laughed. "Maybe we can cadge some leftovers. At least you are getting back to normal."

She kissed me and turned out the light.

I cried a little that she was so thoughtful.

The next day was a day of soreness . . . of body, of mind, of heart. I was finished with my crying jag, but it seemed to me that half the people I knew had suffered serious losses in the last few weeks.

I thought of the old adage: Finders keepers, losers weepers. But that implied some sort of balance. At least some people found, even if others had to lose. The events of the recent past didn't seem to be working that way.

Marie Catlett had to be the worst hit. To lose a child—an only child—had to be the lowest blow you could get. It went against all the rules of nature. Parents died after a gentle old age, comforted and loved by their children. Marie would not.

Along with leaving a demolished mother, Reed had left three children in emotional and financial limbo, having not yet recovered from the loss of their mother. Now dealing with a stepmother about as different from Frances as she could get. And the stepmother was now widowed herself, however much that may have affected her. And I wasn't halfway through my list.

If I kept this up, I'd be weeping again.

Cindy was out with Fargo, getting the papers. I grabbed my jacket and coffee and went out to trim the hydrangea. It was one of those misleading, summerish September days that fools you into thinking winter isn't coming this year. I rapidly shed the jacket, and the hydrangea rapidly shed it branches. I was stuffing them into a plastic bag when Mom and Aunt Mae arrived. With food, bless 'em.

Fargo arrived next. He probably smelled Mom's meatloaf three blocks away, but Cindy wasn't far behind with papers and croissants. We had just sat down to what would probably be our last outdoor breakfast of the year, when the Tellman sisters arrived. Between them, they lugged a cooler filled with lobster, caviar and three bottles of wine, all together, worth about what I make in a week.

Fortunately, Cindy had shopped generously, and after fresh coffee and goodies all around, one of those sudden silences settled over our group. A couple of us laughed softly. Several throats were cleared, and finally Jan spoke up.

"First of all, I'm grateful we are all here in good health. Secondly, Betsy and I need some advice. Jeanne, Mae, I know you can help us with this. We were supposed to leave tomorrow, but things keep changing and we keep needing to be here a bit longer."

"Like certain people making your lovely old barn burn down," I said bitterly.

"And certain other people keeping it an unfortunate occurrence, rather than a tragic death scene!" Betsy added with asperity. "But I admit, the old stone chimney just wouldn't let us go. We decided to keep the property around the barn and build a cottage to use in the summers. We can't use the stones again in a chimney, but we can put them elsewhere. A façade or perhaps a patio or garden. We'll see."

Mom took a sip of her coffee and laughed. "Betsy, you don't seem to need advice, you seem to need a little time without high drama."

"That, too." Betsy smiled. "But here's where the advice comes in. We, or the business, actually, had a hundred thousand dollar insurance policy on Charlie as a highly valued employee. We plan to keep half of it to reimburse us for actual expenses we will incur due to her . . . absence. We could legally keep the other fifty. We do still maintain the corporation and have certain other interests, but we would rather it went someplace where it's needed, preferably local."

"Charlie's mother could surely use a portion of it," Aunt Mae piped up immediately. "Especially now with Charlie gone. She's not poverty stricken, but she certainly counts every penny. And that's not just an expression. An extra thousand or so would be a help. But I don't know how she'd feel about taking it."

"Don't tell her," Cindy said. "Just say it was Charlie's policy, bought through the company. If the insurance company won't issue a check to the mother, route it through the bank."

Jan looked at Betsy. "Well, there's part of it solved. Next."

"Could you give me a day or two?" I asked. "I have an idea, but I need to check a couple of things."

"I don't see why not," Jan said. "It seems we will be here. And now, our second question: Do we attend Reed's funeral or not? We really have no desire to go, but we don't wish to insult the family, either. What do we do?"

"I imagine half the people in Ptown are asking that question this morning," I said and lit a cigarette and managed not to cough before I put it out.

"You do not attend," Aunt Mae said firmly. "It will be in the local paper tomorrow. The funeral is private, for the immediate family only. I stopped by their house this morning to see if I could help in any way.

"God, you're brave," Cindy murmured.

"Courage is different in each of us, dear. Actually, they're holding up well. Marie's friend arrived this morning. Zoe will be home this afternoon. Rob and Merrilou are real champions."

I almost choked on my coffee. "Rob and Merrilou are champions? I'm surprised at that. I though she'd be on her way back to Dixie by now, clutching large T-notes."

"No, Merrilou apparently has taken over, but gently so. She called a conference early this morning. She says she will keep the house, at least until Marvin is ready for college, or the Marines, if that idea lasts. She says the children need an anchor—a headquarters—to call home, and while they may not ever be the ideal family, at least they can be friends. If Zoe wants to live with Marie, fine. If not, which seems more sensible, there will be no controversy about how she leads her life in Provincetown. And she's going to remodel the master suite so Marie and Barb can have a little private apartment anytime they want to visit or just

241

come to the Cape."

"Merrilou hasn't suffered a recent blow to the head, has she?" I couldn't resist.

"No, and she has not been walking along the road to Damascus lately, either." Aunt Mae could field a good one when she tried. "No one in this town exactly welcomed her, and she handled it badly, I'm sure she would admit. But she was right about the kidnapping originally being a trick. If Reed hadn't tried to turn it into a nasty, abusive experience, it would all have fizzled out in a day or so. This entire mess could have been avoided."

Thoroughly chastised, I was aware of some dim idea circling my own jolted brain. I'd nail it down when I had some quiet time.

Our little impromptu gathering dispersed shortly after that. I supposed all of us—except Aunt Mae—were thinking that we hadn't exactly cut Merrilou much slack. I personally remembered referring to her as "a money-grabbing sexpot, offset by also managing to be a religious hysteric who would gladly reinstate her own version of the Inquisition." Somehow, it no longer had the same ring to it as it had at the time I so cleverly said it.

As I cleared the tables, Cindy checked the ice in the cooler and pronounced it adequate. "And we've certainly got an entire dinner here." It seemed that the Tellmans had included a fresh-cut salad, dinner rolls and petit fours with the lobster and deviled eggs with caviar. Mom's and Aunt Mae's more pedestrian fare went into the freezer.

"Why don't you bring in one of those bottles of wine and let's crack it," I suggested. "There's a couple of things I'd like to talk to you about."

"I wondered how long it would take you to sample the most expensive wine we'll probably ever drink."

"Would you prefer we save it for our fiftieth anniversary?" I asked sweetly.

"Actually, I've been wracking my brain to think of a reason we ought to open one of them."

So we got out two of our best wine glasses, put some ice in our best wine cooler, I carefully wielded the corkscrew, and we took them all into the dining room to our little table-for-two by the window.

And we talked.

Chapter 28

We talked and we talked, letting our thoughts roam until they solidified. After an hour or so, we felt they could not be improved upon, so I changed into a fresh shirt and started my rounds. We needed a few answers before we could have the pleasure of helping the Tellmans distribute their largesse.

Fargo reminded me that he hadn't had much attention for the last day or so. I said, "Okay, you can come," and he bolted for the car.

My first stop was Karen Maddock's. I found her and Harry at their kitchen table, munching tuna sandwiches with little enthusiasm. I was using the fact that Reed's funeral was to be private as an excuse for stopping by, although certainly Karen would eventually wonder why I didn't simply pick up the phone to relay such mundane information. Then I asked Harry if I could please speak to his mother alone.

He shrugged and took his plate into the living room, closely followed by Fargo, who loved tuna fish. Shortly, I heard the TV come on.

I hoped I didn't find myself on the sidewalk wearing the remains of Karen's lunch in my hair after I asked my question.

"Karen, is it true that you and Charlie were having an affair and that Charlie had found a little house for the two of you to share?"

She actually laughed aloud and said, "Lord, no! Alex. Who on earth dreamed that one up?"

"Matter of fact, it was your husband. He was telling Sonny and me the events at Tellman's Gallery. He said you had served some big fancy dinner, complete with champagne, and made the announcement. First, you told them of the catering business with Rosie and Charlie. Then you told them you were in love with Charlie, that you were made for each other, that Charlie had found a place for you to live, and that you wanted a divorce. Mark was especially upset you had said all this in front of Harry."

"As no doubt he should have been if it were true." She waved her hands as if she were clearing steam away from a boiling pot. "Alex, anyone in my family, certainly including Mark, can tell you that when I get excited, I tend to overstatement . . . and then some."

She got up and poured us both a mug of coffee. "First of all, I am not gay. If I were, I certainly hope I would have found a better way to tell Harry than at a family dinner with Mark present."

I sipped my coffee, tried not to wince, and nodded my understanding.

"Secondly," she said, "I may have said that the three of us were meant for each other and that I just loved Charlie to pieces. And Charlie had found a little restaurant that was closing down for good, with most of the equipment we needed. We would have rented it and worked out of it. Certainly none of us would, or could, have lived in it." She shook her head in disbelief.

"What about the divorce?" I asked

"Oh, I think Mark said something about not sitting still while

245

I got involved with a bunch of gays—queers, he said. I told him I wasn't about to give up this chance to be independent. If he didn't want to sit still for it, he could move. I meant it. I imagine a divorce might well have been the end result, but the word wasn't even used at the time."

I smiled. "That about clears it all up. Neither Sonny nor I could believe what Mark was saying."

"Mistaken or not, he still killed her. None of us will ever get over that." Karen sighed. "Poor Charlie is dead, and Ruthie and I are sad and disappointed to boot. And Harry is heartbroken that his father is a murderer."

"It may not be quite as bad as it seems now, Karen. For one thing—don't tell Harry until it's certain—it may turn out to have been some kind of accidental shooting. Manslaughter, yes, but that's better than murder."

Her face brightened as I stood. We gave each other a farewell hug.

And I moved on to visit number two. Fargo leaned against me in the car. He reeked of tuna fish, not one of my favorite perfumes.

"What are you? A cat? Real dogs don't eat tuna fish." He gave me a look that said this one did, and sighed heavily into my face.

We pulled into the Catlett driveway, and Fargo immediately looked happier, doubtless recalling the croissants of his last visit. A maid admitted us, looking askance at his presence. She led us into the dining room. The family was gathered around brunch remains, eerily recollective of my first visit, minus Reed, plus Zoe and Marie's friend Barb.

Their greetings to us were much warmer than before. Even Merrilou managed a pat for the dog and asked if he could have a piece of bacon. I figured it would be a wonderful breath freshener and readily agreed.

Aside from Marie, who looked completely drained, and Zoe, who still seemed a little spacey, the household seemed in some quiet way, happier, as if a splinter had been removed from the constant pressure against a sore thumb.

I accepted coffee—delicious in this house—and a cranberry muffin. Conversation was general, with Marie and Zoe thanking me again for my help last night. I was getting embarrassed and wondering how I could separate Merrilou from the crowd, when she did it for me.

"Alex, could Rob and I see you in the office for a moment?"

"Sure." I noticed it was now the office, not Reed's.

Settled in a comfortable leather chair, I waited. Rob nodded to his stepmother, and she began.

"May I assume you've heard the rumors that Reed was somehow involved in a fraudulent construction scam on certain state buildings in the area?"

I nodded. She continued. "John Frost called early this morning to warn us that an investigation was imminent. Reed's business and personal assets will probably be frozen. We can't do anything about the business, but we have taken certain steps to protect the personal ones."

Rob continued. "I'll be at the bank first thing tomorrow to clear out the safety deposit box. Dad always kept enough cash to run on for two or three months. I'll get that and any personal papers out. I'm listed for access."

I muttered, "Unhuh," and pulled out my cigarettes, looking at Merrilou questioningly. She grinned and motioned for Rob to crack a window.

Replacing the pack and lighter in my pocket, I held up a cautionary hand. "Don't tell me anything you're doing that is illegal. If I know it, someday I may have to testify to it. But I can tell you this. Stick with John Frost. He will look out for your interests to the last penny, and he can make Sherman's March to the Sea look like mischievous trespass."

"Right. I had that feeling. Thank you." Merrilou gave me a keen look. "Trust funds and insurance policies are okay. Reed did not shoot himself to avoid prosecution." She gave a sour smirk.

"The house is in my name and—"

"How so?" I interrupted. "The will can't possibly have been probated."

She laughed bitterly. "A week or so after we came here from our honeymoon, Reed was so busy he had to work on a Saturday. Good little bride that I was, I took him his lunch, all dolled up in a wicker basket with a ribbon! He was busy, all right, on the couch with one of his female draftspeople! They were so busy they never even heard me. I snapped a photo on my cell phone and left his lunch in the hall with a note that the house was to be in my name by Tuesday, or I'd sue for divorce, naming the—married—lady, on Wednesday."

"My God, you and Reed had been married almost no time."

"Yes, not quite a month. Of course he swore never to do it again, and I forgave him. But the house is mine, and was so long before any business fraud was mentioned anywhere."

"Good for you!"

"I don't recommend it as a way to start a marriage," she replied. "However, to wrap this up"—she pointed across the room—"Just academically, do you know a good bank in Nassau or thereabouts?" She looked pointedly at the safe standing in the corner.

I felt my heart beat a little faster. According to Choate Ellis, Reed had finally come up with over half a million dollars in cash. Where was it? Not the bank, he had brought it here, with his two gorillas, to Reed. Only a hundred thousand had gone to the Tweedles. Merrilou interrupted my thoughts.

"Alex, I swear to you on the Bible, I do not know the combination to that safe. I have never seen what is in it. For all I know, it may be full of old Snickers bars."

"Good enough." I deliberately did not look at Rob as I dug out my cell phone and called home.

When Cindy answered I said, "This is purely hypothetical . . . a bet with a friend over a drink. Can you name three banks in Nassau?"

"What the . . . oh, yeah, sure."

I scribbled them down as she rattled them off and handed the list to Merrilou. "Thanks, honey. Forget this call. Oh, did you see Ellen?"

"Yep, all is well. See you later." She hung up.

I tucked the phone back into my pocket and looked at Rob. "I do not wish to know any more about any of this, okay? Now, could I boot you out for just a few minutes?"

"No prob. Thanks for your help. All of it along the way. And don't hesitate to send us a nice fat bill." He smiled.

"My pleasure," I said to his retreating back.

I turned to Merrilou. "What did you major in at college?"

Her eyebrows went up, but she answered easily. "Business. Why?"

"So managing a small business would be within your capabilities?"

"I would think so. Again, why?"

"Just one more question," I temporized. "What about sales?"

"You mean selling? Honey, if it's made, I can peddle it." She smiled at me and blinked her big blue eyes, and I believed her. "Now, you gonna let me know what business I am in or not? I'm beginnin' to be afraid to ask."

I told her. She was thrilled.

"You know, I was going to look for a job. I'd go crazy just sittin' and knittin' in this mausoleum. But I knew this was a bad time of year. This is wonderful."

"You'll have the winter to cut your teeth on small stuff. Cindy and I are booking the first party. Others will come along, with your expertise, and by summer, you'll all three be pros. But what about dealing with gays, Merrilou? There will be a lot of them."

"My dear Alex, business is business. That is the first commandment. I am discovering not all gays are so bad, after all. Don't ask, don't tell. That is the second."

"Good enough." I laughed. "I'll have Karen call you.

• • •

249

Cindy and I finally got our lobster and caviar and finished off the bottle of truly excellent wine we had started that afternoon.

Cindy told me of her visit to Ellen Hall to explain the plans that Betsy and Jan had for Charlie's insurance policy. The Tellmans wanted to be sure Ellen didn't perchance need some of it herself. Not all people who seem to be making it big, really are. But Ellen didn't need it and was happy to see it do some practical good for local people.

"I'm particularly glad about Charlie's mother," she had said. "It was hard enough for her to let Charlie do little things for her. I'm sure she wouldn't have let me help at all, though I'd have been happy to."

So we were able to call the Tellmans and forward Ellen's suggestion of thirty thousand to Charlie's mother, ten thousand to the catering group to help them get off the ground, and ten thousand to Harry Maddock's college fund.

Then we looked at each other. Were we really at home together with no one we had to call, no place we had to go?

Cindy sighed. "There are at least some winners in this. Frankly, except for poor Marie, there are no real losers in the Catlett fold."

"Ellen," I named the next on my list.

"A loser for now," Cindy agreed. "But her business is thriving, and she's good folks. She'll meet someone before too long. Then there's Karen."

"A mixture," I said. "Some pain around Mark, naturally, and I know she feels for Harry, although he's better off outside Mark's sphere of influence. How about the Tweedles?"

Cindy laughed aloud. "Oh, winners all the way. Who do you think is going to run the little shop in St. Lucie for Betsy and Jan?"

"You think so?"

"Betcha." She finished her wine and yawned.

"How about we go to bed and watch some TV?" I asked.

"Sounds good to me."

And so we did. I pushed a button on the remote and we watched the screen come to life. I pushed another button and we watched it go blank.

As Cindy turned into my arms, I thought, we have lost a friend in this, and feel the grief of some others. But we have each other, and with that, we will never be losers.

Chapter 29

There was another "finder" in our little Provincetown nursery rhyme, but his find did not come to light until long after our lovely fall had given way to the monochrome drear of December.

I was battling the blahs and trying to make out two Christmas card lists, one for Cindy and me, one for my business contacts. I welcomed the interruption of the phone.

I particularly welcomed Sonny on the other end, advising me that the Provincetown Police Department had finally cut a check reimbursing me for my tuxedo, demolished in their behalf.

He added that if I would meet him at the Wharf Rat Bar at noon sharp, he would treat me to lunch. I gushed my acceptance of this rare invitation, ignoring the forecast of sleet for the afternoon, and wondering why my brother had twice underscored my being on time. I'm usually prompt anyway, but today I arrived at the Rat fifteen minutes early.

Sonny was already at the bar, and only one stool beside him

was empty. I took it, and a couple of people standing at the end of the bar glared at me. I judged that Sonny had flashed a gold badge to save it. Before I could order a beer, Joe set a bourbon Old Fashioned in front of me.

As I started to thank my brother for the unusual generosity, he advised me that he had ordered a seafood platter for both of us. "I figured I'd better order. Billie's going to be busy around here."

At that remark, I realized that not only was the bar filled, so were most of the tables. A rarity this time of year. "What's going on?"

"That's what I want to know!" said a voice behind us. Billie, Joe's wife and the Wharf Rat's excellent cook, went on, "Weather like this and everybody gone for the season, and we're full with a sleet storm coming, when in the summer a drop of rain meant nobody was here when they were here." Conversation with Billie always left me with a slight buzzing in my ears. But she was a sweetie, and her seafood platters were masterpieces.

"Hang in there, Billie. If you get swamped, I'll help you clear."

"Thanks, Alex. I appreciate your help even if I don't take it." She hurried on.

"Can you understand her?" Sonny whispered.

"Perfectly."

"Now that scares me. Ah, here's the noon news. Let's watch it."

"I sat silently watching and listening, without knowing why, to a male and a female anchor reciting the disasters du jour. Looking around, I saw that most of the Rat's customers were doing the same thing. Bored, and very close to being irritated at my brother's mysterious smug smile, I almost missed the beginning of why we were here.

The video showed the governor pinning medals on two men, saying something about the Good Citizens Award and their help in initiating an investigation regarding fraudulent practices in state construction.

Suddenly I recognized Harmon and his brother-in-law, looking strange and uncomfortable in double-breasted suits and stylish haircuts.

At the same moment, a shout came from the Rat's front table, where Harmon and his Blues Brothers cronies hung out. "Look, everybody! Look at that! I'm on the TV. I'll be damned, they said we would be on TV, but I didn't believe them. Look at that!" Harmon, now in familiar jeans and work shirt, but with a medal pinned to the shirt pocket, had leapt to his feet and was pointing at the screen, where the grinning governor stood between the two men and raised their hands like triumphant boxers.

Applause, cheers and whistles broke out around the Rat, as the news went on to lesser stories. Harmon made his way around the room, stopping a moment here, shaking hands there, smiling, as if he were the governor himself.

When he reached us, he stopped and thanked Sonny, with tears in his eyes, for reporting his tip to the State Police. "I just love the both of you," he said. "You are good people. I wish you had been with us yesterday. It was something. They put the governor and us in this nice room until they were ready to make that little movie. They called it the green room, though there wasn't nothing green it. But there was a big table and leather chairs and all kinds of drinks. Hard and soft. The governor, he made us all a stiff one. I figured maybe he was nervous about being made a movie of." Harmon tilted his bottle of beer for a genteel sip.

"Anyway, just to settle him down," Harmon continued, "I told him some of my crime experiences. He was especially interested in that alligator with the naked lady. And I can tell you . . . I have to say it . . . he was plumb amazed. Nice man, but don't know much about the drug picture."

Sonny grinned. "I'm sure you set him straight."

"I did," Harmon said. "Anyway, here I rattle on, and what I want to say is to the two of you. I know how hard you both work when a case is tough. I've seen you both tired and worried, but

I've just gone on about my own business. Well, I want you to know, from now on, I'm not going to be so selfish! This medal really means somethin' to me. I'm gonna be Johnny-on-the-spot to help you both in every way I can. And that's a promise."

He rested a large, warm paw on each of our shoulders.

Sonny looked stricken.

I managed a reply, quite probably tearful.

"Harmon, you cannot imagine what that promise means to us."

Publications from

BELLA BOOKS, INC.

The best in contemporary lesbian fiction

P.O. Box 10543, Tallahassee, FL 32302

Phone: 800-729-4992

www.bellabooks.com

WITHOUT WARNING: Book one in the Shaken series by KG MacGregor. *Without Warning* is the story of their courageous journey through adversity, and their promise of steadfast love. 978-1-59493-120-8 $13.95

THE CANDIDATE by Tracey Richardson. Presidential candidate Jane Kincaid had always expected the road to the White House would exact a high personal toll. She just never knew how high until forced to choose between her heart and her political destiny. 978-1-59493-133-8 $13.95

TALL IN THE SADDLE by Karin Kallmaker, Barbara Johnson, Therese Szymanski and Julia Watts. The playful quartet that penned the acclaimed *Once Upon A Dyke* and *Stake Through the Heart* are back and now turning to the Wild (and Very Hot) West to bring you another collection of erotically charged, action-packed, tales. 978-1-59493-106-2 $15.95

IN THE NAME OF THE FATHER by Gerri Hill. In this highly anticipated sequel to *Hunter's Way*, Dallas homicide detectives Tori Hunter and Samantha Kennedy investigate the murder of a Catholic priest who is found naked and strangled to death. 978-1-59493-108-6 $13.95

IT'S ALL SMOKE AND MIRRORS: The First Chronicles of Shawn Donnelly by Therese Szymanski. Join Therese Szymanski as she takes a walk on the sillier side of the gritty crime-scene detective novel and introduces readers to her newest alternate personality—Shawn Donnelly. 978-1-59493-117-8 $13.95

THE ROAD HOME by Frankie J. Jones. As Lynn finds herself in one adventure after another, she discovers that true wealth may have very little to do with money after all. 978-1-59493-110-9 $13.95

IN DEEP WATERS: CRUISING THE SEAS by Karin Kallmaker and Radclyffe. Book passage on a deliciously sensual Mediterranean cruise with tour guides Radclyffe and Karin Kallmaker. 978-1-59493-111-6 $15.95

ALL THAT GLITTERS by Peggy J. Herring. Life is good for retired Army colonel Marcel Robicheaux. Marcel is unprepared for the turn her life will take. She soon finds herself in the pursuit of a lifetime—searching for her missing mother and lover. 978-1-59493-107-9 $13.95

OUT OF LOVE by KG MacGregor. For Carmen Delallo and Judith O'Shea, falling in love proves to be the easy part. 978-1-59493-105-5 $13.95

BORDERLINE by Terri Breneman. Assistant prosecuting attorney Toni Barston returns in the sequel to *Anticipation*. 978-1-59493-99-7 $13.95